Titles by Laurie Cass

No Paw to Stand On

A BOOKMOBILE CAT MYSTERY

Laurie Cass

BERKLEY PRIME CRIME
New York

BERKLEY PRIME CRIME
Published by Berkley
An imprint of Penguin Random House LLC
penguinrandomhouse.com

ISBN: 9780593547441

First Edition: August 2024

Printed in the United States of America
1   3   5   7   9   10   8   6   4   2

*To Mark and Phil, who,
except for their regrettable tendency
to bring up the Steak Knife Incident,
are the best brothers anyone could have.*

Chapter 1

There were days in my life when I woke up perky and cheerful. When I bounced out of bed with a smile on my face and a song in my heart. When the sun shone through windows that didn't show a single streak, when my annoyingly curly hair cooperated, and when the peanut butter didn't tear up the bread as I made my lunch. When from morning to night things got done and fun was had by all.

This was not one of those days.

"It's hot."

I looked over at Julia Beaton. Now in her mid-sixties, a few years ago Julia had retired to her hometown in northwest lower Michigan after a successful career on Broadway. She wasn't the type who could sit around and do nothing but enjoy herself, so it hadn't been long before I'd hired her as my part-time bookmobile clerk. She charmed everyone from infants to octogenarians and beyond, she was the best-ever storyteller, and she laughed at my jokes.

But she didn't like the heat.

And neither did I.

We were sitting on folding lawn chairs in the shade cast by the bookmobile's awning. The vehicle itself, all thirty-one feet, twenty-odd thousand pounds, and three thousand books of it, was sitting in the shade of a maple tree and its air-conditioning had been working just fine its entire life. Until today.

How long had the bookmobile been on the road? More than three years, but not four, I was pretty sure of that. My half-melted brain tried to do the math and then quickly gave up.

"Too hot," I murmured.

Julia nodded, waving her face with the fan she'd made out of a local restaurant's take-out menu. Though she'd put her long strawberry blond hair up into a twisted bun, and tendrils had escaped onto the nape of her neck, sticking to her skin. It was actually a good look on her, as pretty much everything was, but she looked miserable with the heat and humidity.

Our first sign of pending air conditioning doom had been a whine from Eddie, my black-and-white tabby cat. Eddie had stowed away on the bookmobile's very first voyage, and now if he wasn't on every trip, he would receive get-well cards from patrons by snail mail, e-mail, and text message.

Twenty minutes ago, there had been an odd *click* from somewhere inside the rooftop air-conditioning unit.

"Rrr," Eddie had said from his current favorite spot inside the storage cupboard.

Julia and I had been busy setting up for the day's first afternoon stop and hadn't realized what he'd meant. Sure, I knew he usually said "mrr," not "rrr," but what I didn't know was that he was tuned in to the bookmobile's mechanical innards and was trying to warn us.

Well, that or a far more likely explanation, which was that at three in the morning he'd howled so much and for so long for no known reason that the missing "m" was the feline equivalent of laryngitis.

"Rrr," he said now.

I looked over my shoulder. My cat was flopped in the open doorway, stretched flat from one side of the door to the other, but with his head rotated so his chin was on the very edge of the top step. How he managed that without his head falling off, I had no idea.

"Sorry, pal," I said. "That fur coat of yours probably isn't helping, is it?"

"Rrr."

Julie waved her menu fan in Eddie's direction. "Deepest apologies for the weather, Sir Edward," she said in an upper-crust English accent. "I take full responsibility."

He heaved a deep sigh and his body went even flatter, something I wouldn't have thought possible.

"Want to bet on how many people show up at this stop?" I asked.

The movement of Julia's fan slowed as she considered. "Twice as many as the last one."

More math? The woman was cruel. "No one showed up."

"And two times no one is?"

"A big fat zero." I slid down in my chair and wished I had my own menu from Fat Boys Pizza to fold into a fan.

When we'd discovered the air-conditioning was out, I'd called Josh Hadden, the library's IT guy, and asked him to send out a mass text to all the bookmobile patrons to let them know what was going on. He'd grumbled, saying that we were perfectly capable of doing it ourselves with the hot spot he'd set up, but I told him we were on the east side of Tonedagana County, outside of the hills and valleys and lakes of the county's western side. Although we were in the county's flatlands, it was also sparsely populated, so telecommunications were routinely inconsistent and spotty. Josh had given one more obligatory grumble, said I owed him one, and hung up.

The end result was Julia and Eddie and I sitting in the gravel parking lot of a small white clapboard church, waiting for a breeze that wasn't coming.

"Just like Godot," I muttered, but not very loudly, because otherwise Julia would have started quoting the play, and I'd never once been able to sit through a production of Samuel Beckett's most famous work without falling asleep. It was, without a doubt, a character flaw, but so far it was one I'd managed to hide from my coworker, and I hoped to continue to hide it ad infinitum. Which was undoubtedly another character flaw.

"Snow," Julia said weakly. "Remember snow? A bare five months ago this land was covered in a bleak blanket of white. Damp cold pierced our bones and we longed for spring. For summer. And now?" She sighed. "Oh, the trickery of a wish granted."

I expended some energy to turn my head. She didn't look like she was quoting from something, but it could be hard to tell. "Was that you or a character?" I asked.

"No idea." She flapped the fan in her face. "Too hot to remember."

"Rrr."

I slid down in the folding chair so far that my chin was almost touching my chest. Sighing, I wondered how much of the scheduled stop time was left. Once we got back inside, battened down the hatches, and got rolling, at least we'd have some breeze from the open windows.

My phone was in the pocket of my cropped pants, which were made marginally professional because I always wore a belt. I thought about pulling it out to see what time it was but didn't want to risk working up a sweat. If I started sweating, it would be hard to stop. Soon the only thing left of me would be a puddle of perspiration, and who would be left to drive the bookmobile back to Chilson?

Julia had never wanted to go through the training to get her commercial driver's license, a requirement of the library, though not of the state of Michigan, so she was out. Eddie didn't have the license either, but he also didn't have opposable thumbs or legs long enough to reach the pedals.

I closed my eyes, smiling at the image of Eddie driving the bookmobile. If he could, he surely would, because rules and regulations, whether state, federal, local, library, or mine, didn't mean much to a cat.

"Hey, Minnie?"

My eyelids opened slightly. "What?"

"It's hot. I'm . . . hot."

I sat up. Julia, the indefatigable and indomitable perpetual optimist, the instigator of many a "Minnie, pull up your big-girl panties and do what you need to do" conversation, sounded different. If I hadn't known better, I would have said she sounded human.

This could not be allowed to go on. It was time to abandon the heat-and-humidity-inspired ennui.

And I knew exactly what to do.

Half an hour later, Julia was smiling. "Brilliance," she said. "Sheer brilliance."

I shrugged. The move had more self-preservation than genius, but I was feeling pretty pleased with myself. Now, instead of sitting on a flat windless plain in an empty parking lot, we were sitting in a crowded parking lot with a gentle breeze and an outstanding view of Lake Michigan, with a temperature fully ten degrees lower than where we'd been.

Waves rolled onto the sandy beach, seagulls squawked, and the big lake's flat horizon gave no hint of the distant Wisconsin. It was Chilson in August, and we were at the beach. Nothing on earth could be better, because we were also, thanks to the city of Chilson's concession stand, snarfing down ice cream sandwiches faster than they were melting, no mean feat in this weather.

"You know," Julia said, chasing a drip down the outside of her hand, "we could set up shop here for the rest of the day."

The thought had already occurred to me, but there was this little issue of needing a library card to check out materials. I surveyed the mass of humanity. People on the sidewalk, people on the lighthouse pier, people on the sand, people in the water. People, people everywhere. "You think any of them are locals?"

"One way to find out." Julia popped the last bit of her ice cream into her mouth and stood. "Finally, all those years of cheerleading are coming in handy," she said, then held her hands to her mouth, megaphone-style, and shouted. "Two bits, four bits, six bits a dollar, all for Chilson, stand up and holler!"

A woman walking past with her children gave Julia a wide-eyed look and hurried her tots along. Other than that, most people ignored the cheer, but a few laughed, and two or three actually stood up and hollered.

This, of course, encouraged She Who Didn't Have an Introverted Bone in Her Body. Julia stood superhero-style, hands at her waist and feet wide. "Calling all Chilson residents!" she shouted. "Come aboard the magical Chilson bookmobile! Meet Eddie, the bookmobile cat! Discover books of fun and fancy! No learning required! It's summer!"

"You sound like one of those carnival barkers," I murmured when she paused for breath.

"Well, darn," she said. "And here I was trying for Lady Macbeth." Her cheeks were tinged a healthy rosy red, a much better color than her earlier washed-out paleness.

A family was picking their way across the beach, heading in our direction. Something about the group looked familiar, and I squinted thoughtfully, counting. Seven people total. One dad, six kids.

Three girls and . . . and then I knew who they were. "Well, would you look at that! It's the Engstrom family, come to pay a call."

It had been Ethan Engstrom, the youngest boy, who had freed a hidden Eddie on the very first bookmobile trip. At the time, I'd been trying to keep my cat's presence a secret, as my then boss had been an absolute stickler for the rules, even rules that weren't actually in place. Chad, the father, homeschooled the three sets of fraternal twins, and he seemed to manage that amazing feat through an efficient combination of humor and military precision, along with a hefty dollop of reality.

"Miss Minnie, Miss Minnie!" Emma, the youngest girl, who had to be nine now, skipped up the steps and threw her arms around my middle. "It's been, like, forever since we've seen you!"

Ethan came up beside her. "Is Eddie still here? Where is he?"

The middle set of twins, now twelve, were next inside. "He's on the console. See?" Cara pointed while Patrick made a beeline for the mystery section. Firstborn twins Rose and Trevor, who were shockingly tall at fifteen, said a polite hello to me and Julia and went to the biography and mystery sections, respectively.

Chad Engstrom, about a decade older than my thirty-five, climbed the stairs. "Thought you could get rid of us, did you?" he said in a fake sneer. "Not so fast, my pretty. We may move downstate for the school year these days, but we'll come back. We'll always come back. Heh heh heh."

"Daaad," Cara said, drawing the three-letter

word out into forty-six syllables. "You are sooo embarrassing."

He tugged on the bill of his ball cap. "Just doing my job, missy."

I laughed. It was good to have the Engstroms on the bookmobile again. Five of the six kids had already pulled out books and were sitting on the carpeted step that ran along the bottom of the bookshelves, serving as seat and step to reach the upper shelves for anyone who, such as myself, had vertical efficiency. The sixth child, Ethan, was up front with Eddie, tickling his furry white belly.

Chad noted my glance. "Eddie going to be okay with that? I can have Eath stop."

I snorted. "He's more than okay. Hear those purrs?" Because over the mutterings of the Engstrom kids, over Julia's tapping on the computer keyboard, and over the water and human noises wafting in the open doorway, the rumbling of Eddie's purrs wafted in and around us.

More than once, I'd wondered if cat purrs had healing powers. I didn't wonder out loud, though, because I didn't have a tenth of Julia's self-confidence and might never recover from the social ridicule if that thought got out into public consumption, but on my inside I speculated on what, exactly, it was about a purr that made me go all squishy.

I could ask Rafe, though. My soon-to-be husband, Rafe Niswander, might laugh at me, but he also had the power to make me go squishy on the inside, so maybe there was a correlation.

Chad pointed at the ring finger of my left hand. "Big day coming soon?"

And there I went, all soggy inside, and probably some of my outside, too. It happened almost every time I truly looked at my engagement ring. After we were officially engaged, I'd gone ringless for some time. This had bothered Julia more than it had bothered me, but the wait turned out to be worth it.

What I wore on my finger now was a reimagined version of the high school class ring I'd lost years ago on this very beach. Rafe had convinced a friend with a metal detector to spend hours and hours walking up and down the sandy stretch, and in a minor miracle, he'd actually found it. Rafe had taken the poor beaten-up thing to the city's jeweler, and had it reworked into my engagement ring.

I still could barely believe that, one, he'd even remembered that I'd lost the ring; two, that he'd gone to so much trouble to find it; three, that he actually *had* found it; and four, that he'd followed the jeweler's advice for the design instead of going with his initial request for an exact re-creation of my old ring.

"Yes," I said to Chad. "Third Saturday in September."

The date, which had once seemed so far away we barely had to pay attention to it, was now rushing toward us faster than we were prepared for. Wedding and reception details were all in hand, thanks to the efforts of my aunt Frances, but the idea of becoming half of a whole was taking some getting used to.

"Where are you having it?" Chad asked. "Downstate? You're from Dearborn, aren't you?"

"It made more sense to have it here." Chilson

was my adopted town, the place where I'd spent childhood summers with my dad's sister, the place where I'd found my dream job as assistant director of the Chilson District Library soon after graduate school. And it was the place where I'd lost my heart to the middle school principal.

"Mrr."

Chilson was also the place where I'd found Eddie one absurdly warm April day when I'd abandoned all chores and went for a walk. The fact that we'd met in a cemetery probably meant something, but I still hadn't worked out what.

"The wedding itself," I told Chad, "is going to be in the library's community room. The reception will be at Uncle Chip's Marina, with tents in case of whatever weather. My friend Kristen is doing all the food, but since Three Seasons isn't set up for catering, we're using the bookmobile to transport and serve."

Chad's face lit up. "That's outstanding," he said, laughing. "I can't think of anything more appropriate."

In retrospect, our venue choices were inevitable. In reality, it had taken us a bizarrely long time to get there. We'd tried hard to get my aunt to take over every single solitary decision, but she'd balked at venue, attire, and the attendants and guest list. Attendants were easy, as we were only having two each. Kristen was my matron of honor and my college roommate Lauren was my bridesmaid. Rafe's best man and groomsman were his college roommates.

Aunt Frances had encouraged us to have more attendants, but we'd flat-out refused. Going beyond those four would require moving friends from Level Four to Level Five, and that would require a selection process we weren't prepared to endure.

I'd been introduced to Rafe's friendship levels some time ago, and it hadn't taken long for me to fully embrace the concept. Level Five friends were the kind of friends that might as well be family, and if you had more than one or two in your life, you counted yourself lucky. Level Four were good friends, the people you did things with on a regular basis, people you'd call for a ride to the airport, people you'd help move. Level Three friends were people you'd make sure to look up if you happened to be in the same town, Level Twos were people you'd stop and talk to if you ran into them on the street, but you didn't have their phone number in your contacts list, and Level Ones were people you liked but had met only once and probably never would again.

When Rafe had first explained the levels to me, I'd found it very Rafe-like and hadn't thought about it much more. In time, though, I'd come to understand the value of the divisions. It had helped with our Christmas card list and the wedding guest list, and I could see it having a cascading impact on whom we vacationed with the rest of our lives.

By the time the Engstrom crew made their book selections, the bookmobile was beginning to get crowded. I averted my eyes from the sand being tracked inside and gave myself over to enjoying the unusual mix of patrons, some of whom I'd never seen outside the bricks-and-mortar library.

Eddie, not a fan of crowds, squeezed himself into the space under the passenger's seat, a spot that had up until then seemed far too small for a thirteen-pound cat. I bent down every so often to make sure he was still breathing, and every time was reassured by the dulcet tones of his snores.

On occasion, his snores were not so dulcet, and patrons glanced around, puzzled. "Is that Eddie?" a fit and fiftyish woman asked, her arms full of do-it-yourself books ranging from plumbing to landscaping. "I can't believe he's sleeping through this."

"Eddie," I said, "has many talents. Snoring his way through thunderstorms happens to be one of them." Along with shredding full rolls of paper towels, disappearing my favorite pen, and hacking up hair balls—loudly—when I was in the middle of any video meeting I ever had at home.

The woman, whose name was Rebecca, laughed. "An all-purpose cat."

If there was such a thing, Eddie would be an excellent candidate. Although maybe he didn't qualify, as I'd long thought that he was a species all to himself. *Felis eddicus.* And thanks to a small procedure at Dr. Joe's veterinary clinic, no little Eddies would ever be set loose on the world.

This sometimes made me a bit sad. I'd never had the chance to experience a kitten-size Eddie, since we'd met when he was full-grown. How adorable he must have been, prancing around with a short tail straight up, experiencing life for the first time.

Then again, except for the short-tail thing, he was like that most days. Just that morning he'd been shocked by the microwave's beep, something he'd heard every morning for more than three years. I sometimes suspected it was all an act, that he jumped so high because he enjoyed coming down so much, but I hadn't come up with a way to prove my theory. Not yet, anyway.

I ran Rebecca's heap of instructional books through checkout. We chatted throughout, and I discovered that she and her husband had just bought a house to fix up and rent.

"Long term only," she said. "I know we could make a lot of money if we went the short-term rental route, but we'll still turn a profit doing it this way." She looked at the stack of books and smiled. "Assuming these help, of course."

We started discussing the worth of instructional books compared to online video instructions and were agreeing that both had value, when my cell phone started vibrating. I ignored it until Rebecca was gone, then pulled it out.

I blinked. Kristen had left a voice mail, then sent half a dozen text messages, each increasing in the number of capital letters and exclamation points. The final one read *CALL ME NOW!!!*

My stomach tightened into a small knot. I waved my phone at Julia and pointed outside. She nodded, and I hurried down the stairs and around the far side of the bookmobile, tapping the phone as I went.

"Are the kids okay?" I asked as soon as Kristen answered.

"The . . . what?"

"Your babies," I said, frowning. "The twins. Are they okay?"

"Oh. Right. They're fine. But . . . ah . . . I need to talk to you. Can you come over?"

My frown deepened. Kristen sounded hesitant. Indecisive, even, which was not like her. "Sure," I said. "Tonight, after dinner?"

"Um. How about . . . now?"

The stomach-centered knot hardened into a rock. Kristen never cried wolf. Ever. "I can be there in half an hour."

"Okay," she whispered. "But can you hurry?"

After a quick, quiet consultation with Julia, we shooed everyone out of the bookmobile, tucked everything away, and drove to the library. The two of us hauled the returned books into the building, Julia said she'd take care of the checking in, and Eddie and I got in my car and drove out to the farmhouse where Kristen, her husband, and their twin not-quite-four-month-old babies lived.

For northwest lower Michigan, it was an old building, built soon after the Civil War, when people were moving up from downstate to homestead and farm. Though many of those farmhouses were gone, and almost all the farms had vanished, this particular house had survived long enough to have been purchased, years ago, as a summer place for a New York City–based chef with a nationally syndicated television cooking show, *Trock's Troubles*.

Trock Farrand (not his real name) updated the entire place—which included a massive kitchen addition—but overall, he kept a low profile in Chilson. He and his son, Scruffy (not his real name) Gronkowski (real), were the producers of the popular *Trock's Troubles*. The show centered around a problem that Trock was having in the kitchen, and he would go to restaurants all across the country for help in solving his problem of the day.

One fateful summer Trock decided he didn't want to travel to do a show. He told Scruffy to find a local restaurant, the Scruff came across Kristen's place, Three Seasons, and now I was driving to the farmhouse Trock had vacated for the sake of Scruffy, Kristen, and their twins, Eloise and Lloyd, more commonly called Cooper, because Kristen had been the size of a small car her last few weeks of pregnancy.

It was all working out, because as Trock aged, he was spending less and less time wandering the country and more time on the East Coast, producing the television show. Kristen and Scruffy were starting to do the same thing, with Kristen turning more of her restaurant's management over to her staff, but the arrival of the twins was bringing up a lot of question marks.

I drove down the gravel road to the farmhouse, dust pluming behind, wondering why Kristen had called out an SOS. Sure, I'd learn soon enough, but there was no way I could keep myself from conjuring up possibilities, each one worse than the last.

She'd said the kids were fine. Okay. What defined "fine"? It could mean they were fine for now but had been diagnosed with something horrific that would manifest later in life.

Or it could be something about Scruffy. As far as I knew, the Scruff, whose ironic nickname came from his seeming ability to walk out of a neck-deep mud puddle with a white shirt, was in perfect health. But maybe he'd been diagnosed with something.

Or . . . I pulled in a short, sharp breath. Maybe something was wrong with Kristen.

I shook my head. No, that couldn't be it. Kristen Jurek was a rock. A six-foot-tall blond rock. I'd met her when I was twelve, the first year I'd been sent north to spend the summer with my aunt Frances. We'd bonded over the making of sand castles, and she'd been the one who'd convinced me to expand our duo to include Rafe, now my almost-husband.

Summer upon summer I'd come north, and my friendship with Kristen had deepened every year. We'd drifted apart a bit during college, and during Kristen's bleak time. She'd majored in biochemistry, working hard to earn her PhD, and sailed off to work for a major pharmaceutical company in another state. Not long into the job, she'd come to the conclusion that she hated it, and in a typically Kristen move, she'd quit immediately and come home. Not long after that, she found the funding to open Three Seasons, a fine-dining restaurant open—go figure—three seasons of the year, serving strictly farm-to-table ingredients, spices being the only exception.

Spring, summer, and fall she'd worked long, hard hours, and come late October, she'd fled Chilson's gray skies for the sunny ones of Key West, where she'd tended bar and taken on the self-imposed task of determining once and for all the design of the perfect hammock.

Post-marriage, she'd been spending less time in Florida and Chilson and more time in New York, and I'd begun steeling myself for the news that she was going to sell Three Seasons to Misty, her head chef, and that the young family's home base would henceforth be on the Eastern Seaboard, with the eventual result of Chilson being a summer place they were frequenting less and less often.

I shook my head, told myself not to borrow trouble, and parked in the driveway. I grabbed the cat carrier and hurried to the house, the cheerful attraction of its bright white clapboard and wide bay windows lost on me, and opened the solid wood front door. "Kristen? It's me. And Eddie. Where are you?"

I'd assumed she'd be in the kitchen, which was where she was ninety-nine percent of the time she was awake and not tending to a small human, so I put the cat carrier on the wide wood planks of the entryway and headed in that direction when she answered my question.

"Out here."

Well, that was weird. I tacked, altering course from kitchen-bound, and went to the sliding glass door that went from dining room to deck, now open with its screen door doing nothing to keep the air-conditioned cool inside and the heat outside where it belonged.

Tall, long-legged Kristen was sitting on the deck's railing, wearing shorts, T-shirt, and flip-flops. Her cell phone was to her left, the baby monitor to her right, and she was staring at . . . at I had no idea what.

"The kids are okay?" I asked. "Scruffy? Parents?"

Not looking away from whatever, she nodded.

"And you? You're okay, too?"

There was a short, heart-stopping pause, but she nodded a second time. The iron grip of tension that had been squeezing my neck released and I was able to take a deep breath and consider what next to say.

I didn't want to tell her that whatever it was, things would be fine, because although Kristen milked every ounce of drama she could out of every minute of the day, she did that because she thought it was fun, not because she truly thought days needed more drama added to them. No, whatever was going on was serious, and I didn't want to make light of it.

So instead of saying anything, I climbed up on the railing and sat next to her.

And waited.

A lifetime or two later, she sighed. "It's the restaurant."

"Okay."

"I have no idea what happened," she whispered. "It just doesn't make sense. I must have done something wrong, but . . . I don't know. I don't know what to do."

Kristen was being indecisive, and she was doubting herself? She was right, this didn't make sense. "What happened?" I asked gently.

"The ice cream cones," she said. "It had to be that. That's the only thing they all had."

A shiver of unease tingled down the back of my neck. "The ice cream?"

"The cones we've been giving away. Didn't I tell you? Last year Scruffy and I went to London, remember? We got hooked on the 99 they have over there. Soft-serve vanilla in a cone with a piece of milk chocolate on the top. I worked out a recipe for a gluten-free waffle cone and we use scooped vanilla ice cream. We've been calling them 77s. When the temperature is seventy-seven degrees or higher, we offer them to people on their way out the door. But . . ." Her voice trailed to nothing.

"But?" I asked softly.

She blew out a whuff of breath. "Today eight people who walked away with cones had allergic reactions. Two of them are at the hospital."

There was a beat of silence as I tried to absorb the news.

"Minnie?" she asked, her voice cracking. "What did I do wrong? How did this happen? I don't know what to do."

She might not, but I did.

I pulled out my phone and tapped a few buttons.

"Tonedagana County Sheriff's Office," said the friendly voice. "How can I help you?"

"Deputy Ash Wolverson, please. I'd like to report a mass poisoning."

Chapter 2

It took some time to convince the young man who answered the phone that I didn't need to call 911, that no one was in immediate danger, that it was a suspected poisoning from earlier in the day, and that the two people who might be in danger were in the hospital under medical supervision.

Eventually, I answered his questions. I was connected to the desk phone of my friend Ash, and I was heartily wishing that I'd kept my mouth shut until reaching Ash. Or that Ash's fiancée, Chelsea, who also worked at the sheriff's office, had answered the phone. Or that I'd called Ash's personal cell phone even though the detective in training typically didn't answer his personal phone when on duty.

As was sadly usual when I was irritated by the dumb things I'd done, I made matters worse when he picked up the phone.

"Why aren't you looking into what happened at Three Seasons?" I demanded.

"Good afternoon to you, too," Ash said. "My day has been going just fine, thanks for asking, although I have a feeling it's about to take a hard turn in the other direction."

"Do you even know what I'm talking about?"

"Are you going to give me a clue?"

"Which means that no, you don't know." I blew out a breath, pulled in another one, and gave him a three-sentence summary.

After a moment of silence, he said, "Minnie, we'll get involved if the health department contacts us. And of course we'll be involved if there are suspicions of criminal behavior. We don't have either one of those things right now. Besides, no offense to Kristen, but accidental food poisoning is far more likely than intentional—what did you call it? Mass poisoning?"

"But . . ." I sighed. He was right. It was just that Kristen was acting so weird I'd wanted to do something to help.

I glanced at my friend because I'd expected her to interrupt my conversation with Ash long before. But instead of paying any attention to me, she was tapping on her cell phone at the speed of light. Which, by itself, meant little, as that was her usual operational speed for doing anything. Given the circumstances, though, I wondered who—and what—she was texting. "Thanks," I said to Ash. "Um, you'll let me know if you hear anything?"

"If it's something I can share, sure, if I remember."

Though it could be helpful to have a former boyfriend, now a solid friend, in the sheriff's office, the honesty inherent in such a relationship could also be a hindrance.

When I thumbed off the phone, I looked at Kristen. "Something going on?" I asked.

"Scruffy needs to get back here," she said distractedly, still texting. "He went to Petoskey for a chamber presentation on child care, go figure, but I have to get to the restaurant. The traffic will be summer horrible and he'll take forever to get here . . ." She bit her lip and kept texting.

I swallowed. "Um, I can watch the twins, if you want."

Kristen's thumbs stopped moving. She slewed a glance my way. "You sure?"

"Sure," I said, trying to project confidence and competence, two things that you'd think would go together but I'd found didn't always. "Scruffy will be here in, what, half an hour? Forty-five minutes tops."

Kristen's blue eyes stared at me with an intensity she'd usually reserved for entree-plating presentations. After a long moment, during which I realized that I had very little experience with infants and certainly shouldn't be trusted with two of them at the same time, she nodded and slid off the railing.

"You know where everything is," she said. "If anything happens, you have Scruffy's number. He'll be on the road in five minutes."

I jumped down, grabbed the baby monitor, and followed her inside, watching as she snatched her purse off the kitchen counter. She headed to the door that led to the garage, reaching inside her purse for her car keys as she went. "Is there anything else I can do?" I asked.

She stopped abruptly. "Yes," she said, turning

around, and reached out with her arms. "I could really use a hug."

"Well, that's easy enough." I hurried over and gave her the biggest one I could. "There. Any better?"

"A little." She released me. "You're the best friend ever. I know that you find watching my kids a terrifying prospect."

I shrugged. "True, but now I have time to teach the kids bad habits before your husband gets here."

Kristen didn't react to my almost-funny statement. "I called the health department an hour ago," she said, and though she was looking at me, I got the distinct feeling she didn't see me at all. "I just got a text that the inspector has pulled in. With so many people sick, they're going to . . . going to . . ."

My throat tightened as I silently finished the sentence. *They're going to close the restaurant.* The restaurant she'd created herself. The place she'd devoted so much time, money, and energy to. The restaurant that was an anchor to our town and was a destination for people from Calumet to Chicago.

I gave her a gentle push. "Go. We'll be fine."

She gave me another hug, then ran to the door.

I trotted upstairs and, from the window in the twins' bedroom, watched her drive off. I was still up there, watching their small chests going up and down and up and down, when Scruffy got home.

After we shared notes, it turned out that he didn't know any more about what was going on at the restaurant than I did. We made a pact to contact each other the minute we heard anything, and Eddie and I made our way back to Chilson.

Driving, I thought about what Ash had said, that

the sheriff's office would get involved if the health department contacted them. Had they done that? Would any of the people who got sick hit Kristen with a lawsuit? And what had made them sick, anyway? The whole thing was weird. And troubling.

Rafe, principal of the middle school, had gone to work that morning, but since it was early August, he hadn't exactly worked a full day. When Eddie and I came in the back door, he looked up from whatever he was cutting up on the kitchen island and smiled. "Hey, sugar beet, what's . . ." His voice trailed off as he absorbed the look on my face. "What's wrong?"

I put Eddie's carrier on the floor and hunkered down to open his wire door. "It's Kristen," I said, and was startled to hear a quiver in my voice. "The restaurant."

There was a clatter of cutlery, and next thing I knew Rafe was pulling me upright and wrapping his arms around me.

I cried for a bit, then I pulled away, blew my nose, and told him everything that had happened, from the text message from Kristen I'd picked up on the bookmobile, to what Ash had said, to the chilling possibility of Three Seasons being closed by the health department.

"What does that mean?" Rafe asked. "For a restaurant to be closed down? How long will it take to open up again?"

"No idea." I added it to my ever-increasing list of things I didn't know anything about. "And right now I don't want to ask. I have no idea what Kristen thinks happened, but I don't see how it could be anything other than some sort of poison."

"Mrr!"

Rafe and I looked down at Eddie, who was doing figure eights around our ankles.

"Well, of course no one at Three Seasons did it," I said to him. And to Rafe. "They're all too good at what they do for accidental food poisoning. And of course no one there would have done it intentionally. Kristen pays more than any restaurant in town. Kristen's staff loves her and their jobs."

"Not a single disgruntled employee?" Rafe's eyebrows went up.

"They're all extremely gruntled," I said firmly.

My beloved gave me a look. "Is that a word? Gruntled?"

I had no idea. "How could you have disgruntled without first having gruntled? Trust me. I'm a librarian. I read books and I know things."

Rafe grinned, his teeth showing white against skin that looked perpetually tan, an inheritance from long-ago Native American ancestors. "You said that so convincingly I'm not even going to call for a fact-check."

"What I'm mostly worried about," I said, moving on, "are the restaurant review websites. If word gets out about a poisoning, it's going to take forever to get her reputation back."

"If?" Rafe shook his head. "More like when. But The Blond will get through it. She's almost as tough as you are." He gave me a quick squishing hug. "And speaking of tough, that's what our chicken is going to be if I don't get it out of the oven."

I watched as he went back to chopping up the salad-bound vegetables. He was right about the "when" thing. There were probably social media posts about the poisoned desserts already. But I also knew that I was right: No one who worked at Kristen's restaurant had done anything wrong.

And if the reputation of Three Seasons was going to get kicked into the mud, I was going to pull it out, polish it up, and make it shinier than ever.

Because that's what friends did.

The next morning, I put the Eddie-filled carrier into my car and backed out of the garage.

"Did you see that sunrise?" I asked him. "No? Well, it came up all big and red-orangey. Pretty, but you know it's going to be another round of the classic summer triple H. Heat, haze, and humidity. Darren stopped by the bookmobile last night and did something magical to the air-conditioning, so it's working now, but with this heat, I'm wondering if I should leave you home."

I looked at the carrier, strapped into the passenger's seat. Eddie's gaze was fastened on me. "If you have something to say, say it."

Nothing from the cat side of the car.

"Okay. I'll say it for you. Darren is the best mechanic ever, and if he said it's fixed, fixed it is, and I shouldn't worry."

"Mrr!"

With that settled, I was able to look around and appreciate the quiet streets of Chilson, which would stay quiet for maybe another hour. I couldn't quite see the wide waterfront sidewalk, but I knew it would soon be busy with people taking advantage of the relatively cool air, running, walking, and exercising their dogs.

I drove through the heart of downtown, looking

up and around at the various building types that
blended together to make a happy whole that could
never have been planned. Brick mixed with clapboard, fieldstone mixed with stucco, single story
next to three stories. Antiques stores, restaurants,
gift shops. Toy store, pharmacy, wine store, bakery,
candy store, jeweler, bookstore, general store.

Almost everything I'd ever wanted—and absolutely everything I'd ever needed—was here in this
small town, including the best library ever.

I parked in the back parking lot of the Chilson
District Library, where Julia and the part-time
bookmobile driver, Hunter Morales, were ready to
roll. I'd already texted them the good news that the
air-conditioning was fixed, so I handed the cat carrier to Hunter.

"He's been quiet this morning," I said. "Not sure
what that means. Could be bad for you."

Hunter and his wife, Abigail, both in their mid-
twenties, were two of the hardest-working people I
knew. Abigail was an office manager by day and a
bartender at night. Hunter was taking business
classes, working on the bookmobile part time, and
trying to establish a welding business. Happily for
them, his business was starting to take off, and I
wasn't sure how much longer he'd be with the bookmobile.

Of every three pennies they earned, one went to
their current expenses, one went to build the business, and the third went to a savings account dedi-
cated to the down payment for their first house.
They were living with Abigail's parents, and while
that was working, from what Hunter had told me on

long bookmobile drives, it was becoming clear that it would be better for everyone when they moved out.

My own living arrangements, until recently, had been deep in the unusual category. From mid-October through April, I'd lived with my aunt Frances in the large and rambling hundred-year-old home that had been in her first husband's family since it had been built. Then, when the weather warmed, I'd been cheerfully kicked out to make room for her summer boarders, and made my way down the hill to Uncle Chip's Marina and my adorable little houseboat.

But that was all in the past. Aunt Frances had married Otto Bingham and sold the boardinghouse to Cousin Celeste, who was hiring a contractor to renovate the place into long-term rental apartments. Rafe had proposed to me, and I'd moved into his large Shingle-style house across from the marina.

When he'd bought the place, it had been a disaster. Tiny apartments carved out of roomy spaces with cheap paneling and even cheaper fixtures. The irony that Rafe had removed apartments from an old house and that Celeste was creating them was not lost on me. Sometimes, though, that was the way things went. And maybe the fact that I was renting my houseboat to Isabella and Corey Moncada, a young couple who were poised to take on management of a downtown candy store in the fall, made up for it.

I sighed. Right now, Corey worked downtown at Shomin's Deli, but Isabella worked for Kristen. I hadn't heard from Kristen, so I didn't know anything more now than I had when she'd left me in charge of the twins. Though I didn't want to borrow trouble by assuming the worst about the restaurant, it was hard to keep my thoughts out of the worry rut. If Three Seasons closed temporarily, I was sure Kristen would try to keep paying her staff. But that could go on only so long.

It only took a minute to tell Julia, who'd become friendly with Kristen, what had happened.

She took it all in and was silent for a beat. "Well, whatever happened, I'm sure you'll figure it out."

"Me?" I blinked. "What are you talking about?"

"Because that's what you do." She smiled her stage smile, the one that could be seen from the top row of the second balcony. "Minnie will ride to the rescue and save the day."

I made a rude noise in the back of my throat. "Off with you. And if the air-conditioning goes out again, come on back. I don't want either of you to get heat stroke."

"Mrr!"

"And," I added smoothly, "I don't want the feline of the group to suffer an ounce of discomfort."

"Mrr."

I waved them off into the wild hazy yonder and pulled out my phone to see if cats could even get heat stroke. Since they were mammals, it seemed to make sense that they could, but . . . I tapped away and soon discovered that, yes, cats can get both heat stroke and heat exhaustion.

"Well, there you go." I texted that little tidbit to Julia and Hunter and pocketed my phone, secure in the knowledge that they'd take care of Eddie as if he was their own. Better, maybe, since they were both inclined to give him more treats than I did.

I approached the library and, as I tried to do every time I approached but usually didn't remember because my brain was occupied with a zillion other things, looked at the building with deep appreciation.

A couple of years before I was hired as assistant director, the good citizens of Chilson approved a millage to take a vacant school and turn it into the best small-town library in the world. The building had excellent bones to start with—high ceilings, oak beams, and a multitude of details in the Arts and Crafts architecture style—and the millage money had allowed an expansion in that same style. Dark brass fixtures, metallic mosaic tiles, massive pendant lights hanging in the old gymnasium turned main stacks, and the best thing of all, a working fireplace in the reading room, which included a deep upholstered window seat.

Well, it was the best thing in winter, anyway. Not so much a draw on a hot August day.

I walked past the still-dark rooms and headed straight to the staff break room and kitchen. There weren't any other cars in the parking lot this early and I was free to make the first pot of coffee. Though caffeine was the staff of life, it didn't have to be strong enough to melt braces off your teeth, which was how Kelsey Lyons, one of our part-time clerks, always brewed it, so it was often a race to make the first pot.

The happy brown stream had just begun when I heard footsteps. From the noise, I could tell it wasn't Kelsey or Holly Terpening, the other clerk on duty today, or Josh Hadden, our IT guy. Gareth Dibona, maintenance guy extraordinaire, had his own coffeepot, so there was only one person it could be at this time in the morning.

I turned as Graydon Cain, library director and my boss, walked in. Many people had tried to convince me to apply for the director job, but I'd decided to opt out. I'd spent a few months as interim director and had quickly learned that if I got the big job, I'd have to give up driving the bookmobile, and I wasn't ready to do that. Graydon, in his mid-forties, thin-faced and pleasant, had been director for a year and a half, and I'd been ready to anoint him Best Boss Ever within weeks of his arrival.

"Good morning." I smiled and gestured at the coffee. "Kelsey-free."

"Thanks." He took a mug from the cabinet and filled it.

I frowned because he'd chosen the mug no one ever used. It was small, it had a chip in the rim, it was an unfortunate shade of overly bright orange, and we all knew it had once upon a time belonged to a former library director no one missed.

"Um, is something wrong?" I asked hesitantly. Graydon was a fantastic boss, but our personal lives didn't tend to intersect. "Are you okay?"

"Okay?" Graydon suddenly focused on me. "Yes, I'm fine. It's . . ." He shook his head. "I had a phone call from Gareth first thing."

That couldn't be good. My brain leapt straight into bad-scenario territory. "It's not the air-conditioning, is it?"

"What? Oh. No. Everything's fine, structure-

wise. It's something else. We've had some vandalism."

My eyes went wide. Vandalism wasn't a thing for
the library, not in this gorgeous building that was
such a point of pride for the community. We didn't
even bother to lock the library's book bike. Okay,
that was mostly because its weight made theft ex-
ceedingly unlikely, but still. "Where? I didn't see
anything when I came in." My mind shied away
from the idea of graffiti sprayed across the light
brick.

"Out front." Graydon pointed in the direction of
the parking lot, flower beds, and playground. "Half
the irrigation heads have been destroyed, and some
of the lines have been pulled out of the ground."

Which explained why I hadn't seen anything.
The bookmobile, in the back parking lot, was on
the other side of the library. "Any idea who did it?"

He shook his head. "Gareth is with the city police right now. I'll talk to them in a few minutes."

"Kids?"

"Probably." He sipped his coffee. "It could have
been a lot worse, and it's likely nothing to worry
about."

"Sure."

"But it also doesn't hurt to be cautious. I have to
make some phone calls. Tell everyone to keep an
eye out, will you?" He topped off his coffee and
headed up to his second-floor office, where he'd be
calling each and every library board member and
giving them the bad news.

I spent a moment being happy with my status as
assistant director, then my thoughts turned bleak.

The vandalism had taken place last night or early this morning. Yesterday, around lunchtime, free ice cream cones from Three Seasons had made people sick.

Two nasty incidents in one small town within less than twenty-four hours. Unrelated? Or related?

I had no idea. But I needed to figure it out.

Chapter 3

I spoke to the staff working that day about the vandalism and got the expected responses from each
of them. Holly was horrified, Kelsey took it almost
as a personal attack, and Josh, after going out to
look at the damage himself, said that as far as vandalism went, the vandals had a long way to go.

"What are you talking about?" I asked. I'd gone
along with him, and we were standing on the curb
around the main parking lot, looking at the mess.
"It's a mess. Sprinkler heads aren't cheap. And Gareth said this kind is on back order. We may not get
them until winter."

"Yeah, I know." Josh shoved his hands into the
pockets of his cargo pants. "I'm just saying that it
could have been a lot worse. Serious vandals would
have broken windows. Or run over some fencing.
Or busted up sculptures." He nodded at a nearby
metal sailboat that looked so lifelike I was sometimes surprised it hadn't sailed off into Lake
Michigan.

I remembered being anxious about spray paint earlier, and nodded. "So they were stupid vandals?" Which was redundant, but Josh didn't call me on it.

He shrugged. "Or ones without much experience. If it was kids from around here, the city cops will figure it out soon enough. People talk."

People did indeed. Although not always about the things you wanted most to know.

I thought about that for a minute, then started a long text conversation with Kristen. The bad news came first; the health department had closed the restaurant. The not-so-bad news was that the inspectors had already passed them for safe food-handling practices, contamination, and temperature control.

This was surprising to me, since I would have thought determining that would take . . . well, I didn't know how long, but longer than that. But since the only thing I knew about running a restaurant was that I didn't know how to run a restaurant, my ignorance wasn't surprising.

Minnie: *Any idea when you'll be able to reopen?*

Kristen: *waiting for blood test results—should know more Monday*

I winced. Being closed over a summer weekend would be a hit to her cash flow. Still, it could have been a lot worse.

Minnie: *Is the staff working today?*

Kristen: *Most are why*

Minnie: *I'd like to talk to them. See if I can help figure out what happened.*

Kristen (after a pause): *Have at it. I gotta go Cooper crying*

Her texting dots disappeared and I frowned at

my phone. Why wasn't Kristen acting like Kristen? The version I'd known for more than twenty years would have been at the restaurant that minute, ripping the place apart until she found an answer to what had happened. This hesitant Kristen was someone I didn't know at all.

The arrival of twin babies had, understandably, rearranged her priorities, but this . . . this didn't feel like that. Not even close. Which made me even more determined to get to the bottom of the waffle-cone mystery. I wanted my friend back, but even more, her children needed the old Kristen, who was sometimes overbearing but always competent and confident.

The rest of the morning, between vandalism e-mails, text messages, and phone calls to the non-scheduled staff and the Friends of the Library volunteers, I thought about what I was going to say to the Three Seasons staff. I knew the regulars, staff who came back year after year, but I didn't know some of the summer employees at all.

"Start with what you know," I said to myself as I drove down the hill after the standard lunchtime, "and move on from there." Once I heard it out loud, even if it was my own voice, it sounded like good advice, so when I knocked on the back kitchen door and let myself in, I decided to take it.

At this time of year, the Three Seasons kitchen would normally be in a short lull after the lunch rush. The calm before the dinner storm, Kristen always called it, when the noon pots, pans, plates, and silverware were cleaned and being shelved, but before the evening preparations went into full swing.

Post-lunch, staff would be tidying up countertops, triple-checking food supplies, walking through
the dining areas to make sure everything was clean
and tidy, and sharing stories of lunch events, good
and bad. Today, however, there was none of that.
Today, the kitchen staff and the waitstaff were gathered at the main stainless steel counter, sitting on
stools, and not talking. At all.

This was not the time for a joke, which made me
very glad I hadn't brought Rafe with me. I shut the
door behind me and Harvey looked up from a serious contemplation of his thumbnail.

"Oh. Hey, Minnie," he said listlessly.

Harvey was Kristen's sous-chef and had been for
years. Outside of his top-notch skills with cutlery,
he was famous for his capacity to absorb the worst
of Kristen's tirades and turn them back on her in a
way that invariably made her laugh.

I looked at Misty Overbaugh, the head chef, who
was a little shorter than my efficient five feet. She
gave me a brief finger wave, then returned her attention to the cloth napkin she was apparently trying to iron with the flat of her hand.

The rest of them—the maître d', the headwaiter,
waiters, and Isabella, the assistant sous-chef and
my houseboat renter—looked as if they were teeter-
ing at the edge of the abyss.

I knew them all, was good friends with many of
them, and the last thing I wanted was to have any
of them think they were suspected of tampering
with the ice cream. But to help Kristen, I had to
follow through with my plan.

After sucking in a deep breath, I said, "This is
going to be awful, and I'm saying sorry in advance,

but I'd like to talk to each of you, one on one, in Kristen's office, about yesterday."

Harvey was the only one who moved, and even then it was to give a small shrug. "Okay. But why?"

"To figure things out."

The headwaiter frowned. "Isn't the health department going to do that?"

I had no idea. "Probably, but they're looking at it from a different point of view. They're looking to pin blame; I want to find out what really happened."

Finally, there was a widespread stirring of interest.

"You don't think we tried to kill people?" Misty asked, sarcasm in every syllable. "Because that's what social media is saying."

"Social media also says chewing gum will stay in your stomach for ten years," I said. This got a tiny smile out of Misty. "Kristen wants to get out ahead of this as much as possible"—or she would if she was thinking straight—"and getting all of you to think about yesterday is a first step."

Harvey looked up from his thumb. "Because sure as snowflakes, something happened. And we were all here yesterday, so maybe one of us saw . . . something."

"Exactly." I nodded. "Who wants to go first?"

Just under an hour later, I reviewed the notes I'd jotted on paper I'd pulled out of the printer. Everyone I'd talked to had said basically the same thing: We were busy, everything seemed normal, I didn't see anything unusual.

I sighed. I hadn't truly expected to solve the mystery of the ice cream cones right then and there, but I had hoped to unearth at least one piece of information. To see a dawning realization on a staff member's face that the empty plastic bag they'd picked up off the floor and thrown away might have contained poison. To hear at least one comment about seeing someone, preferably a stranger, where they shouldn't have been.

Folding the small stack of papers in half, I tucked them in my purse and made my way down the narrow hall back to the kitchen. This time, the room was empty. I stood at the stainless-steel counter where Kristen and I had eaten many a Sunday night crème brûlée, and looked around. No clues jumped out at me; everything looked the same as it always did. Shiny, clean, and professional.

Sighing, I stood. Just then, I caught a glimpse of something way underneath a wire shelving unit. Something . . . blue. Which didn't make sense because the floor was a terra-cotta color. I crouched down, stretched my arm and fingers out long, and pulled out a knife. A paring knife with a handle of thin layers of different shades of blue, from navy to sky.

I heard voices and poked my head out through the double doors into the largest of the multiple dining areas. Everyone was hauling tables and chairs to one side in what I assumed was preparation for a round of deep cleaning. I showed Harvey the knife. "Found this on the floor back there."

He took it from me and looked at it blankly. "It's a Lee. Not one of ours. A vendor probably dropped it."

"I have to get back to the library," I said. "I didn't learn much, but if someone remembers something later, tell them to give me a call."

"Will do. Did you talk to everyone?"

"Everyone except Misty."

"Oh, right." Harvey nodded. "She went out on some errand. Do you want her to call you?"

"Soon as she can." I rummaged around in my purse and scribbled my cell number on the back of a business card. "You never know what's going to be important. The least little detail can make a huge difference."

He gave a half-hearted smile. "Did Kristen get that from you, or did you get it from her?" When I gave him a blank stare, he said, "That's what she says every time she plates a meal."

It was becoming painfully obvious that the absence of my larger-than-life friend was a gaping hole in the life of her restaurant. I cleared my throat, which had grown suddenly tight.

"It'll be okay," I said, as quietly and as reassuringly as I could.

But I wasn't at all sure it would be.

After the bookmobile returned, safe and sound, I put Eddie in my air-conditioned and tree-shaded car. Julia and Hunter regaled me with tales of the day while the three of us lugged crates of books inside the library and I tried not to be envious of the fun they'd had while I'd talked to everyone and their brother about vandalism and sorted out magazine subscription expiration dates.

With the library chores done, they headed home to their respective spouses, and Eddie and I drove to a shady lakeside county park, the location Kristen and I had agreed upon via text. I wasn't sure if the heat had abated, or if my internal thermostat was adjusting—which would be nice, though a little late now that it was August—but either way I wasn't sweat-sticky from head to toe when I came to a stop in the gravel parking lot.

I looked over at Eddie. "Are you ready for this?"

Things had not gone well the first few times Eddie had met the twins. Wide-eyed stares, ruffled fur, and screeching howls from all three had dominated most of the encounters, but earlier in the summer there'd been a shift, and I hoped it would be a permanent one.

When Kristen pulled in, we were at a picnic table with Eddie snoring in his carrier, me reading *The Sentence* by Louise Erdrich. A few minutes of normal kid-oriented activity later, Kristen and I sat facing each other with one cat and two infants in carriers between us.

"So," Kristen said, adjusting her baseball cap, her long blond hair flowing out above the adjustable band in back. "Did you learn anything?"

I eyed her. Though the words she was saying were the right ones, the tone she used was more along the lines of "I think it's supposed to rain" than "I need to save my restaurant, so tell me everything this minute." The Kristen I'd known for more than twenty years would have been pounding tables and demanding action. I shook away my concern.

"Sort of," I said, and told her that none of the staff I'd talked to had seen anything out of the ordinary.

"Okay." Gently, Kristen rocked Lloyd's carrier up and down, up and down. "You talked to everyone?"

"Everyone but Misty. She was out on an errand."

I made a mental note to catch up with her soon. "But overall, what that tells me is someone outside of the restaurant did something to the ice cream cones."

"Or it was Misty. Or one of the staff was lying to you." She shrugged. "People lie all the time, especially to get themselves out of trouble."

I blinked at the transformed Kristen, not quite squaring her with the version who would have been buttonholing each of her staff herself, giving each of them her sharkiest shark stare, the one with the power to make even the whiniest customer back down and apologize for bothering her.

That Kristen would have been talking to each employee, one by one, glaring them down until she felt sure she had the truth. This Kristen barely seemed to care. I fully understood that having two babies had shifted her priorities, but the knowledge that she was relying on me, Ms. Avoid Confrontation As Much As Possible, to get the truth out of her staff on something so important was hard to grasp.

"You honestly think someone on your staff did something to your 77s?" I tried to keep the incredulity out of my voice and failed epically.

"What?" She sat up straight, frowning. "Of course not. Well," she added, her brief return to her former personality fading quickly, "at least not on purpose. But accidents happen. They can happen to anyone."

I caught a glimpse of what was worrying her. If one of her employees had accidentally poisoned the ice cream cones, she'd have no choice but to fire him. Or her. And the entire summer, she'd said over and over again that this was the best staff she'd ever had. The core employees hadn't changed in years, but many of the waitstaff came and went, and getting a group that worked well together from top to bottom was a gift.

"Accident," I said. "You think that's what happened?"

She started rocking Eloise's baby carrier. "There's no point guessing. The blood work will come back on Monday. We'll know more then."

"I see your point about guessing," I said slowly to the person I was having a hard time recognizing, "but don't you think it might be worth our time to think about possibilities ahead of time?"

Kristen shrugged. "If you want, I guess."

I did want. At some point she was going to wake up and realize that Three Seasons, her professional pride and joy, was on the brink of extinction, and I didn't want the future Kristen to regret not doing everything she could to haul it back from the brink.

"Like I told Ash," I said, "it could be poison. And I don't mean accidental. Maybe someone did it on purpose."

Kristen rolled her eyes. "That's nuts. What, you think someone tiptoed into the kitchen, uncorked a bottle labeled with a skull and crossbones, poured it in the tub of ice cream, stirred it in, then tiptoed out, all without someone noticing?"

"Stranger things have happened," I said, trying to sound ominous, but more likely sounding like I was floundering for a rationale. "Who would want to make some of your customers sick? Who are your enemies?"

"You're serious." She gave me a sidelong glance. "As the *Oxford English Dictionary*."

She blew out a sigh and looked across the waters of Trout Lake, its cottage-lined far shore maybe half a mile away. Finally, she said, "I don't know about enemies, but there are a couple of people who wouldn't mind seeing me fail."

After another sigh, she started talking.

And I opened the memo app on my phone and started taking notes.

Rafe squinted at me over the top of a too-hot-to-eat pizza. "Hang on, *that's* why Kristen and Holly have kept a minimum half-mile distance between them for almost two decades?"

"Apparently." I'd also found it hard to believe, but Kristen had been adamant. Ever since I'd clued in to the fact that my best friend and my library colleague barely spoke to each other, even though they'd graduated from Chilson High School only one year apart, from very small graduating classes, I'd wondered why. Eventually, I'd decided it was just a personality thing and gave up any and all attempts at reconciliation. But in asking Kristen about enemies, the whole story had come out.

First, she'd mentioned Parker McMurray, a failed restaurateur who now worked as manager of the hardware store, as a possible enemy. "Parker wants all restaurants to disappear from the face of the earth," she'd said. "Especially restaurants that are successful."

Although it seemed like a stretch from wacky opinion to poisoning strangers, I'd dutifully tapped the name into my phone.

"But," she'd gone on, "if I have an enemy list, I'd have to say Cherise Joffe is way up there."

I'd paused, then typed in the name. And waited. Eventually the whole story had come out.

Now Rafe was shaking his head. "Tell me again. Because I can't have heard right."

I knew what he was feeling. After Kristen had told me the story, I'd called Holly, and she'd given me the same tale, almost word for word. "You sure you want to hear this a second time?"

Rafe nodded and served me a piece of piping-hot yumminess. We were at Hoppe's Brewing, a place we rarely ate on a summer weekend because the wait time to get a table was ridiculously long. But a couple of weeks ago we'd heard that the owners had implemented an online reservation system, and here we were, even though we'd had to wait until eight thirty to get a table. There were adjustments you had to make when living full time in a place that tripled its population in the summer, and accepting the change from being able to walk into any restaurant and get a table anytime you wanted to having to make a reservation three weeks in advance was one of them.

"Waiting with bated breath," Rafe said.

I nodded and started the story again. "It was about this time of year, back when Kristen was going into her junior year." Or had it been when she was a sophomore? One of those. "Kristen and Holly were trying out for the cross-country team."

He gave me a look. "Not a sport that tends to cut anyone. Some seasons they don't have enough kids to compete at invitationals. And it only takes, what, five?"

I had no idea. "Anyway, the coach had everyone run the school course, and timed it. Somewhere on the back part of the course, Kristen and Holly were running next to each other on a narrow part of the trail. Their feet got tangled up with each other, and they both went down hard."

Rafe raised his hand to ask a question. "Was one of them hurt?"

"No. But it had just rained. They landed in this huge mud puddle, and they came out looking like they'd been wrestling pigs."

The love of my life nodded solemnly. "Wish I'd seen that."

"Both teams, girls and boys, practiced together, so when Kristen and Holly finally showed up at the finish line, everyone was watching. Some guy that Holly had a huge crush on started laughing. Kristen didn't care, but Holly . . . Holly was so embarrassed that she walked off the course and never came back."

"Let me guess. Holly still blames Kristen for her fall into the mud and subsequent humiliation."

I nodded. "And Holly still wants an apology, something Kristen says she'll never do, because she didn't do anything wrong." Rafe made a rude noise that I ignored. "Yes, they're now both fully functioning adults and you'd think they'd have moved on from that day, but apparently not. Everything Kristen does irritates Holly, everything Holly does irritates Kristen, and never the twain shall meet."

"Never is a long time," Rafe said.

"Yes," I said slowly. "But I think it's mostly that their personalities are chalk and cheese, as the English say. I honestly don't see any scenario in which they'll ever do more than tolerate each other."

Rafe waved his fork in a circle. "Okay, that all makes a weird sort of sense, if you know what those two are like, and we do. But how is this involved with what happened to the Three Seasons ice cream cones?"

"I asked Kristen about enemies," I said. "About who might have intentionally done something to it to make Three Seasons look bad."

"Tell me she didn't say Holly."

"She did not." Which was good, because Holly was my friend, and even though she could be prickly, she was a good, kindhearted person and it would take a lot of evidence to convince me that she could do anything that hurtful. "It's Cherise Joffe," I went on. "She manages Angelique's restaurant. Holly and Cherise have been best friends since elementary school."

Rafe looked at my plate, which still had half a pizza slice on it. I shook my head and he served himself another piece. "Still not seeing the connection."

I wasn't sure I did, either. "Kristen is convinced that because of what happened between her and Holly, that Holly has talked Cherise into hating her, too."

Rafe frowned, looking off into the distance, and I let him sort out the pronouns as I ate a couple bites of pizza.

"Okay," he finally said. "Enemy by association, I guess. But it's a big jump from hating your friend's enemy to sprinkling poison—or whatever—into a vat of ice cream."

"Kristen says that when she opened Three Seasons, Cherise walked in, looked at the menu, and told her it would never last. Then, after Three Seasons was on Trock's show and started getting national attention, Cherise has never missed a chance to make snide comments."

"Still." Rafe reached for his pint of beer. "Not sure I'm buying it."

I understood exactly how he felt, because I was feeling the same way. "Kristen's in a bad place," I said. "She doesn't seem to want to do anything about anything until the blood tests from people who had allergic reactions come back. That's Monday, at the earliest. She seems fine with sitting back and waiting for . . . whatever to happen."

Rafe sat back. "Wait, are we talking about the same person? The one who has a five-year plan that she adjusts every calendar quarter? The person who wouldn't recognize indecision if it jumped up and bit her on the kneecap?"

"Yep."

He frowned. "We have to fix this."

I forked off another bite of pizza. "Yep," I said again, and on the inside, I smiled.

Now that we were together on this, nothing would stop us from helping our friend.

Chapter 4

By the time Rafe and I had eaten as much of our pizza as we could, I'd also told him that the word from Kristen's staff was that none of them had seen anything or anyone out of place during the time frame when the ice cream cones must have been tampered with.

"Misty had to leave on some errand," I told him as I slipped the last three pizza pieces into our to-go box, "so I didn't talk to her, but I did to everyone else."

"You believed them?" Rafe reached for a half piece of pepperoni that I'd left behind and popped it into his mouth.

"I did. Yes, I know I'm usually the worst person ever for detecting liars, but this was different. Is different. This is for Kristen. And, anyway, I know these people, so it wasn't like talking to strangers. It was more like being able to tell whether or not, um"—I hunted around for a comparison—"whether or not Reva Shomin was lying."

Rafe's puzzled look smoothed out when I lifted a hand to wave at Reva and her husband, who were being ushered to the table next to us. I wasn't sure what her husband did, and was only mostly sure that his name was David, but Reva owned Shomin's Deli, my favorite downtown lunch place. She was about my age, and she and her kids were regular visitors to the library.

"Hey, Minnie. Rafe." Reva, whom I'd been inclined to like the first time I saw her since her hair was just as black as mine and almost as curly, sat in the chair closest to me and hitched it around to face Rafe and me. "I heard about Three Seasons. How's Kristen doing?" she asked, her face showing nothing but concern and sympathy.

I'd lived Up North long enough that I wasn't surprised that the other restaurateurs in town knew what had happened, but I could still be caught off guard by the kindness and sympathy offered so easily.

After a quick glance at Rafe, who gave me a shrugging nod, I told her the truth. "Not good," I said, and told her what little I knew, leaving out the parts about me talking to the Three Seasons staff and asking Kristen about enemies.

"It's so weird," Reva said, pushing a lock of hair that had escaped her ponytail behind her ear. She paused to tell her husband to order her a two-piece fish fry and a half pint of cider, then turned back to me. "I just can't imagine anyone in Kristen's kitchen making a mistake like that."

I took a breath and plunged in. "Which is why I asked her if she has any enemies."

"Enemies?" Reva sat up straight. "You think somebody *intentionally* poisoned people?"

Rafe nodded. "Needs to be considered."

"Wow." She flopped back against her chair. "That's . . . that's nuts. Not everyone gets along with Kristen. I mean, no one gets along with everybody, right? But to think someone hates her enough to poison people? Are you sure?"

"No," I said. "But what is it they say? That once you eliminate the impossible, the improbable is the only thing left." Or words to that effect.

"Huh." Absently, Reva tucked back the strand of hair that had again escaped. "Anyone who runs a restaurant ends up with unhappy customers. I suppose if one of those happened to be a psychopath . . ."

Her husband looked up from his perusal of the beer list. "Estimates are that thirty percent of us have some level of psychopathy."

Right. A psychologist. That's what Reva's husband was.

I hitched my chair forward and lowered my voice. "Kristen mentioned Parker McMurray." And Cherise Joffe, but I wasn't ready to throw her name out into the open. Not yet, anyway. "Do you know anything about him?"

Reva and her husband looked at each other. "Too much," he muttered.

She touched his arm, saying to me, "David can't make a diagnosis since Mr. McMurray isn't his patient, but I'll tell you for free that McMurray is a miserable excuse for a human being. About ten years ago, he took every penny he had and opened a restaurant without ever having worked in one in his life, and when it failed, he blamed everyone but himself."

"Including Reva," David said darkly.

"And every other restaurant in town." She nodded. "It was our fault for taking away his business, the chamber's fault for not pulling in enough people, the state's fault for having so many regulations, the city's fault for not keeping the streets clean enough."

"He's a shift manager at the hardware store," Rafe said. "I run into him every once in a while. I forgot about his restaurant."

Reva smiled. "Well, it didn't last long. And ever since then, he's made it his life's mission to tell the world that the restaurant scene is decadent and is a sign of the pending apocalypse."

"She's exaggerating," David said. "But not by much."

"If he poisoned Kristen's dessert," Reva said slowly, "is he going to stop? Or is he going to keep going? Is he going to sabotage my place next?"

The four of us looked at each other.

"Um, I didn't mean to scare you," I finally said. "This is nothing but sheer speculation."

"Sure." Reva nodded. "Speculation. That's all." She pushed her chair back and stood. "Honey, I'll be back in a few minutes, okay? I just want to make sure I locked up."

She hurried off. David watched her go. "You know," he said, "it wouldn't hurt to install security cameras at the deli. Can either of you recommend anyone?"

I could not, but Rafe had recently contracted for

upgrades at the middle school. They dove deep into a technical conversation and I half listened, but half wondered if I'd unintentionally started a small restaurant-based panic.

When I woke up the next morning, for a brief and wild moment I had no idea what day it was. My first guess was Thursday, but that couldn't be right because the sun streaming through the windows was way up and by then I should have been long up and gone. I next guessed Friday, which also couldn't be right because Rafe and I had gone out for pizza Friday night, and that had only been the day before; ergo, today was Saturday.

"Excellent," I said, sliding from underneath sheets and Eddie and oozing myself into the bathroom for a quick shower. It had to be quick because downstairs I'd heard breakfast preparation noises and was pretty sure I detected the rejuvenating scent of coffee. Since it was Saturday, Rafe was almost certainly going to some buddy's house to help with something or other and was probably headed out soon.

Because I'd synced our calendars, I lived in the hope that someday he'd start adding those things to his phone and I'd be able to see them and schedule my plans accordingly, but he persisted in not grasping that spending all day Saturday helping a friend was a real appointment.

My last attempt to shift his habits had met with a blank stare and a typical Rafe response. "Why? I'm right here. Just ask me what I'm doing." When I'd patiently pointed out that we weren't always together and sometimes circumstances required that I commit to plans without having time to contact him, he'd shrugged.

"That can't happen very often," he'd said. "Besides, there's no way I'll know weeks in advance when someone might need help on a weekend. Guys don't plan like you do."

They should, but I'd had the sense to keep the thought to myself.

"Anyway," Rafe had gone on. "I'm still doing payback for the help we got in July for working on the gazebo."

Now, as I trotted down the stairs, I smiled at the thought of our gorgeous backyard gazebo. It was perfectly sized for a small table and two chairs, which meant one chair for me, the table for a book, and the other chair for my feet and Eddie, whichever came first.

"For you, madam," Rafe said, pouring coffee into a mug. "Would you like your breakfast served inside, or al fresco?"

I glanced at the outdoor thermometer. Already seventy degrees with a humidity level far past the tolerable status. "Inside," I said, pulling up a stool and reaching out for my mug. "Have I told you lately how wonderful you are?"

"Not since last night," he said, shaking his head sorrowfully.

"Huh." I sipped my coffee, to which he'd already added my happy amount of creamer. "Well, you are. I promise to never take you for granted."

"Yeah?" He flipped the frying eggs. "Works both ways, missy."

"Mrr."

We both looked at Eddie, who was standing in the doorway between the kitchen and dining room. "You're wonderful, too," I told him. "Goes without saying."

"Mrr!"

"But we should say," I added quickly. "Every hour on the hour."

Rafe winced. "Don't tell him that."

"I said 'should.' Not that we would."

"Mrr!!"

"Pretty sure the distinction is lost on him," Rafe said. "Your wonderfulness status just went down a point."

Oddly, I wasn't too concerned with my ratings drop. "Will it go back up if I pay the electric bill today?"

"And back to the top she goes." He slid two eggs onto my plate and three onto his. Turning to the oven, pot holders in hand, he pulled out a sheet pan of cooked bacon and added a few slices to each of our plates.

It didn't take long to snarf down breakfast, and soon Rafe was out the door, tool belt in hand, and I was doing one of my most hated chores: washing greasy things.

"One more reason to be grateful you're a cat," I said to Eddie, who was watching my efforts from a windowsill that wasn't quite deep enough for him. "You never have to do dishes."

He stared at me, unblinking, clearly communicating that there were an infinite number of reasons to be happy about his feline status.

"Well, sure. I get that, and . . ." But I wasn't sure where I was going with that, so I started telling him about the waffle cones, and Kristen, and how so far all I'd done was frighten Reva Shomin.

"Next," I said, "I need to find out more from Misty Overbaugh. Harvey said she'd left to run an errand downtown, and I saw her car outside Pam's store."

My recollection capacity for car makes and models was on the far end of the bell curve. I was okay with colors, but that wasn't much help since most cars seemed to be black, white, or some shade of gray. However, I was excellent at reading bumper stickers, and this year she'd put on a "It's not burned, it's blackened" version, and how many of those could there be in Chilson?

After the dishes were done, I patted Eddie on the head and walked downtown through the wall of humidity. I stood at the glass front door of Pam Fazio's store, Older Than Dirt, and knocked.

Pam's head popped out through the curtains that separated the front from the back. I waved, and she came out to unlock the door.

"Morning, Minnie. Coffee?" She ushered me inside, locked the door behind me, and we went to the back, where the coffee was still dripping. Pam, an Ohio refugee from corporate America, had opened her eclectic retail store a few years ago, and it had been a success from the start. Though her place was primarily antiques, she sold anything that fit her goal of only selling things that made her say, "Hey, that's cool!"

She filled two mugs, handed me the creamer, and asked, "To what do I owe the pleasure? If you want to buy Rafe a wedding present, you've come to the wrong place."

"Oh, I don't know. He's a sucker for plaid lunch boxes."

Pam tipped her head back, her short dark hair rippling as she laughed. "I dare you to buy him one."

The temptation was strong, but I was here on a mission. "Got a question for you. I was hoping to talk to Misty Overbaugh. Did she stop in here yesterday afternoon? I thought I saw her car."

"Sure." Pam nodded. "She was here for quite a while."

"Did she seem upset?"

Pam's eyebrows went up, then she nodded slowly. "That's right. I heard about the troubles at Three Seasons. I wonder if that's why . . ." She trailed off.

"Why what?" I asked.

"Um." Pam shifted from one foot to the other. "Like I said, Misty was here for a while. She said she really likes the kind of things I have here, and she was wondering if I'd done any interior decorating."

I waited, because there had to be more.

"But as we kept talking," Pam said, "it became obvious that she doesn't want to decorate a house. She wants to decorate a restaurant."

That didn't make sense. If Kristen was going to revamp Three Seasons, she would have mentioned it to me.

"And she wasn't talking about Three Seasons," Pam said, blowing out a breath.

"You mean . . ." My stomach clenched.

Pam nodded. "Misty wants to open her own place."

About the last thing Kristen needed right now was a head chef who was about to quit.

I said as much to Eddie, but he was busy cleaning his back feet and didn't respond.

"You could at least pretend to care," I told him, which got me the same response. Absolutely nothing. Sighing, I put my feet up on the extra gazebo chair and tried to clear my mind by admiring the view.

This time of year, Janay Lake was much obscured by the boats in Uncle Chip's Marina, my own little houseboat being one of them. It was comforting to know that in a few weeks most of the boats would be gone and our lake view would be restored, as long as you didn't mind the fact that no boats also meant pending winter. Which I didn't, because I liked snow and how it had the power to change the world overnight.

I let my thoughts wander, through the crisp days of fall, the holidays, ski season, and the muddy maple syrup season, then came back to the topic at hand.

If Misty was opening a restaurant, could she have poisoned the ice cream cones to ruin Kristen's reputation and create a larger clientele for herself? After finishing the thought, I revised it. Because she was head chef, of course she *could* have done it. The question was, *would* she?

Eddie, who in spite of his fur coat didn't seem bothered by the heat, jumped onto the table and looked at me.

"It's too hot to scold you," I said. "Today you get a free pass for sitting where you don't belong. Just don't get used to it."

He promptly curled himself into a cute little ball of Eddie and, seconds later, was snoring.

"Do all cats snore, or is it just you?" I asked, but softly, because I didn't want to disturb his sleep. Silly of me, because Eddie asleep now meant a wide-awake Eddie at three in the morning, but cats had a powerful force field that projected Do Not Disturb, even when asleep.

"Maybe even especially when asleep," I murmured, and smiled as one of his ears twitched.

I had a copy of *Perestroika in Paris* by Jane Smiley on my lap, but even the thought of turning pages made me break out in a trickly sweat, so instead I sat quietly and planned my next steps, investigation-wise.

Until I could talk to Misty myself, I didn't want to tell Kristen anything about the possibility of her head chef taking the leap to go out on her own. So I needed to get hold of Misty.

Then there was Parker McMurray. I needed to learn more about him. If he was as nutty as Reva thought, maybe I could learn something from the sheriff's office, if Ash was in the right mood.

And what I really needed to do, most of all, was make sure Kristen was okay.

I slid my phone out from underneath Eddie's front paws and sent a text message.

Hey. How are you doing? I can come over, if you want.

I watched the phone and saw the triple dots of an incoming reply. Then they stopped.

And though I waited and waited, she never responded.

Chapter 5

That night, I stepped up and took care of dinner all by myself. Rafe had been doing hard physical labor much of the day, so he'd earned a big meal, but the only exercise I'd had was a walk downtown and some half-hearted cleaning. The obvious solution was to order sub sandwiches from Fat Boys Pizza: full Italian for him, veggie for me.

"Pickup or delivery?" asked the voice on the other end of the phone. Fat Boys wasn't far, so it seemed ridiculous to have it delivered, yet three blocks was three blocks. The combination of heat and humidity made walking unattractive, but summer parking issues meant I could wind up in a parking spot that was farther from the restaurant than our garage.

"I'll pick it up," I said, and felt absurdly proud of myself for not giving in to the delivery option. Rafe was about to get in the shower, so I called up the stairs. "I'm walking over to Fat Boys to pick up dinner."

"Okay," his voice floated down. "Take it slow. A melted Minnie will mean another fitting for the wedding dress."

As if. "Duly noted," I muttered, and headed out. There was no way on this green earth that I'd drive all the way to Dearborn for another dress fitting. My mother had insisted on three, which as far as I was concerned was two too many, and called and texted me regularly asking if I'd lost or gained weight.

I tried to understand, and part of me did. Mom and Dad had two children. I was the only girl, and my brother, Matt, older than me by nine years, had married twenty years earlier. It had been a long time since there'd been a Hamilton wedding, and Mom was making the most of it.

It was hard going for her, because Rafe and I had resisted almost all of her efforts to make our wedding a glorious extravaganza. The only things we'd caved on were my shoes and the reception chairs. I'd been fine with using a pair of off-white heeled pumps I hardly ever used and having our guests sit on folding chairs Chris Ballou, the marina's manager, swore would be fully cleaned and dusted. But I was now the owner of a glitzy pair of strappy heels, and a rental place would be delivering white chairs the day before the wedding.

I pushed all that to the back of my brain—especially the part about the chairs, because although someday I'd admit to Mom she was right about them, that day wasn't today—and opened the door to Fat Boys.

Inside, the forty-something night manager was staring at his phone. We were more acquaintances than friends, but even so, it was easy to tell that he was horrified by something.

"Hey, Brendan," I said, going up to the counter. "Something wrong?"

"What?" He lifted his head and blinked me into focus. "Minnie. Right. Your order. It'll be up in a minute."

"Is something wrong?" I asked again, because clearly something was.

"No, all good." He pasted on a smile, but his fearful glance at the phone he'd laid on the counter told a different story.

I leaned over. He'd put down the phone faceup, and I read the upside-down words with growing horror. "Fat Boys Pizza has no business being in business. The kitchen hasn't been cleaned properly in years. And in the time they take to make a pizza, you could fly to Italy and get a real one. You can get better food in an elementary school cafeteria."

"Is that a review site?" I said, my voice rising. "Which one? I'll put up a positive review right now." I pulled out my phone and started typing.

Brendan managed a smile. "Thanks. Appreciate it. But . . . we're not the only ones."

I stopped in the middle of spelling "scrumpdil-lyicious." "What do you mean?"

"Every restaurant in town is getting bad reviews right now. And I don't mean normal bad reviews. Those happen. You get used to it. But this . . ." He turned his phone off, making the bad news go away. "This is different."

"Different how?"

Brendan spun his phone in a wobbly circle. "Most bad reviews talk about something specific. A wrong order. Rude waitstaff. A bill with the wrong amount. These are more general, but more vicious."

"'These'?" I echoed.

"Well, like I said, everyone in town is getting bad reviews. But they're being posted every day. We're getting more bad reviews than we are good ones."

That was beyond weird. "The bad reviews are from different people?"

"Different screen names, anyway. Hard to tell if they're from one person or a bunch of them. An IT person might know, but . . ." He shrugged.

After paying for our dinner, I headed out into the heat, thinking about what Brendan had said, and quickly came up with more questions than answers. Could the wretched reviews be a planned effort? If so, was it one person, or a group? Would Josh be able to figure out if all the postings were from one person? And most of all, were the reviews related to the poisoning?

I was pulling out my phone to call Josh, when it rang in my hand, making me jump.

"Hey, Mom," I said, juggling phone and food, trying not to drop either one. "What's up?"

A huge sigh gusted into the phone. "Oh, honey. We have a problem."

I burst in the front door and shouted for Rafe, who came running. When I told him what Mom had said, he gave me a long look. "To summarize. Mr. Welsh, the minister from your parents' church that we met over the holidays, the guy who was going to marry us, took a bad fall while skateboarding with his kids, broke his leg in three places, and now needs surgery. He can't possibly travel north for the wedding, so we now have no one to officiate."

"Yup." I pulled in and released a shaky breath. "We need to call Aunt Frances."

"After we eat." My beloved took the bag of food from my hand and led me from the front door to the dining room, which was pretty much my favorite room in the house, because the parts that weren't doors or windows were clean white bookshelves. Every book Rafe and I owned was on these shelves (except for the handful scattered around the kitchen, living room, study, bathroom, and bedroom), and the sight of our lifetime accumulation of knowledge and entertainment almost always lifted my spirits.

We inhaled our sandwiches, and I put my phone on speaker, put it in the middle of the table, and called my aunt. "Wondered when you'd call," she said. "Your mom already filled me in."

"And you already have ideas for a replacement?" There was a lift of hope at the end of my question.

"I have one," Rafe said.

"Since when?" I asked, surprised.

"Since right now." He grinned. "My buddy Tank is deejaying the wedding, right?"

I nodded. Rafe's friends came in all shapes, sizes, and breadths of competence and reliability, so initially I hadn't been convinced that Tank was the best choice, but I'd eventually learned that Tank was, in fact, an excellent deejay, proving once again that all things are possible.

"Well," Rafe said, "Tank has one of those online wedding-officiant licenses. He's married a bunch of people."

My aunt didn't say anything, but she didn't have

to. There was only one possible response. "Absolutely not."

The love of my life eyed me. "Why?"

So many reasons, starting with the fact that my mother would have a canary and ending with the fact that I wasn't sure that I'd feel married if one of Rafe's high school friends pronounced us husband and wife. I took his hand. "Tank will be busy setting up his equipment. Adding more jobs would distract him, and you know how he likes to get things right. We'll come up with something else. Right, Aunt Frances?"

The sound of throat clearing emanated from my phone. "Yes. The wedding is six weeks away. Plenty of time to find a new officiant."

The three of us did some brainstorming, with Aunt Frances making a list of names. When the ideas ran dry, she arranged the names in order of desirability and assigned most of the names to herself, a few to me. "We need to start straightaway," she said. "Talk to you soon."

She hung up, and Rafe looked at me. "If all of those fall through, we'll always have Tank."

His eyes were crinkled at the corners, so I assumed he was laughing at me, but I let it go, because I was already writing my mental to-do list for the next day.

Since, if possible, I followed through with any and all plans that I made, after a late and leisurely breakfast the next morning out on the back deck in air that, mercifully, had dropped in humidity, I left Rafe and Eddie behind and headed downtown.

The bells that hung on the door of Gennell

Books & Goods jingled cheerfully as I stepped inside. Carpet muted the sound of my footsteps, and I closed my eyes to pull in my favorite store scent ever: brand-new books. I didn't have to see to know that the walls were lined, floor to ceiling, with heavily laden bookshelves. To me, it was an atmosphere of optimism and hope, and the comfy armchairs and soft lighting I'd already noted only pushed the positivity up a notch.

"Good morning!"

My eyes opened fast. "Um, hi," I said. "Are you Blythe?"

"That's me." The fortyish woman smiled at me. "And you're Minnie Hamilton, the bookmobile cat lady."

By now I was used to Eddie being more famous than I was, so I nodded and returned her smile. "Sorry I haven't introduced myself before now. I've stopped in a couple of times, but you were always busy."

She laughed and came forward to shake hands, flipping her long auburn hair back over her shoulders. "Never too busy to talk about books with the bookmobile lady."

The press releases I'd seen had told me the bare bones about Blythe Gennell. She'd grown up in northwest lower Michigan, left home for the lights of the big city, but had returned to raise her children in a small town. That she seemed to be making an instant success of the best kind of store ever was a huge bonus to me, because the used-book store had closed last winter.

"I need a recommendation," I said. "My, um,

friend was in a skateboarding accident and I'd like to send a book to help him recuperate."

Blythe put a hand to her chest. "Is he going to be okay?"

"Sounds like it."

She blew out a breath. "Good to hear. So. What can you tell me about your little friend?"

After I made it clear that the skateboarding friend was a full-grown man, not a child, and that I barely knew him, Blythe diverted from the path we'd been taking to the middle grade books and we spent a few fun-filled minutes choosing between Agatha Christie's *The A. B. C. Murders*, *A House for Mr Biswas* by V. S. Naipaul, and *An Officer and a Spy* by Robert Harris, settling on Mr Biswas. Blythe told me that she could gift wrap and ship the book, and I happily handed over my credit card. "Next time my wedding officiant has an unfortunate sporting episode, I'll come back to buy more."

"I'll be here," Blythe said. Her laugh was bubbling and contagious, and I felt a sudden certainty that we would become friends.

And one of the things friends did was look out for each other. "Out of curiosity," I said, watching her wrap the book in bright yellow paper patterned with multicolored confetti, "do bookstores get online reviews like restaurants and hotels?"

"Sometimes." She ripped another piece of gift wrap off the thick roll. "More social media posts than review sites, but there are some of those, too."

"You're getting positive ones, I assume?"

"As far as I know. My husband pays more attention to that than I do. I don't believe good ones, and a bad one could send me into a tailspin that takes days to pull out of." She flashed a wide smile. "I figure the best thing is not to read any of them. Ever."

It sounded like a reasonable plan, and I said so.

But I was also wondering if Chilson restaurants might not be the only businesses getting hit with the wretched reviews.

Thoughtfully, I walked back to the house. Since I was a reasonable adult who did her best to refrain from doing tremendously stupid things, I resisted my impulse to yank my phone from my pocket and check for horrific online reviews of non-restaurant Chilson businesses while I was actually walking. Instead, I waited until I reached the safety of our front porch and sat on the top step, tapping and scrolling.

Some indeterminate time later, the door opened and Rafe poked his head outside. "Are you going to stay out there all day, or what?"

"Or what," I said, still scrolling, and explained what I was doing.

"Huh. What did you find out?"

"That a lot of people are willing to say bad things anonymously."

"Keyboard courage." Rafe held out a hand and helped me to my feet.

"Exactly. But none of the bad ones I read are anywhere close to as bad as the ones like Fat Boys has been having. And saying they're bad reviews doesn't come close to what they're like. Those are down-in-the-gutter nasty. They're . . ." I searched for the right description and came up with nothing.

"Vitriolic?" Rafe asked.

"Ooo, good use of a college word." We bumped knuckles to celebrate the occasion. "And now I'm headed over to the farmhouse to talk to Kristen. Are you coming or not?"

The eventual answer was "Not," as he'd been invited by his buddy Tank to go fishing.

"I thought fishing was an early-in-the-morning thing."

Rafe shrugged. "Fishing happens whenever Tank feels like going."

"Going to be crowded out there." I looked pointedly at Janay Lake, which, now that it was closing in on noon on a sunny August Sunday, was busy with boats of all shapes and sizes.

"Always room for one more."

It finally sank into my brain that the point of going out in the boat wasn't necessarily to fish. Far more likely it was a wish to spend a summer day on the water, hanging out with a friend. But most guys don't tend to say things like that, or even to acknowledge them. Instead, they bury their feelings deep and come up with absurdly expensive ways to circumvent the need to say to a friend, "Hey, I'd like to spend time with you today."

A few minutes later, he headed for the public boat ramp, where Tank was dropping his boat into the water, and I got in my car to drive over to Kristen and Scruffy's.

After her uncharacteristic ghosting, I'd wondered what would happen when I reached out this morning, but Kristen had come back fast with an apology and a flurry of explanations, all related to baby Lloyd, many of which involved bodily fluids about which I would have been perfectly happy to live the rest of my life in complete ignorance.

I parked in the driveway and, after ringing the doorbell once and knocking twice—our prearranged signal—I let myself in. "Yoo-hoo! Is anyone home?"

"In the kitchen," Kristen called. "And yoo-hoo? Seriously? How old are you, a hundred and ten?"

Now, that sounded more like the friend I'd known and loved for so long. A Kristen who wasn't snarky wasn't much of a Kristen at all. Smiling, I went back to her bright and sunshiny lair. The twins were on the breakfast nook table, in what looked like infant-size reclining chairs. A gift from Grandpa Trock, no doubt. Though their eyes were mostly closed, they were still tracking their mom's movements, which was easy, because she was standing at the long countertop, staring at an array of mixing bowls and an equal number of odd-looking waffle irons.

"Um, what are you doing?" I asked.

"This is the batter for the ice cream cones," she said, nodding at the mixing bowls. "And these are the same kind of waffle-cone maker I have in the restaurant. I was going to figure out if an overcooking, then fast cooling, could have created a chemical reaction that could have triggered an allergic reaction in my customers."

There were a lot of "coulds" in there. But Kristen's background in biochemistry meant she thought about cooking differently than pretty much anyone, so it only made sense she was running experiments. There was one problem, though. "'Was'?" I asked. "You mean you're not going to test this out?"

She gave a short, hard shake of her head. "Waste of time. Nothing accidental could have made that happen. The reactions aren't possible."

My hope that she'd pulled out of her funk died a quick death. "Don't lots of discoveries happen through accidents?" I ran through my mental store of chemical history and came up with a grand total of two examples. "Penicillin. Teflon. How can you be so sure about this?"

Kristen took two mixing bowls and poured the batter down the sink. "Because I have a PhD in biochemistry, that's how."

Her tone was beyond snark. I blinked. "Hey. That's—"

"Sorry," she said, her shoulders sagging. "Sorry, sorry, sorry. I don't know what's wrong with me."

"You have twin infants and a restaurant that's . . . that's going through some trouble. You're stressed, that's all. Cut yourself some slack."

She opened the dishwasher. "Can't. Slippery slope."

Kristen was the most driven person I knew. If anyone could juggle twins and a roaringly successful business, it was her. Still, everyone had a breaking point.

"You know," I said quietly, "that you can always talk to me. I'm a good listener."

"Best ever." Kristen flashed a small smile over her shoulder as she put the bowls into the dishwasher. "Thanks, but I'm okay. Honest."

She wasn't. Obviously. I had to wait for her, though. Pushing her wouldn't help. "Okay. Just remember that I'm here for you. Always." I pulled a stool up to the kitchen island. "Now. Which do you want first? Investigation news or wedding news?"

"Investigation." She reached for two more mixing bowls. "Then wedding."

I nodded and told her what I'd learned. Which, even though I told her every detail I could remember, wasn't all that much. "What I'm going to do next," I said, "is find out more about Parker McMurray, talk to Cherise Joffe, read more review websites, and talk to more downtown businesses and find out if they've had any incidents."

"Do you know how much I appreciate you doing all this? Because I do. A lot."

"Well, um, sure," I said awkwardly. "Thanks." Effusive Kristen was even weirder than Super-Snarky Kristen. "You'll let me know when you hear about the blood tests?"

"Soon as I can. And I now forbid any further talk about my problems." She poured more batter down the sink. "On to the wedding!"

"Well, about that. There's a little problem with the officiant."

That story took even less time to tell, and when I was done, she was glaring at me in straight-up Kristen style. "When I asked for the wedding news second, I thought I was setting myself up for good news last. This is so not that."

"Nope. But it'll be fine," I said hurriedly. "You don't need to worry about this. Truly. Aunt Frances is on it, and things will work out. I'm sure of it."

Her face went a little twisty. If it had been anyone other than Kristen, it would have looked like she was trying not to cry. "And here I thought the matron of honor was supposed to be taking care of wedding emergencies."

"No worries," I said. "There's lots of time for something else to go wrong."

"She said with confidence." Kristen smiled.

I smiled back. "And whatever it is, you'll be the first to know."

But given the fatigue and strain writ so clearly on my best friend's face, I hoped that the next wedding emergency would be a very, very small one.

Chapter 6

Rafe, as I should have predicted, was not concerned about finding someone to marry us.

"You're joking, right?" I asked.

In spite of the fact that he'd been out in the sun all day, catching fewer fish than he'd consumed adult beverages, he must have caught my flat tone, because he looked up at me over our dinner of grilled cheese sandwiches and salad. "Not yet. Should I have been?"

"Who, exactly, is going to be available? The wedding is less than two months away!"

Rafe pointed at his face, which was fat with a huge bite of sandwich.

"No," I said. "You took that big bite on purpose so you wouldn't have to answer me, and anyway, you've never let your mouth being full stop you from talking before, so don't pretend you're starting now."

He chewed, chewed some more, and swallowed.

"Not going to believe that I'm trying to be a better human since we're about to become a married couple? That I'm trying to establish better habits?"

"No," I repeated. "And if you are, let me know, because I'd like to weigh in on which habits you should start working on. First would be cleaning out the bathroom sink after you shave."

Rafe put the remains of the sandwich on the plate and reached for my hand. "Minnie, it'll be okay. Things will work out."

I nodded and rubbed my silly eyes, which were starting to blink fast and leak moisture. "Thanks. Sorry for snapping at you. I know you're just trying to help."

"Do you want me to conjure up a cousin that can marry us?"

"That would be great." I smiled. "And it would be fantastic if she's taller than Kristen."

Rafe started drawing up an imaginary list of officiant qualifications, and, after a minute, I started to feel better.

The next day was a library day. On my way out of the house, I found Eddie languishing in a parallelogram of sunshine he'd found on the floor of the entryway.

"You do realize," I said, "that within a few minutes, one of two things is going to happen. Either the sun moves and you're left in the shade, or you have to move to follow the sunshine."

My cat opened one eye, then closed it again.

Since I'd hoped for more interaction—Rafe had left early and I hadn't yet spoken a single word to anyone that morning, I gave him a few thumping pats on his hip. "Hello? Anyone in there? Say 'Mrr' for yes, and 'Mrr' for no."

"Mrr." He flopped his head down and squinched his eyes shut.

I kept that amusing image in my head through downtown, quiet and dark this early in the morning, up the hill to the library, and all the way inside to the staff break room, where I started coffee.

"Morning, Minnie. Graydon here yet?"

Over my shoulder, I saw Gareth standing in the doorway. "Didn't see his car when I came in. Um, are you okay?"

I asked the question because he wasn't smiling, he hadn't made a remark about Kelsey coffee, and he wasn't making eye contact. If only one of the three things had been going, my spidey sense wouldn't have been triggered, but three for three meant a problem. The last time he'd looked like this had been during a super-duper cold snap last winter when a water pipe had frozen.

Gareth shifted from one foot to the other. "We've had another one."

"Another?" The penny dropped. "More vandalism?"

He made a come along gesture with his chin. I quickly poured a cup of coffee and followed him out of the kitchen, down the wide hallway, through the outside doors, and out onto the sidewalk. I slowed, expecting to stop there, but Gareth kept going, so I did, too.

We walked along the edge of the building—I fully regretting my decision to fill a coffee mug so close to the brim—took a hard left at the building's corner, and came to a stop.

Silently, Gareth pointed.

The row of rosebushes, mature shrubs that bloomed spectacularly in June, each of which was a different variety with names I could never remember, the roses that were the pride and joy of the Chilson Garden Club, had been yanked out of the ground in a shocking display of wanton destruction. Large and small branches were broken. Great globs of dirt were scattered hither and yon. Leaves had been shredded to bits of green confetti.

The vandals had struck again.

Gareth and I were still standing there, staring at the raw display, when Graydon hurried around the corner of the building.

"Got your text," he said, hurrying our way. "What's the . . . oh. Oh, no."

And then it was three of us standing there, staring at the ugliness of destroyed rosebushes. Suddenly, I was glad I had a nearly full mug of coffee in my hand. Its warmth, even on this balmy summer morning, was comforting, and the caffeine could only be a help.

It could have been a minute later, or it could have been hours later, when Graydon gave a sharp nod. "Right. Gar, take pictures and send them to me and Minnie. I'll contact the police and the board. Minnie?"

I nodded slowly. This was more serious than a few sprinkler heads. This was damage to a much-loved part of the library. I'd been told that roses preferred the conditions on that side of the building, and since apparently it's nearly impossible to convince a rosebush to bloom where it doesn't want to, that's where they were put when they'd been transplanted from the old library.

This time I needed to step up and support my boss by doing more than the easy stuff. "If you want, I can call the garden club. And I'll tell the staff. Do you want me to do anything else? Write a media release?"

"Good idea," Graydon said. "Sketch one out. After I talk to the police and Trent, I'll let you know whether or not to publish the release. And maybe the police will want to see this, and maybe they won't, but until then we need to leave it alone." He gave Gareth a half smile. "I know it will be physically painful for you. Sorry about that."

"Understood." Gareth was already taking pictures. "The one good thing is this is on the side of the building that people walk past the least."

Which made no sense at all from what I assumed vandals wanted, which was to have their work seen and admired. But since I'd never vandalized anything in my life, I was no expert.

Graydon was on the phone to the city police chief by the time we reached the door. He went upstairs to his office, still talking, and I went to my office to be an assistant director.

I didn't typically make early morning phone calls to people I knew were retired, but this was an exception. I fired up my computer and found the phone number of the current garden club president, Patsy Bissell. Patsy, another of my role models, was a tall, active, and vivacious woman approaching eighty. She had more energy than most people half her age, and there was no job too big or too small for her to tackle.

Even so, this was not going to be an easy phone call, and I was shamefully disappointed when she answered with a cheery hello, because for possibly the first time ever, I had a voice mail message all composed in my head and ready to roll out. "Good morning, Patsy. This is Minnie Hamilton from the library."

"Well, hello, Minnie Hamilton from the library. What can I do for you on this lovely morning?"

I looked out my office window. Right. It *was* nice out. I'd almost forgotten. I turned away from the lure of the blue sky, partly because my window was right above the desecrated rosebushes, and said, "Patsy, I have some bad news for you."

Patsy's first reaction had been to swear a bluer streak than I'd heard in quite some time, reminding me that she'd spent decades in the construction business, partnering with her husband in Bissell Building and Development. Then she sighed and started asking the practical questions. I promised to e-mail her Gareth's photos and told her I'd contact her as soon as we got word from the police that it wasn't a crime scene any longer and that it would be okay to fix the garden.

"You really think the police are going to spend their time investigating a case of minor vandalism?" Her tone was half sarcasm and half hope.

My expectations for a police solve were about the same, but I was assistant director and needed to be positive. "If they don't," I said, "we will. One way or another, we'll find out what's going on."

I said the same thing to Holly, Josh, Donna, and Kelsey, and everyone else I found at the library, including patrons. The reaction of elderly Mr. Goodwin, everyone's favorite patron, if we had favorites, which we didn't, was a fierce frown. "Never fear, Minnie dear," he said, swiping his cane at an imaginary foe. "I'll protect the library with my last breath!"

Stepping out of the way, I said, "Appreciate the gesture, Mr. Goodwin, but I'm pretty sure the police have it covered."

He nodded but kept thrusting the tip of his cane into the air. "Take that, you rascal! I'll teach you to uproot our rosebushes!"

I wondered if anyone ever truly grew up. Then I wondered what would happen if we all did, because what implications would that have for the world? It was a big question, and hours later, I was still wondering (and coming to no conclusion) as I walked downtown for lunch.

My plan was to grab a quick sandwich from Shomin's Deli, then pop into whatever stores weren't super busy and chat with the owner or manager to see if they'd had recent nasty online reviews or any other variety of bad publicity.

I was thinking about stopping in at the chamber of commerce office to see if they'd heard anything, when a distant shout caught my attention. It wasn't a random "Hey" kind of shout, but more a prolonged chant, like you'd hear at a football game. Or, I realized as I drew closer to the sound's origin, a protest.

"Shut. It. Down! Shut. It. Down!"

Mystified, I made my way through the summer crowds and finally saw what was going on. A fifty-ish man in jeans and polo shirt, stocky, with brown hair so short it was almost invisible, was parading up and down the sidewalk, holding up a handmade sign. I couldn't make out the words at first, but then he turned and they were all too clear.

THREE SEASONS = HEALTH HAZARD. SHUT IT DOWN FOREVER!

Fear shot up the back of my neck, burrowed into my skin, and started to trickle throughout my body.

This was not good. Seriously not good.

I sidled up next to Cookie Tom, who was standing in front of his store, arms folded, glaring at the man.

"Hey, Tom," I said. "Who is that guy, do you know?" Though he looked vaguely familiar, I couldn't place him.

"Sadly, yes." Using his chin, Tom gestured across the street. "That's Parker McMurray."

I pulled out my phone and called Kristen. She picked up immediately and said, "Harvey told me. McMurray's been out there for half an hour."

"Did you call the city police?"

"I did," she said. "Turns out there's this thing called the First Amendment. Remember that free-speech part we learned about in high school? It's real. As long as he's not interfering with pedestrian traffic, there's nothing they can do."

"It's slander!" My voice was loud, and I got a few curious looks from passersby. More quietly, I said, "Since when is slander legal?"

"It's not legal, but it's not a criminal offense. This would be a civil case. I was recommended to contact my attorney."

"What did she say?"

"It's a him, but I haven't called."

"After you talk to him, call me right away and tell me what he said."

"Oh, I don't know." She sighed, and all the good feeling I'd had yesterday that Kristen was waking up and starting to fight for her restaurant vanished. "Either this will blow over or it won't. I'm not sure racking up a huge attorney bill is going to help anything."

I made a mental note to contact Leese Lacombe, my attorney friend. She specialized in elder and real estate law, but she was bound to know something about slander. "Have you heard from the health department?" I asked.

"Not yet. Hey, Minnie, I have to go. One of the kids is waking up."

"Sure, but—" I suddenly clued into the fact that I was talking to a thick rectangle of metal and plastic that wasn't connected to my friend.

"Kristen okay?" Cookie Tom asked.

Shaking my head, I slid my phone into my pocket. "Hard to say."

"Well, there's one good thing." He nodded in the direction of the protesting Parker McMurray. "No one seems to be paying any attention to anything he's saying."

I studied the scene. Tom was right. "And," I said, "he seems to be losing his voice."

"Sometimes things just work out. Tell Kristen that we're all rooting for her." Tom patted me on the shoulder and went back to tend to his business.

That Parker's chants were being ignored and growing raspy and hoarse made me feel a bit better, but not enough. I abandoned my intent to talk to downtown businesses—with the streets so crowded they'd likely be too busy to talk to me anyway—and headed for the sheriff's office.

Inside the front door, I stood in front of the glass window. Chelsea Stille, office manager extraordinaire, was at her desk, frowning at her computer screen and typing madly at the keyboard. I waited a moment, then knocked on the glass window to catch her attention.

She looked up, eyes wide in classic deer-in-the-headlights style, and smiled. Standing, she came around her desk and slid the glass window open. "Hey, stranger. What's up?"

"Want to compare wedding-planning woes?"

"Like I want another hole in my head," she said promptly. "If my sisters don't stop arguing about what color they want for the bridesmaid dresses, I'm going to make the decision myself, and lately my favorite color is fluorescent green.

I laughed. "Now, that I'd like to see."

"Speaking of seeing, who are you here for? Detective Inwood is out on lunch, and the sheriff and the undersheriff are in union negotiations."

"How about Deputy Wolverson?"

Chelsea made a face. "He's in the wedding doghouse along with my sisters because he won't help me make a decision about the food. But he's in his office, writing reports. Go on back. I may or may not warn him that you're on your way."

Laughing again, I went to the interior door, waited for her to hit the lock release, and went through and into the long hallway. I passed the interview room, where I'd spent a surprising number of hours, and walked back to the small office he shared with Detective Hal Inwood.

He, too, was tapping away at his computer, and looked up only when I knocked on the metal doorframe.

"Did Chelsea tell you I was here?" I asked.

"Sort of. She said someone was coming back, but she didn't name names." He pointed at an open chair and I sat. "Let me guess. You want to know what we're doing about the poisoning at Three Seasons."

"Poisoning?" I asked. "That's really what you're calling it?" I had been, but it was different coming from law enforcement.

"We kind of have to call it poisoning when the blood tests came back showing the same substance in each of the victims."

"You mean a real *poison* poison? It wasn't an accidental thing?"

He shook his head. "It was something called triticale. The waffle cones were supposed to be gluten-free, but these had triticale cooked into them. People who have allergic reactions to gluten react to this stuff, too."

"But . . ." My mouth hung open. "That's awful. Does Kristen know?"

Ash gave me a look. "This is now officially a crime. You know what that means."

"That you can't talk about it," I said mechanically, then promptly ignored what I'd said. "Did Kristen tell you about her enemies? Parker Mc-Murray and Cherise Joffe? And did you hear that Parker is on Main Street right now, holding up a sign about Three Seasons and chanting that it should be closed forever?"

He nodded. "Joel over at the city police gave me a call. I'll talk to McMurray later on today."

"So you are investigating this?"

"Of course we are. Like I told you," he said, impatience edging into his tone, "we had to wait for the health department to contact us. We can't just poke our noses into things willy-nilly like some people do."

I patted my nose. "My nose is right here, not poking into anything. And 'willy-nilly'? Have you been hanging around my cousin Celeste? Because that sounds like something she'd say."

He grinned, and once again I was reminded what an attractive human being he was. "You know what she said the other day?"

Just like that, we were off the topic of the Three Seasons investigation. I let it happen, because if Ash was determined to keep me out of the investigative loop, outside the loop was where I'd stay.

But more than that, I was concerned about Kristen. What with the twins and running her restaurant, she was being pulled into a long, thin wire, and thin wires had a terrifying tendency to break. Would knowing someone had poisoned her customers stretch her too far?

Chapter 7

I tried to shake off my worries about Kristen. Like my aunt Frances said, if there's a problem you can do something about, get busy doing something. If there's a problem you can't do something about, worrying isn't going to change a thing, so why waste your time and energy worrying?

"Minnie?"

I looked up. Ash had his hands on his desk, clearly about to push himself back, stand, and go check more things off his detective-in-training to-do list.

"Right," I said. "Since we can't talk about Three Seasons or that tri . . . tri . . . that stuff—I have a vandalism question."

Ash mimicked writing notes. "All Three Seasons staff completely innocent. Got it. Thanks for the tip—that'll save me a lot of time." He rolled his eyes in a very undetective-like way. "Now, what's that about vandalism?"

I showed him the pictures Gareth had texted.

"And the other day some sprinkler heads were destroyed and irrigation lines pulled out of the ground."

"Those the same bushes they made all the fuss about transplanting from the old library?"

"The very ones."

"Huh." He rubbed his chin. "Graydon's talked to the city police?"

"Both times. I haven't seen him since this morning, so I don't know what they said. Here." I texted him the photos. "So I was wondering if there'd been other vandalism cases around the county."

"There's always vandalism," he said. "But this has a different feel. Can't quite put my finger on it, though."

"What, you're having a gut feeling?" Feigning shock, I looked over my shoulder. "Don't tell Hal Inwood. He'll write you up, complete with capital letters and exclamation points, and put it in your personnel file."

"You're too hard on Hal," Ash said, but there was a half smile on his face when he said it, which made me happy, because there had been times when I'd feared he was becoming more Hal-like than Ash-like.

Hal Inwood had moved to Chilson with his irrepressibly cheerful wife, Tabitha, after retiring from a downstate detective position, and it hadn't taken long for her to shove him out of the house and into the Tonedagana County Sheriff's Office. Tabitha, who'd retired from a career as a legislative policy analyst, was someone else I wanted to be like when I grew up. How she and the dour Hal had stayed married for so long, I had absolutely no idea, but as long as Ash stayed Ash and didn't turn into Mr. By the Book and Nothing but the Book Inwood, all would be well.

"Is there something else?" Ash asked, standing.

I gave him a long, serious look. "We need to talk about your wedding meal planning. I recommend steak and lobster, with appetizers of caviar and—"

"Out." He pointed at his office door, like a Ghost of Christmas Past with speaking powers of single syllables. "Now."

Laughing, I headed out into the sunshiny sidewalk, leaving behind an irritated Ash and an amused Chelsea. My job there was done for the day.

I stopped at Shomin's Deli and picked up a turkey wrap with avocado and dried cherries to go, and made my way to the narrow pocket park the city had shoehorned into a tiny space between the toy store and Seven Street, a fine-dining restaurant I'd been into all of twice. High-end restaurants were not something I tended to spend much time patronizing, because assistant library directors did not tend to make the kind of income required to make visiting them a regular thing.

I sat on a shady bench and unwrapped my wrap from its paper. Halfway through my first bite, the *click* of high heels approached.

"Minnie Hamilton, I thought that was you!"

As quickly as I could, I chewed and swallowed. "Hey, Bianca. It's been a while. What's new?"

The blond real estate agent dropped onto the bench, kicked off her heels, and started massaging her feet. "Not much and everything at the same time, if you know what I mean."

I laughed. "Actually, I do."

"Might be time to ditch the heels," she murmured. "Is this a sign that I'm getting old?"

"Not a chance," I said, confidence clear in every consonant and vowel. "Because that would mean I am, too, and that can't be the case."

She held out her fist and we bumped knuckles. "Good call."

Bianca Sims, now Bianca Koyne, was one of the most successful real estate agents in the area. She'd married Mitchell Koyne not long ago, and against all expectations, the marriage seemed to be flourishing. Mitchell had been a classic Up North slacker, making a living by cobbling together seasonal jobs in landscaping, snowplowing, ski-lift operating, and construction. Then he and Bianca had met, and next thing we knew, Mitchell was managing Chilson's toy store and making a huge success of it.

Though I was now accustomed to the concept of Mitchell as a fully functioning adult, a teensy part of me missed the slacker Mitchell who had the library's largest ever amount in overdue fines and who spent half the winter next to the fireplace in the library's reading room.

"How's Mitchell doing?" I asked. "Toy store busy this summer?"

Bianca nodded. "Best ever, he says."

"And you?"

Her face curled into a satisfied smile. "No complaints. Matter of fact, I just listed this place." She tipped her head backward.

I'd been about to take another bite of my lunch but lowered it. "Seven Street is for sale?"

"As of ten minutes ago." Bianca glanced at her watch. "No, I'm a liar. Eleven. Might take a while to sell, since I couldn't talk Harold down from what he thinks it's worth, but we'll get there."

She asked about the bookmobile and our upcoming wedding. I must have given reasonable responses, because she didn't stare at me with concern for my sanity, but I was mostly thinking one thing.

Could the sale of Seven Street be related to the trouble with Kristen's waffle cones?

That night, Eddie was bouncing off the walls.

Literally.

I was in our small study, trying to do the adult thing of paying bills on time, but my attention kept getting pulled away from dollars and cents because my cat kept galloping into the small room, coming close to the far wall, flopping down in a sliding stop that ended with a thump at the baseboard, jumping up and running out into the entryway, then doing a cat-size U-turn and starting the process all over again.

After it became clear that Eddie was going to continue his antics for the foreseeable future, I gave up and wandered into the kitchen, where Rafe was cooking smashed hamburgers for our dinner. A dish of coleslaw was on the counter ready for serving, and I was nearly certain it had grocery store origins, but did I care about that? I did not.

"What do you know about Harold Calkins?" I asked, pulling a stool up to the kitchen island as Rafe topped the meat patties with cheese.

"That the guy who owns Seven Street?"

"Sort of. I ran into Bianca today, and she just listed the property."

"Huh." Rafe prodded a patty. "That's interesting."

"Exactly what I've been thinking."

"Conclusions?"

I reached for the bag of potato chips that Rafe had left open on the counter, but he pulled it away from me. "Dinner food, not snack food. But I'll let you have one if you tell me what's going on in that busy brain of yours."

"Probably the same thing that's going on in yours. Does selling his restaurant give Harold Calkins a motive for destroying the reputation of the other restaurants in Chilson? Bianca said he was firm on a listing price, even though she doesn't think it will sell for that."

"Bianca knows what she's doing." Rafe turned and switched off the toaster oven, where he'd put two buns to warm and get just the right amount of toasting. "But I'd guess people are always thinking their property is worth more than it really is."

"Probably. But that's why I was asking what you knew about Harold Calkins. I've never met him, and I don't know anything about him, other than that he owns a restaurant where your average person can't afford to eat."

Rafe pulled two plates out of the cupboard and loaded them with the burger buns. As he continued doling out our food, he said, "Calkins is maybe seventy years old, maybe a little less. He grew up here, left for a while, and came back about twenty years ago with enough cash to buy the building that became Seven Street. Bought it outright, no loans."

Even twenty years ago that must have been a big

pile of dollars. "Do we know where his money came from?"

"You know how people talk." Rafe shrugged. "Lots of guesses. He made a killing on the stock market. He was lucky with real estate investments. A rich relative died and left him a ton of money. He was tied up with the mob."

"The mob?" I laughed. "Seriously?"

"Just telling you what people said."

It was also what people were probably still saying. And even if they weren't, they would when the For Sale signs went up in the Seven Street windows.

"But that isn't the kind of thing I need to know," I said. "What is he like as a person?"

"You mean, is he the kind of guy who would sneak into the kitchen at Three Seasons and add some triticale to ice cream cones?"

When he put it like that, it sounded stupid, but I said, "Yes, that's exactly what I mean."

By now, Rafe had topped our burgers with mustard, ketchup, mayonnaise, and for me, pickles, spooned coleslaw onto our plates, and added a small pile of potato chips. He slid the plates across the counter and came around to sit on the stool next to me, saying, "Calkins didn't come back north after his kids were grown, and they've stayed downstate, so if they have their own kids, they're not in Chilson. I don't know the guy."

"And here I thought hanging out with the middle school principal would be helpful."

"Joke's on you." He grinned and my heart went a little mushy. "But I do know one thing about him. He has a boat over at the marina."

I frowned. "No, he doesn't." I knew all the Uncle Chip's boat owners, and I'd never once run into him.

"New this summer." Rafe bit into his burger.

"Oh. Well." That made sense. Now that I was renting my houseboat out, I didn't attend the regular Friday night potluck parties. I'd been told Rafe and I were more than welcome to come on over, but it would have felt . . . weird, so we hadn't.

After chewing and swallowing, Rafe said, "Maybe buying the boat pushed him into thinking about retiring. Hard to spend much time on a boat when you have to run a restaurant, and from what I hear he's pretty hands-on with the place."

"So he'd know his way around a commercial kitchen."

"Even still, it seems like a stretch. If the guy has the money for a new thirty-six-foot Baja, why would he need to jack up the price of his restaurant?"

"Because that's why he needed to bump the price. To pay off his boat."

Rafe considered this, then nodded. "That sort of makes sense. But it seems like a big risk for a gain that may or may not happen."

"Anyone who owns a restaurant, especially one up here when there are almost no customers seven months out of the year, has to have a high tolerance for risk."

"That," my fiancé said through a bite of coleslaw, "is a very good point."

I gave him a regal nod. "Thank you."

And I moved Harold Calkins to the top of my mental suspects list.

After I did the dishes, we went for a walk. Rafe and I often took a walk in the evening, but this one

had a bigger point to it than exercise, companion-
ship, and fresh air. On this particular walk I wanted
to get a good look at the boat Harold Calkins
owned, and to get any information I could about
the man himself.

I was keeping an eye out for Louisa Axford, my
former next-door dock neighbor, because Louisa
was the marina's unofficial welcomer to new slip
owners, but Rafe tugged me in the direction of the
marina's office.

"Don't want to," I murmured. "You know what's
going to happen."

Rafe gave me a look of wide-eyed innocence
that wouldn't have fooled a two-year-old. "I have
no idea what you're talking about." In his very
next breath he called out, "Hey, Skeeter. Chris.
What's up?"

Chris Ballou, the marina's manager, and Skeeter
Conlin, perennial marina rat, were probably ten
years apart in age, with Chris pushing fifty, but they
could have passed for brothers with their lanky
frames, weather-beaten skin, and permanent summer attire of shorts, T-shirts, and flip-flops. They
were both sitting on white plastic chairs and were
both holding cans.

From this distance, I couldn't quite make out the
can's pattern. "What are they drinking?"

"Labatt Light," Rafe said promptly.

The man I was soon to marry had many skills,
talents, and abilities, one of which was identifying
beer cans from a remarkable distance. His best effort was a Heineken can in an expressway ditch
from a quarter mile away, but I was still mostly sure
that had been a lucky guess.

Skeeter's feet were propped up on a cooler. As we came closer, Chris reached out with one long leg and shoved Skeeter's feet off and onto the concrete sidewalk. "Down to our last ten, so don't get greedy."

I rolled my eyes, but Rafe gave Chris a serious nod. He gave me a questioning look as he reached into the cooler. I shook my head, and he pulled out a single can. "Orange whip?" he asked, looking at his two partners in beer.

The origins of the phrase were lost on me, but they all knew it meant "Do you want another one?" Chris and Skeeter shook their heads. Rafe replaced the cooler's cover, and Skeeter's feet returned to their resting position.

If I didn't get the conversation moving in the right direction, we'd end up finding two more chairs, sitting down, and being there all night. Rafe would be fine with that, but I was getting itchy to Do Something.

"I didn't hear until today that Harold Calkins got a slip here this summer," I said. "Who left?"

Chris lowered his beer and wiped his mouth with the back of his hand. "Guy down on dock three. He went upscale and got a slip out at the point."

"La-di-dah." Skeeter snorted. "Twice the money and half the fun with all the rules they have. Don't get it, myself."

No. I was not going to let this shift to a hate-on-rich-people session. "What's Harold like?" I asked. "Does he fit in?"

Fitting into the culture at Uncle Chip's was important. In general, boaters were fun-loving people, so things tended to work out. However, not everyone was ready to have super-friendly neighbors living so close for such long stretches of time.

"Maybe, maybe not," Skeeter said. "Jury's still out."

Chris nodded. "He's not here much. Busy running that pricey restaurant. But sounds like he's retiring from that, so maybe next year we'll get a handle on him."

"He drinks beer." Skeeter tapped his can. "But from what I saw, it was that craft stuff."

The three men cogitated that statement. This time I kept my eye roll to myself. If they wanted to go all reverse snobbery with preferring cheap mass-produced beer over quality locally made beer, I truly did not care. "Which boat is his?" I asked.

Chris gave me the slip number, and I headed in that direction. "Be right with you!" Rafe called, which I believed in an "ish" sort of way.

Before I set foot on the dock, my phone rang. Aunt Frances.

"Good news?" I asked.

"Some."

Which could only mean the overall news was bad. "Tell me."

"If you recall, your first choice of a replacement wedding officiant was Rafe's childhood minister. The good news is I was able to track him down. He's moved churches a few times, and he retired five years ago, but he remembered Rafe with some degree of fondness."

That was good to know. I wouldn't have been surprised to learn that Rafe, never one to be cowed by figures of authority, had been tossed out of Sunday school and forbidden to return. "And?"

"The bad news is he's marrying his granddaughter the weekend of your wedding. In South Carolina."

I waited a beat, but that was apparently it. "Huh." Then, because I couldn't think of anything else to say, I said it again.

"This is not yet a serious problem," Aunt Frances said. "We have a long list of possibilities. Have you heard back from the people you contacted?"

"Not yet." Mainly because I hadn't reached out to anyone, as I'd been anticipating success from my aunt.

"Well, we have lots of time. No need to worry. Certainly no need to panic."

But her breezy tone didn't fool me. She was worried.

And if my über-calm aunt was worried, we had a serious problem.

After ending the call, I went to the end of the nearest dock and sat down to gaze at Janay Lake, soaking in the sights and sounds of summer until I felt better. Sunlight sparking off the water, seagulls flitting around, boats zipping back and forth, sailboats slicing their way from wherever they'd been to wherever they were going.

It was watching the sailboats that soothed me. I wasn't sure they'd ever had that effect on me before, but then again I'd never been down an officiant right before my wedding, either.

"Well, this isn't getting the cows milked," I said, quoting a great-uncle who'd died before I was born, and climbed to my feet. A glance at the clock on my phone told me I'd been sitting for longer than I'd realized. It was after eight, and the sun would be down below the horizon in about half an hour. There'd be some dusky twilight for another forty-five minutes past that, but most boats would be off the water soon, if they weren't already.

I dusted off the seat of my shorts and hunted down the slip number Chris had rattled off. Empty, which, given my luck of the day, I should have expected.

"Don't do that," I muttered out loud, because I was feeling my spirits sliding in a steep downward direction. Kristen, even if she didn't know it, needed me to repair her restaurant's reputation, and staying optimistic was essential to . . . well, to making any positive change.

Not that I was trying to change the world. That was a task far beyond my capabilities. But I could try to fix my little corner, and right now that meant finding who'd added triticale to Kristen's waffle cones.

One of the things I'd taken away from my time in graduate school was how to take a great big topic I knew nothing about and create small, manageable tasks that would eventually lead to a conclusion. The research topic at hand was far more real than any academic paper, but the process was the same and, in a nutshell, was to figure out a way forward and get going.

Tonight's small step had been to learn more about Harold Calkins. The tidbits we'd learned were mundane, but you never knew what might be important later on, so I didn't discount the knowledge about his beer-drinking habits. Not completely, anyway. And the knowledge that he'd been talking about imminent retirement since June might also come into play.

I sighed because I didn't see how either one of those things had anything to do with Kristen's waffle cones. After giving the dock piling at Harold's slip a mild irritable kick, I walked around the docks to the Axfords' slip, but their boat was battened down and dark. Even my own houseboat, rented for the summer to Corey and Isabella Moncada, was empty of life.

"No one's home," said a male voice.

I turned. "Hey, Eric. Rafe's over at the office with Chris and Skeeter. The cooler was still half-full when I left, half an hour ago."

"Not tonight," he said with a sigh. "I'm headed home first thing in the morning. Surgery in the afternoon."

Dr. Eric Apney was a few years older than me and was a very successful downstate cardiac surgeon. He'd bought a big cruising boat when he and his wife divorced, moved from marina to marina for a while, and finally landed in Chilson, where he acclimated to the Uncle Chip's crowd faster than anyone ever.

Which meant that he might also be a good person to talk to about Harold Calkins. "I hear there's a new guy in slip seventeen," I said, climbing aboard at Eric's invitation and settling into one of the clean-as-new canvas director's chairs scattered around his back deck. "What's he like?"

Eric squinted in that direction. "Harold's okay, far as I know. He hasn't been around much, but he says it'll be different next summer, because his restaurant will be long sold by then."

Apparently I was the last one in town to learn that Harold Calkins was selling Seven Street. "Bianca Koyne just listed it. Sounded like she thinks the price is too high and it might take a while to sell."

"Yeah?" Eric shrugged. "All I know is that Des Pyken said he's thinking about buying it, and he sounded pretty serious."

"Who?"

"Des Pyken," he repeated. "Desmond. He moved up here last summer, from Grand Rapids, I think it was."

The name was unfamiliar. "Is he a restaurant guy?"

"All I know is he's a golf guy. Met him up at the country club. He's a little weak at putting, but dang, the man can hit them out of the sand traps like no one I've ever golfed with."

Before Eric could descend into a golf-only conversation, which would have been a very one-sided talk because I knew little about the sport, I got up, saying I had to get back to Rafe, and made my good-byes.

When I got back to the marina office, Rafe was deep in a discussion about the upcoming college football season. I caught his eye and pointed at me and at the house. He nodded and flashed both of his hands, our signal for ten minutes. I nodded, not believing him, and headed home.

"What do you think?" I asked Eddie as I shut the front door. "There's no way he's going to be home in ten minutes, so what's your guess for the multiplier? Two? Three?"

"Mrr," Eddie said, bumping the top of his head up against my shin. "Mrr."

"Two? You could be right. Chris is a Wisconsin fan, and Rafe said Skeeter is a Pac-12 guy, so he might be back sooner rather than later." My soon-to-be husband had a master's degree from Michigan State University and so of course he was a die-hard Spartan and Big Ten fan. "But three is the number of suspects, right?" I counted on my fingers as I went into the living room.

"There's Parker McMurray and Cherise Joffe. And Harold Calkins, too, although that's more conjecture than anything else." I sank onto the couch and picked up the copy of *Gift from the Sea* by Anne Morrow Lindbergh that I'd left there the night before. Eddie jumped onto the coffee table and sat upright, Egyptian statue–style, staring at me with unblinking eyes.

"Stop that," I told him. "But then there's Misty. You know, Kristen's head chef who's probably starting her own restaurant? She's the only staff member I haven't talked to."

I sighed. Misty was fun, smart, and talented. I didn't want her to leave Three Seasons. And I certainly didn't want her to have had anything to do with the triticale.

But to help Kristen, I couldn't assume anything. Every suspect had to be investigated, even the one I most wanted to be innocent.

Chapter 8

The next day was Tuesday, and a full bookmobile day. The weather was gorgeous and being out on the road would have been more fun than people should be allowed to have, but I'd begged Hunter, my backup driver, to come in. Trent Ross, the library board chair, had called a special board meeting and Graydon wanted me to attend.

I wasn't going to fuss about that, though, because there would be other fine bookmobile days, Eddie hadn't tried to sleep on my feet and thus mess with my sleep patterns, and in the middle of the night Kristen had texted with the blood test results. She'd apologized for not telling me earlier, but Eloise had been running a slight fever so she hadn't been watching her phone for anything other than messages from the doctor's office.

"So," I said to Eddie as I strapped his carrier into the passenger's seat of my car, "like Aunt Frances is always telling me, time spent worrying is time wasted. Kristen wasn't dodging me or the restaurant issues at all. She's busy with the twins, is all, which is as it should be.

"But at some point," I said as I belted myself into the driver's seat, "she'll be back to focusing on Three Seasons." That was my strong belief, anyway. Sure, it was possible that she'd be so consumed with her job as a mother that she'd lose interest in the restaurant she'd created with her blood, sweat, and tears, but I didn't think so. I thought that as soon as the kids were a little older, when she grew accustomed to the weight of motherhood, she'd come back to Three Seasons, full of life and gusto and ready to take on the world.

"Mrr?"

"Exactly. The best thing I can do for Kristen is find out how triticale got into her waffle cones. Sure, the health department and the sheriff's office will be doing their own investigations, but I have something they don't have."

"Mrr!"

"Um. Sure. Right. I have you." I also cared a lot more than any health officer or detective did. Yes, Ash was a friend of Kristen's, but I was her best friend. He didn't know how hard she'd had to work to convince the bank to finance Three Seasons. He didn't know that she'd worked eighteen hours a day for months to get the place up and running. He didn't know how much time and effort she spent on developing new recipes. And he didn't know how deep she went into background checks when she hired staff.

"And," I told Eddie as we pulled up next to the bookmobile, "that's another reason I don't think any Three Seasons employee would have done anything to the waffle cones. She does everything but talk to their kindergarten teachers." She did, in fact, talk to the middle school teachers if it happened to be a local hire, but that just meant talking to Rafe.

"Morning," Hunter said. "What kind of mood is he in today?" he asked, nodding at our furry friend.

I peered in through the slots of the plastic carrier. Eddie peered back. "On the way up, I was pretty sure he was finally revealing the truth about Area 51, but now he's gone quiet."

"Mrr!"

Julia laughed. "He just has to put you in the wrong, doesn't he?"

It was a classic Eddie move. Probably a classic cat move, too, but since Eddie was the only cat I'd ever known up close and personal, I had no proof of that.

I gave him an air-kiss. "Be good today, buddy. The reputation of the Chilson District Library rests on your shoulders. And on your tail."

"And fur," Julia said.

Hunter nodded. "Not to mention his claws."

I winced. "Let's not go there." To date, Eddie had been the perfect cat gentleman when dealing with patrons, even the small ones who tended to pull his tail, and I devoutly hoped it would stay that way.

After waving good-bye to everyone on the bookmobile, even the four-legged one who couldn't see me and wouldn't have returned my wave even if he could, I walked around the far corner of the building to check up on the rosebush vandalism. Yesterday afternoon, after a quick visit from the city police, Gareth and the garden club had been given a thumbs-up to replant and repair.

They'd done a lot of work in a short period of time. So much work that I pulled out my phone to compare yesterday's photos to today's smoothed dirt and tidy plants. Yes, there were fewer bushes now than before, but other than that, everything looked fine.

I was standing there, comparing yesterday to today, when my phone vibrated. Startled, I dropped it. "Silly," I muttered to myself, picking it up, and was surprised to see Misty Overbaugh's name as the incoming caller.

"Hey, Misty. Thanks for calling me back." I'd left her at least three messages the last couple of days, saying that she was the last Three Seasons staffer I needed to interview about the day of the allergic reactions, and could she please contact me as soon as possible.

"Minnie, I can't . . ." She pulled in a juddering breath. "I'm so . . . it's not . . ."

"Whatever it is," I said, "first thing you need to do is take a deep breath, okay? No, that wasn't deep enough. Try again. There you go, much better. Now one more, because you can never have too much air in your lungs. How's that?"

"Better," she said. "Thanks. I was having a little minute, there."

"All good. Happens to everyone. So what's up?"

For a moment, all I heard was her soft breaths going in and out. Then, just as I was about to ask if she was okay, she said, "Kristen told us that triticale was added to a batch of the waffle cones. That doesn't make any sense at all. We don't have any triticale in the restaurant."

"Yes. That's why I wanted to talk to everyone. Do you remember seeing anything unusual that day? Seeing anyone who shouldn't have been there?"

"No, but . . . here's the thing." She gave a deep sniff, and I was suddenly sure she was crying. "Kristen came in to make the cones, and we served them the next day. I was the last one in the kitchen, and last one in the building the day she made them. And I was first in the next morning."

She stopped talking. I waited. Waited some more.

Finally, through a tearstained voice, she said, "Minnie, I'd left the kitchen door unlocked."

I stared, unseeing, at the replanted rosebushes. If the kitchen had been left unlocked, anyone could have walked in and messed with the waffle cones. And, just like at the library, Kristen had never installed security cameras. "What's there to steal?" she'd once asked, shrugging.

"Please don't tell Kristen," Misty begged. "I don't know how I forgot to lock the door, I never forget, not ever. Except this once, and now they closed Three Seasons and it's all my fault and Kristen can't keep paying us much longer without being open and I don't know how I'll be able to look her in the eye ever again because it's my fault, all of it and—"

I interrupted the stream-of-consciousness dialogue. "Misty," I said gently. "People make mistakes. She'll understand, you know she will. Okay, she might yell at first, but she'll understand."

"You really think so?"

"I know so," I said. "She may yell and scold, but at the end of it, she'll forgive you."

After a few more sniffs, she said, "Okay. I'll tell her. Today. I'll do it today."

"Good. But there's one other phone call you have to make."

"Yeah?" she said. "What's that?"

"You have to call the sheriff's office."

Convincing her took longer than I'd expected. I finished communing with the rosebushes, walked inside, stowed my backpack in my desk, started coffee, watched it drip, and added creamer and nicely hot caffeine to my Association of Bookmobile and Outreach Services mug, at which point I wore her down and she agreed to call Deputy Ash Wolverson and tell him what she'd told me.

"Tell him I sent you," I told her. "No, strike that. It's best if you don't admit to knowing me. Not even my name. Do that and he'll make all sorts of assumptions about you."

Misty laughed. Not a very big laugh, but still a laugh.

When I slipped my phone into my pocket, I was back in my office, sitting down at my desk, ready to start my day. The board meeting wouldn't start for an hour, so I had time to answer a few e-mails. Then again, I'd expected to be out all day on the bookmobile, so there was nothing urgent that needed doing right that very second. Which meant . . .

Smiling inside and out, I picked up my steaming mug of happiness and left my office. Every so often, I liked to wander through the library before anyone else showed up. It was just me, the books, and everything the books contained.

I walked through the main stacks, from the high Dewey numbers to the low, moved over to biographies, then past fiction. The room was silent except for my footsteps and the faint hum of the HVAC system. Silent now, but think how noisy it would be if all the people in the books could talk. If they were all talking at the same time. If they could talk to each other.

"Just think," I murmured, smiling. Because I'd love to hear what Abigail Adams and Amelia Earhart would say to each other. And there was no way Sherlock Holmes and Temperance Brennan would get along, but it sure would be fun to hear them go at it.

"You're doing it, aren't you?"

I looked up. Graydon was sitting on top of the reference desk, legs dangling, his heels bumping lightly against the wood. He was in full board summer meeting gear of khaki dress pants, tie and white shirt, and a navy blue sport coat so dark it looked black. He was also wearing running shoes, which was why I wasn't scolding him for marking the furniture, because he left his dress shoes in his office until the minute before the meeting.

"Who was talking?" he asked. "I was thinking Alexander the Great and Elvis Presley."

Last winter, Graydon had caught me in the middle of one of my morning wanders, only then I'd been actively participating in one of my imaginary conversations. I'd turned a hot shade of red and stammered out an embarrassing explanation. But

Graydon being Graydon, he'd bought into my imaginings and started playing the game himself.

I laughed. "Elvis and Alexander? Hard to think of two people who'd have less in common."

"Exactly." Graydon slid off the desk and we started walking upstairs. "One of two things would happen if they met. Either they'd stare at each other and not have a thing to say, or they'd become best friends because both of them, in their own way, conquered the world."

That was an interesting point of view, and I kept thinking about it as we met up with Gareth outside the boardroom. As per usual, I took a deep relaxing breath before walking into the room, because part of me was still a scared five-year-old about to tell my parents that I'd broken the candy dish that had been a wedding present from my dad's great aunt.

I hadn't recognized the connection until a couple of board meetings ago, when Sondra Luth, the board's current vice chair, had pulled out a piece of butterscotch candy in clear cellophane, winked at me, and unwrapped it.

Then I'd remembered. Sneaking into the living room for a piece of forbidden butterscotch candy. The top of the candy dish slipping out of my small hand, crashing down, cracking the dish and shattering the top into multiple pieces.

It had happened in a living room with a leather couch the exact same color as the boardroom chairs, something I hadn't remembered until Sondra unwrapped her candy. However, although I now recognized the source of my boardroom intimidation, the intimidation hadn't disappeared.

Clearly, life was not like all the half-hour sitcoms I'd watched.

Trent Ross, the library board president, was already sitting at the end of the long, polished table, chatting with Graydon, who was taking the chair opposite. Gareth and I took chairs that flanked Graydon, and the rest of the board members trickled in.

"It's nine o'clock," Trent said, glancing at his heavy-looking watch. "Thank you for attending this special meeting. Our sole agenda item is the recent vandalism. Graydon, could you please summarize?"

My boss nodded. "Thank you, Trent, and I second his thanks to everyone. If it's all right with the board, I'll defer my summary to our maintenance director." He scanned the group for assent, then nodded at Gareth.

"Um, okay." Gareth cleared his throat. "I'm not much for public speaking, but Minnie said I could tell you that I can't be worse than she is, so . . ." He shrugged and the board laughed, which had been my intent, and I saw Gareth's face loosen.

"Okay," he said again, this time with more confidence. "The sprinkler heads were the first thing."

I settled back and listened.

Less than an hour later, I was telling the staff what had happened at the board meeting. Which, as it turned out, wasn't much.

"They didn't decide anything?" Holly asked, frowning.

I shrugged. "Depends on how you look at it. They listened to Gareth, then they listened to Graydon when he told them what the city police had said." Which also wasn't much, but you could only do what you could do.

"And then they didn't do anything," Josh said. He, too, was probably frowning, but I couldn't tell because his back was to me as he filled the handled stainless-steel vat he called a mug with coffee, creamer, and sugar.

"And then," I corrected, "they told Graydon to come up with a solution and gave him financial authority to go ahead and do it, with Trent's approval, and retroactive board approval."

I could see Holly's attention starting to wander the second I started talking about the money end of it, but I was so pleased I could almost feel my skin glowing.

Giving Graydon that kind of latitude with such minimal oversight meant the board trusted him. A board that trusted their director often meant a board that trusted all the staff. And that could easily mean that the staff trusted the board, and that could easily mean that the entire organization ran smoothly and respectfully to fulfill our mission.

"So what's he going to do?" Josh turned, still stirring the glop in his coffee vat.

I looked at him blankly.

"About the vandalism?" he asked, oh so patiently. "You know, what you were talking about five seconds ago?"

Since I wasn't about to tell him the truth, that in those few seconds I'd created a fantasy library where everyone was happy all the time and sang in four-part harmony every morning, I told him another truth. "No idea. He and Gareth are working on it."

"We've never had any vandalism before," Holly said. "If the police catch whoever did it, we wouldn't have to do anything."

Josh slurped up his first caffeine hit. "If it happened once, it'll happen again."

To keep the two from degenerating into a sibling-style spat, I turned to Josh. "Before I forget, I have a nonlibrary IT question."

"My favorite kind." He grinned.

"Those online review sites. Most people use screen names to post reviews. Do you have any way of finding their real names?"

"You mean, like digging into the programming code, diving into the dark web, following ISP addresses all over the world, tracking them back here, and finding out the call is coming from inside the house?"

"Yes," I said, nodding eagerly. "Exactly like that."

Josh shook his head. "Sorry to burst your bubble, but no. Maybe the NSA can, but I can't."

Holly laughed. "An IT guy who can't track a hacker? You sure you deserve all that money you're getting paid?"

"Yeah, well, at least I know how to get to work on time. When was the last day you got here before nine? The day you started working here?"

In a heartbeat, they were squabbling like two-year-olds, and my happy-fantasy-library bubble burst.

But as I watched them trade insults back and

forth, I started smiling, because I'd just come to the odd conclusion that I was okay with a popped bubble.

Late that morning, I decided to take the next step in the investigation and talk to Cherise Joffe, the manager of Angelique's, and the only person other than Parker McMurray that Kristen had named as an enemy.

Since Holly and Cherise were good friends, it sort of made sense to talk to Holly before approaching Cherise. Then again, Holly knew I was best friends with Kristen, and she was sure to know that Three Seasons was closed, so if I asked Holly any leading questions about Cherise . . .

Nope. I was not going to go there. I valued my current relationship with Holly too much to jeopardize it by trying to pump her for information about her own best friend. It wouldn't be right.

Instead, in that restaurant lull that came after lunch but before the dinner prep got really rolling, I trotted myself down to Angelique's. I only knew Cherise from her occasional stop at the library to meet up with Holly, so before I left I took a quick look on LinkedIn to refresh my memory of what she looked like.

Mid-thirties, round face, really long dark hair pulled back in a tidy ponytail . . . got it.

I nodded at her image, then made my way down the hill to downtown and onto a side street to a storefront where, a number of years ago, a women's clothing store had been. Now it was the elegant Angelique's, with furnishings of mismatched antique chairs, white linen tablecloths, and fabric-covered walls hung with pastel-based landscape paintings. I peeked in the front window and saw that only one table was occupied with customers, and they were in the act of putting napkins on their plates.

Perfect.

I reached out to open the door, then backed away. Maybe a back-door approach would be better. Restaurant back doors were where deliveries arrived, where staff tended to park, and where staff entered. The odds of my finding someone who would talk to me would be way higher out of sight of customers.

Angelique's was close to the end of the block, and it didn't take me long to round the last building and return through the alley. It was surprisingly hard to figure out what business was what from their back entries—a restaurant looks a lot like an insurance agency when the doors are both flat gray metal—but I was able to pick out Angelique's easily enough, since Cherise herself was out there, tossing garbage bags into a dumpster.

"Hi," I said, smiling. "You're Cherise, right?"

"That's me. What can I do for you?" She tossed over one last bag, her waist-length ponytail swinging back and forth with the effort.

"I'm Minnie Hamilton. From the library. I work with Holly Terpening."

She flopped the dumpster lid over with a bang. "Minnie. You do the bookmobile. With the cat."

The way she said "cat" stiffened my spine, but I kept my smile going. "That's right. I was wondering if you had a minute to—"

"And you," she said, ignoring my outstretched hand, "are good friends with Kristen Gronkowski. No, wait. She still goes by Jurek, doesn't she?"

Kristen hadn't taken Scruffy's name for a number of reasons, none of which were any of this woman's business. I put my hand in my pocket. "This is a small town, so I'm sure you know that Kristen's having some problems. I was wondering if—"

"If I was cheering?" Cherise laughed. "You bet I am. What is it they say, that bad things can happen to good people? Well, this time something bad happened to a bad person."

"Bad?" I echoed. "What are you talking about? Kristen's the opposite of bad."

Cherise rolled her eyes. "You have got to be kidding. All she cares about is herself. That's all she's ever cared about. So now something bad happened to pooooor little Kristen?" She snorted. "I call it karma."

My vision tunneled. The alley, the buildings, even the dumpster disappeared. All I could see was Cherise Joffe. All I could hear were her words echoing in my head. "So you're not interested in finding out who poisoned the waffle cones? You don't care what happens to a fellow business owner? A fellow restaurateur?"

"You have got to be kidding. I wouldn't help that woman if she was the last person on earth. What has she ever done for me?"

"The success of Three Seasons has brought hundreds of people to Chilson," I said as evenly as I could. "More visitors means more business for everyone."

"As if," Cherise scoffed. "What she's done is stolen my best customers. Who does that? Bad people is who does that. I feel sorry for those kids. With a mother like her, they don't stand a chance." She snorted out another laugh, turned, and walked away from me.

It was her mention of the twins that sent my temper into the red zone. I strode after her.

"Let me make sure I understand your point of view," I said loudly, climbing the back steps, going through the door and into Angelique's. "You don't believe it's part of your obligation as a human being to help others? Whatever happened to the social contract?"

Cherise whirled on me. "I didn't sign any contract with Kristen!" she shouted, her face bright red. "And get out of my kitchen! You have no right to be here. Leave now or I'll call nine-one-one. I mean it. Out. Right now."

But at that point I wasn't paying any attention to what she was saying. I pushed past her, ignoring her outraged shouts. Because on the floor, out of Cherise's view, just past a run of cabinets, there was an outstretched hand.

I hurried forward, rounding the cabinet run, and saw a woman on the floor, lying on her side, not moving. I touched her neck, feeling for a pulse.

Behind me, Cherise gasped. "Remi! Remi, are you okay?"

"Call nine-one-one," I said quietly.

What I didn't say was there was no reason for them to hurry. Remi didn't have a pulse. She also had a very large blue-handled knife sticking out of her chest.

Chapter 9

The ambulance came. The city police came. The city police chief showed up, as did deputies from the sheriff's office, quickly followed by Detective Hal Inwood and Detective-in-Training Ash Wolverson. Somewhere in the middle of all that, I texted Graydon.

Minnie: *Sorry, but something's come up. I'm going to be out for a while longer.*

Graydon: *Nothing bad, I hope.*

Minnie (after thinking about an appropriate response): *I'll fill you in when I'm back at the library.*

Graydon: *Sounds good.*

I slipped my phone back into my pocket and started practicing what I'd say to Graydon. Something like: I was out back of Angelique's, yelling at the manager, who'd insulted my best friend, barged into the kitchen, and tripped over a murder victim. Only I had to say it in a way that didn't make me sound like an unstable loose cannon who couldn't be trusted to tie her own shoes, let alone drive a library vehicle that cost deep into six figures.

"Minnie."

I looked up from my shoes—tied nice and tight, excellent job, Minnie!—and saw a uniformed officer looking at me. This one, unlike all the others milling about, was female, and her badge had a different label. "Sheriff," I said. "Yes, ma'am?"

Sheriff Kit Richardson had been elected sheriff before I'd moved to Chilson, and she'd been reelected by the proverbial landslide every time her name went on the ballot. She was in her mid-fifties, had short, distinguished graying hair, and was, of course, taller than I was. She exuded competence and authority, and most people were intimidated by her. I had been, too, until I'd seen her early one morning on her front porch in a ratty bathrobe, cuddling my cat.

"How do you manage it?" the sheriff asked, tipping her head at the kitchen. "The vast majority of people in this country manage to get through their lives without seeing a single dead body outside of a hospital or funeral home. And then there's you."

"Um." I gave my shoes a quick glance. Still tied. Which was too bad, because a small diversion right then would have been handy.

"Sometimes I wonder what it is about you that you keep getting involved with murder. But then my head starts to hurt, so I stop thinking about it." Sheriff Richardson ran her fingers through her hair. "I suppose you're working today."

"Yes, but I texted my boss that I'd be late getting back."

She gave me a long look. "Detective!" she called.

Hal Inwood, who'd been in the kitchen, poked his head into the room. "Yes, Sheriff?"

"Why haven't you interviewed Ms. Hamilton?"

"I was waiting for—"

"Do it now," she commanded calmly. "Minnie here has a job to get back to, although personally I would recommend she take the rest of the day off. Either way, we don't need to make her day any harder than it's already been. Take her statement and get her out of here."

"Yes, ma'am." He nodded and gestured at a nearby table. "Ms. Hamilton, have a seat. I'll be with you in a moment."

Sheriff Richardson winked at me. "See you later, Minnie. Maybe next time we run into each other it won't be over a murder victim."

I smiled. Sort of. "That would be great."

The table Detective Inwood had pointed to was far too close to the kitchen for my taste, so when the sheriff left me to my own devices, I crossed the room and pulled out a wooden chair at the table near the window. I was pretty sure it was the same table where I'd once had dinner with my aunt Frances and Otto, which had been one of the few times I'd eaten at Angelique's since it was in the same price range as Seven Street. And Three Seasons, if you didn't have the Best Friend discount.

Not much later, Hal Inwood sank into the chair opposite me. I looked around. "We're not waiting for Ash?" I really, truly tried not to sound hopeful, but I must have failed, because Hal gave me a sour look.

"Deputy Wolverson is getting instruction from the medical examiner investigator about best practices for taking photos."

"Understood," I said brightly before he went into any more detail. Some things are best left unsaid, because otherwise they could sink somewhere inside me and get pulled out in the middle of the night in a creepy dream that would end up with me wide awake, sweating, with a pounding heart and the certainty that doom was imminent.

"So," he said, pulling a small notebook out of his inside jacket pocket. "Tell me what happened here this afternoon."

"Outside of someone being killed, you mean?"

"Yes. Outside of that."

I gave him a suspicious look. If he was making fun of me, he was doing an excellent job of hiding his smile. "Okay," I said, and told him everything I could remember, starting with talking to Cherise Joffe in the alley and ending with finding one of her employees dead on the kitchen floor.

"How long were you talking to Ms. Joffe?" he asked, writing in a script so tidy it could have been used as an example in a penmanship class.

This was something I actually knew, within a couple of minutes. I'd checked my phone when I left the library so I could make sure to return in an hour, and I'd noted the time when I'd called 911. "Between six and eight minutes," I said, and explained why I knew so exactly.

He wrote down the numbers. "Dispatch will confirm the call-in time. Is there anything else?"

"Um." I looked toward the kitchen, then quickly averted my eyes from the sight of a gurney wheeling past. "Can you tell me anything? About the victim, I mean?"

The detective flipped the notebook shut and tucked it into his pocket. "Remi Bayliss, aged forty-seven. She had been an employee here at Angelique's since it opened. The manager considered her a key employee."

"Did she have kids? Was she married? Do you have any suspects?"

"No, divorced, and the investigation is underway. Do you have anything else to add?"

Just something that was so obvious I couldn't believe he hadn't said anything already. "This murder and the poisoning at Three Seasons. They have to be related. It only makes sense."

"Correlation is not causation, Ms. Hamilton." Hal stood. "But you can rest assured that we'll look into the possibility. I'll e-mail a draft of your statement within twenty-four hours. Please review and DocuSign at your earliest convenience."

He returned to the kitchen, going back to work.

And, after a moment, so did I.

Graydon and Holly both reacted about the same when I told them what had happened down at Angelique's: expressions of horror, then flat statements of "You should go home." Josh, after blinking at the news, eyed me. "You told Graydon about this? What about Holly?"

I nodded. "They both think I should go home."

"If you were a normal person, then yeah." He shrugged. "But you don't look traumatized."

And I wasn't. I was sad, of course, and shocked that something like this had happened, but I hadn't known Remi, and as Sheriff Richardson had sort of said, this wasn't the first time I'd come face-to-face with violent death. "I promised Graydon that if I started shaking, I'd call Rafe to come get me."

"How's that going?"

I held out my hands. "Rock solid. I could do brain surgery, if I knew how to do brain surgery."

"Good to know," Josh said. "I'll keep you in mind if I need someone to thread a needle for me."

"Pretty sure the last time I did that was . . ." I squinted. "Actually, I have no idea."

"What do you do if you lose a button? Throw the shirt away?"

"I put it in my suitcase, and when we go downstate, I give my mom a pile of mending to fix."

Josh walked off, shaking his head.

The mention of my mom reminded me of her now-daily text messages about finding a new wedding officiant. On my aunt's list, one of the names in the Minnie Needs to Contact column was a college friend who'd gone into the ministry. Last night, after ten minutes of Internet sleuthing, I'd tracked down the website of the church where she was serving.

I'd sent her an e-mail that morning, so it was possible she'd already responded. I pulled out my phone, and lo and behold, there was a return e-mail from her.

My heart beat unaccountably fast as I clicked it open.

So good to hear from you. We really need to catch up! And I so wish I could help you and

your Rafe, but next week I'm headed out on a
two-month missionary trip, and—

Nope. I wasn't going to read the rest of it. I'd
read the full e-mail later. Right now, I just couldn't.

I slid the phone into my pocket and headed back
to my office to put the finishing touches on the September bookmobile schedule. Thirty seconds later,
I pulled out my phone. I needed to tell Kristen what
had happened at Angelique's, and it wasn't a texting conversation. This had to be a phone call.

After pushing the button with her tiny picture
on it, I listened to the phone ring. Three rings later,
I got dumped into her voice mail.

"Hey," I said, and gave her a quick rundown.
"Just wanted you to know. I told Hal Inwood that
Remi's murder and the poisoning of the waffle
cones have to be related, so we'll see what happens." I could feel myself starting to babble, always
a hazard when I was leaving a message. "Right.
Give me a call later, okay?"

This time when I pushed my phone away, it skid-
ded way farther than I intended, zipping all the way
across my desk, off the edge, and onto the floor.

"Why am I so stupid!" I jumped to my feet and
charged around the desk. "Why can't I do anything
right?" I asked, glaring at the phone, tempted to
kick it. "Why can't I do the simplest thing?"

"Because," Graydon said from my office doorway, "you've had a traumatic event today."

I snatched up the phone and transferred my
glare from it to my boss. "Not nearly as traumatic
as it was for Remi Bayliss."

"No, but that doesn't mean it wasn't hard for you. Minnie. Please go home."

"But—" My eyes suddenly filled with tears. I turned away, ashamed and embarrassed by my behavior. "But Eddie's out on the bookmobile. I need to wait for him."

"I know where you live, remember? I can bring him home."

"But they won't be back until six, and the books need to be unloaded, and—"

"And I'm pretty sure I can manage to lug a few crates of books. Go home. Talk to that aunt of yours. Talk to your fiancé. Find a book to read and go sit in the sunshine. Or just sit in the sunshine."

I rubbed at my eyes with my fingertips, then turned around. "You're not going to stop bugging me until I leave, are you?"

"For someone who self-proclaimed herself as stupid a minute ago, you're pretty smart." He picked up my backpack, which I'd dropped on my spare chair, and held it out. "Besides, it's almost four o'clock. If you go home now I'm only losing a couple hours of work."

"Well, in that case." I took the backpack. "Thanks," I said, not looking at him. "I appreciate that you took the time to—"

"Out," he said, pointing to the door.

So I went.

By the time I got home, I'd decided to do something useful with my extra couple of hours by doing some mindless cleaning chores, but the third time I found myself standing in a room with no idea why I was there, I decided that Graydon was right. I'd suffered a traumatic event, and I should accept that I needed some time.

Rafe was busy at school, so I didn't want to bother him, and besides, he'd be home soon. So maybe a talk with Aunt Frances would be helpful. It certainly wouldn't hurt, anyway, since my aunt was one of my favorite people in the world.

The walk from our house, at near-lake level, up to where my aunt and Otto lived included maybe a hundred feet of elevation change. It also included fifteen minutes of mild exercise in the summer sun, helping me to clear my head of its darkest thoughts.

Five seconds after I rang the doorbell, the door was flung open.

"Minnie!" Aunt Frances looked down at me from her position of being eight inches taller than I was. "What's this I hear about my favorite niece tripping over a dead body? And what are you doing on my doorstep? Don't you have a job?"

"If she's your favorite," Otto called from the kitchen, "why is she still on the porch?"

By this time I was inside, but I appreciated his comment.

"Because," my beloved aunt said, "she's also my least favorite niece."

"And the funniest." I scrunched up my face.

"Also the least funny," she said, ignoring me and leading the way back to the sunny kitchen, where Otto was chopping away at vegetables. I slid into the bench seat in their breakfast nook and watched.

Though they'd been married less than two years, the way they worked together made it look like they'd been together for decades. Without any audible discussion, tasks were allocated, ingredients assembled, pots pulled, and utensils wielded.

My aunt, who had the rangy build and cheekbones of Katharine Hepburn, and Otto, who could be mistaken for Paul Newman's brother, weaved around each other with comfort and ease, and the occasional loving touch on a shoulder. It was a pleasure to watch them work, and I wondered if Rafe and I would ever look like that. Of course, that would mean I had to cook more. Well, there was always a downside to everything.

"You're not talking," Aunt Frances said. "And before you ask, yes, I'm still reaching out to ministers about your wedding. I'll text you as soon as I know anything, like you did about your college friend. Talk about today."

Right. I straightened out of the slouch I'd slipped into. "It happened after lunch," I started, and told them the gist of the sad tale in a few short sentences.

"Remi Bayliss," my aunt mused. "Is she related to Deb Bayliss, out on Lake Road?"

"No idea. I don't know her. And no library card." Which made me a little sad, because my biased self thought everyone would be happier if they visited a library. "I called Kristen to tell her but had to leave a message."

Otto gave me a long look. "It can't be easy to find a murder victim, even if you didn't know her."

"No," I said. Violent death is a tragedy in so many ways, one of those being how it impacts those left behind. "I should talk to Holly. She's a friend of Cherise, the manager I was with. Holly can probably help her."

I knew, of course, that Otto was talking about

me, not Cherise, so I smiled at him. I'm okay, the smile said. Honest. Thanks for caring.

"What I don't understand," my aunt said, wielding a shiny and massive metal spoon in a frighteningly competent way, "is why you were at Angelique's in the first place. Yes, I noticed that you glossed over that part of the story, so no trying to weasel out of the explanation."

I squirmed a bit. "What have I told you about the waffle cones at Three Seasons?"

The spoon pointed itself right at me. "Basically nothing."

"Oh. Really? I could have sworn . . . never mind," I said hurriedly, and proceeded to tell them everything I could remember.

At the end of it, I said, "And that's why I was talking to Cherise Joffe. Kristen considers her a serious suspect, but Holly swears up and down that she'd never do anything like that. I don't know her, so I figured I'd stop by and ask a few questions."

My aunt continued to give me a Look.

"It's not like I planned on finding a murder victim," I said. "Believe me, I would never have gone there if I'd known."

But I had, and I'd found Remi. And now I was developing a new sense of responsibility. My brain was correlating finding her body with a need to find her killer, and said brain was already thinking of steps to do that very thing. Though the sheriff's office would be doing their best, it was summer and they were stretched thin with the extra work always brought on by the multitude of visitors. Anything I could do to find a local killer, even if it was a small thing, was bound to be helpful.

"That's not it," Aunt Frances said slowly. "It's Harold Calkins. He's on your suspect list because he wants to retire, is selling the restaurant, and it's possible that he's destroying Kristen's reputation to artificially raise the sale price."

"Possible."

"Do you think the poisoning is related to Remi's murder?"

"Maybe." I sighed. "I told Hal Inwood they had to be related, because to me it doesn't make sense that they're not, but . . ."

"But you have no proof whatsoever."

"Correct."

"Hmm." Aunt Frances stirred whatever it was she was mixing up. "There's something I need to tell you," she said, stirring away. "About Harold Calkins."

"You know him?"

"For longer than I've known you, dearest niece."

Otto looked up from the vegetable cutting. "Wait. Is he better-looking than I am?"

My elegant aunt made a snorting noise. "That's your question?"

He shrugged. "First one that came to mind."

"What I need to tell you," she said to me, ignoring her husband's grin, "is about the last time I ran into Harold. It was at the post office, and we got chatting, like you do when you haven't seen an acquaintance in a few months."

Otto looked at me. "Hear that? Acquaintance. Not a former love interest."

I nodded agreement. "I'd say you're safe. For now, at least."

"As I was saying," Aunt Frances said loudly, "we

stopped to chat. I asked how he was doing, and he was all smiles, sunshine, lollipops, and rainbows. He said, and this is a direct quote, 'Sometimes things work out just the way you planned.'"

Huh. "And this was when? What day?"

"Not even a week ago. Friday, maybe?"

The very day that the health department slapped a CLOSED sign on Three Seasons. Once again, Harold Calkins was at the top of my suspect list. There was a huge caveat, though. Did he have any reason whatsoever to kill Remi Bayliss?

I didn't know. But I was going to do my best to find out.

Chapter 10

The next day was another bookmobile day, and since my board meeting obligations had been fulfilled, Graydon had freed me to move about Tonedagana County bringing cheer, goodwill, and books to all.

Clouds and the threat of rain had descended upon us, the threat shifting from my phone's vague forecast of fifty percent chance to actual precipitation before we'd arrived at the first stop.

"This isn't nearly as much fun as I thought it would be," Julia said, sliding down in the passenger's seat low enough that a stickler for vehicular safety would have told her to sit up because in case of an accident, her safety belt wouldn't work properly.

Sometimes I was indeed a stickler, but even though rain was starting to pelt down, the road was wide and straight, there was no traffic, and I'd never once seen a deer on this stretch of road. Sure, there were deer pretty much everywhere, even in town, but deer also typically kept to their same narrow paths over and over again, so I just kept a sharp eye out and let Julia play whatever role she was inhabiting today.

"You sound like a sulky twelve-year-old," I said.

"Huh." She folded her arms across her chest. "I'm slipping. This morning I decided to be thirteen again, just to see what it felt like."

"Why would you want to do that? That was . . ." I thought back and winced. Some life periods were best left in the past. "That was thick glasses because my parents wouldn't let me get contacts until I was sixteen. That was the beginning of acne. Of being socially awkward. Of being afraid that one bad grade would go on my permanent record and ruin my life forever."

"Exactly," she said, sitting up and dropping her aggrieved tone, shedding the teenage persona in one second flat. "Just wanted to remind myself that youth wasn't all sunshine, puppies, and kittens. A lot of it was awful."

"Maybe you need to remind yourself because you're so old. I don't need reminding because I'm so many years closer to thirteen."

"Hear that?" Julia tapped her toes on Eddie's carrier. "Your mom is making fun of my age. What do you think of that?"

"Mrr!"

Julia looked at me. "He said it'll be your turn soon enough, so you should stop with the age references."

"Really?" I flicked on the turn signal and we pulled off the road and into the shade of a massive maple tree that edged the parking lot of a small church. "Pretty sure he said he should get treats as soon as I put the transmission into park."

"Is that true, big guy?" Julie crooned. As we were now stationary, she unlatched the wire door of the carrier.

I was rotating the driver's seat around to face the back and flipping down the work surface that became the front checkout station. Looking over, I saw that my cat had assumed one of his favorite postures: the napping pose.

"If it was," I said, "it isn't now. Hear that snoring?"

Julia peered in. "Wish I could fall asleep as easily as that. The boy has a gift."

He had something, all right. And if I ever figured out a way to monetize it, I'd be able to retire by the time I turned forty.

As we readied the bookmobile for patrons—turning on the computers, hooking up to the Internet, double-checking the shelf full of hold books, unstrapping Julia's chair—we guessed what patrons would brave the rain, which was now falling in round drops big enough to make your clothes stick to your skin if you were out in it for more than ten seconds.

"Those new folks might," I mused. "You know, Bob and Jean? They didn't check out that many books last time because the grandkids were coming up, so I bet they're fresh out." But I wasn't sure they'd show, because it was raining hard, and who would voluntarily traipse out into a monsoon?

"Mr. Zonne will be here," Julia said, nodding and exuding confidence.

Lawrence Zonne, who had achieved octogenarian status years before, was another person who unknowingly served as one of my role models. He was smart, funny, and active, and his memory was a better resource than any computer search engine ever.

He was also one of the bookmobile's most loyal patrons. The only time I could remember him missing a stop was when he'd had to drive to the Traverse City airport to pick up his brother. Afterward, he'd grumbled about it for weeks, saying that next time his little brother wanted to come north, he'd have to pay more attention to the bookmobile's schedule.

The door opened and the man himself hurried inside and slammed the door shut. "If we get any more rain we'll need to research how to build an ark. I had to dash between those raindrops like a knife through butter." He made slicing motions with both hands, karate-like.

Mr. Zonne's comment about knifing through the rain mushed together with the knife expertise Otto had demonstrated yesterday, and something in my brain went *ping!*

"The knives," I said out loud.

"Pardon me?" Mr. Zonne asked. My thoughts had rolled around so fast that he was still shaking the water from his coat. "And pardon me for making a mess of your lovely bookmobile. Oh, dear, look at all that water."

Julia bustled toward him, flourishing a roll of paper towels. "Not to worry, my dear Lawrence."

As the two of them started cleanup operations— Mr. Zonne trying to swipe up what he'd dripped on the small entrance mat and Julia trying to pat dry the back of Mr. Zonne's shirt—I pulled my phone from my pocket.

Minnie: *Question. Are all your knives at Three Seasons made by that manufacturer that starts with a Z?*

Kristen: *Yup.*

Minnie: *Any reason at all you'd have a different brand of knife in the kitchen?*

Kristen: *Never ever. Part of the deal when I hire. Why?*

Minnie: *Checking on something. I'll tell you later.*

After swiping the texting app away, I opened a search engine and typed in the name of Kristen's knives. All had black handles. Not a single one was anything other than black. Fast as I could, I typed in knife details. Professional, chef, layered handle, navy blue, light blue.

I stared at the results.

Then I called Ash.

He didn't grasp the implication the first time I told him, so I decided to say it all over again. That ran the risk of boring him, but there was no help for it. What would have helped was Julia's acting and storytelling abilities. One of these days I'd absorb some of her skills.

"It's like this," I said, slowly, so he could get every word down in his horrendous handwriting. "Wait, you are taking notes, aren't you?"

"Every time you call."

I squinted in the direction of Chilson, wishing for the millionth time that I had superpower X-ray vision, because if I did, I'd be able to see if he was, in fact, writing anything down, and if he was, what kind of writing it might be. I suspected that he was telling the literal truth, that he was writing things down, but I also very strongly suspected that his notes ran along the lines of "Minnie called. Again. Doesn't she have anything better to do?" and were accompanied by doodles of him whacking his head against his desk.

"Anyway," I said, moving on, "it's about the knives. A lot of chefs are fussy about their knives. Whatever kind they like, they never use anything else. And you know how Kristen can be a real control freak in the kitchen? I asked her about her restaurant knives, and she only uses one kind."

"So you're saying . . ."

"What I'm saying is that the knife I saw there that day was a Lee. It wasn't a Three Seasons knife, so it was probably accidentally left behind by whoever added triticale to the waffle cones." Okay, Harvey had said a vendor, but that didn't make any sense to me.

"It's a commercial kitchen," Ash said. "They have to have dozens of knives."

"Sure, but that's not the point. It's the manufacturer that matters here." I tried to come up with a car analogy. "It would be like a Ford guy going out and buying a Chevy. It just wouldn't happen."

"Huh."

"And," I went on, "whoever killed Remi used the same brand of knife."

An odd scratching noise came through the phone. Since we'd known each other for a long time—once upon a time we'd briefly dated—I knew that he was scraping his chin with the cap to a pen, a habit I'd always found tremendously annoying. In this case, however, it was easy to curb my irritation, because I also knew that the pen-cap action meant he was thinking.

After a short eternity, the scraping stopped. "It's worth looking into," he said.

"You'll talk to Cherise?" Because I was still convinced she had motive to poison the waffle cones and, if Remi had come across evidence of that, she might have killed Remi to keep her quiet. And maybe she'd been coming back to the dumpster in preparation for getting rid of the body. The inside of my skin started itching at the thought, and I really wished my brain hadn't gone there.

"It's worth looking into," he repeated, going all Detective Inwood on me. Though I tried to pry more information out of him—was he going to look into it as soon as he got off the phone? was he going to talk to the owner of Angelique's, because maybe she mandated knife brands? how was he going to research where Lee knives could be purchased?— he wouldn't budge from the line of "You know I can't talk about an active investigation."

At the end, however, he did say, "Thanks for the information, Minnie. They didn't find any DNA on the murder weapon, so this might end up being helpful," so I put the call in the Win category. Not that I was done trying to help Kristen, of course. I'd decided on next steps for doing that in the middle of talking to Ash, and when we got back to Chilson, I took Eddie home and started the first one.

For a few days now, I'd been meaning to talk to other restaurants about any recent history of bad online reviews. I wanted to be considerate and stop in when they weren't busy, but that was hard to do

at any time in the summer, so if I wanted to help
Kristen, I needed to get going, and today was going
to be the day. It was midweek, and it was still raining, which I'd been told meant visitors tended to eat
in restaurants less and do more ordering of delivery
pizza.

I didn't see any harm in popping into a few places
and seeing if they had time to answer a few questions, and maybe, just maybe, I'd learn something
that would help.

My first stop was Shomin's Deli. Now that Reva
had my houseboat renter Corey Moncada as manager, she'd been able to expand their hours into
early evening. As I stepped inside and shook the
rain off my windbreaker, I was pleased to see that
the place was almost as busy as it was at lunchtime.

The young man running the cash register didn't
look familiar, and neither did either of the young
women in the back who were busy putting sandwiches together. I craned my neck around, trying to
see into the back, where I knew Reva had a small
office, and caught sight of her peering at her phone.

"Reva!" I waved madly, and she looked up. "Do
you have a minute?"

She made a Come On Back gesture, and I made
my way around the end of the counter.

"You heard about Remi Bayliss?" she asked in a
low voice as I entered the room. "My staff is freaking out. I keep sending group texts to reassure
them, but I must not be doing a very good job. I've
had two people quit, and two more are on the
edge."

The concept that other Chilson restaurateurs

and their employees would be impacted by Remi's murder hadn't occurred to me, and it should have.

"This must be hard," I said. "For everyone."

Reva put her phone down. "First the poisoning at Three Seasons, which was bad enough, but now this?" She sighed and shook her head. "What's happening, Minnie? You work with the sheriff's office—do you know anything?"

I hesitated. My knife theory was in Ash's hands, and it didn't feel appropriate to talk about it to anyone else. But there was one thing I should probably tell her, because if I didn't, she'd hear about it sooner or later and wonder why I hadn't told her. "Um, well, I was with Cherise Joffe. We were the ones who found Remi."

Reva went very still. "Oh, Minnie. I'm so sorry. That must have been awful." She touched my hand. "Are you okay?"

"Mostly." I smiled. Sort of. "But right now I'm worried about Three Seasons. About Kristen. Someone is behind all this, right? Someone who has it in for restaurants in general, maybe, and I was wondering if you'd had a run of bad online reviews lately. Fat Boys has. Some of them were really nasty."

She glanced at her phone, then at her desktop computer. "Tell you the truth, I don't pay much attention to those. Too busy, most of the time. But you might ask Corey. I think he's been keeping an eye out."

After thanking her, I went back out into the rain and stopped at Hoppe's Brewing, Corner Coffee, and the Round Table. I got the same response from all three. Remi's murder was making everyone nervous, and in summer no one was taking the time to read online reviews.

This wasn't a huge surprise. The rhythm of Up North life for those in the hospitality industry was slow from October through mid-May, then flat-out. The old adage of having 100 days to make their money had, over the last decade, stretched out to be closer to 150, but the concept was still the same. Not much to do all winter, too busy to breathe all summer. If there were any clues online, I'd have to track them down myself.

I walked home, taking what shelter was offered by building awnings and overhangs. Though the rain had slowed to a drizzle, the wind had gusted up, and in spite of the facts that it was the middle of August and that we'd had a spell of icky hot and humid weather just a few days earlier, I could have sworn I felt a hint of winter whispering in my ear, wrapping around the back of my neck and down my spine.

The thought became an image and I wished, once again, that I had the ability to draw things more complicated than stick figures. Then again, the wind image was more than a little creepy, and why would I want to immortalize that?

Idly, I wondered if my life might have turned out differently if I'd had an artistic bone in my body. If I'd been able to draw, would I be somewhere else, doing something else, with someone else?

"Stop that," I murmured, because I was scaring myself. Too many what-ifs could ruin a person's day, and none of them mattered because I was in Chilson with Rafe, working in the library and driving the bookmobile. Exactly where I should be. With the man—and the cat—I should be with.

The wind shifted and the rain pounded down. I hurried under the awning of Gennell Books & Goods and backed up against the brick wall, waiting out the deluge. I glanced through the window and saw Blythe at the front counter, chatting with a pair of customers. Since the rain continued to pelt down with no indication that it was ever going to let up, I continued to stand there.

At first I wondered about the customers—where they were from, whether or not they had friends or relatives in Chilson, what did they think of our town, did they plan to come back—but then I noticed Blythe.

It was nearly six o'clock, her weeknight closing time, and she looked exhausted. Her shoulders drooped, her smile looked forced, even her hair looked tired, the auburn strands that had escaped her long braid flat and straggly against the sides of her face.

The woman desperately needed some employees, but so did almost everyone in town. This summer there wasn't a retail shop, hotel, or restaurant around without a HELP WANTED sign in a window.

But a bookstore? Surely that had to be the best possible retail job out there. Low pay, sure, but who wouldn't want to work in a bookstore, seeing the catalogs of upcoming titles, unpacking boxes of stories, helping choose books for gifts and wrapping them up in pretty packages?

It had to be a lot like working in a library, come to think of it, only you got to put books in bags instead of just pushing them across a counter.

The rain slackened and I rushed off, hoping to make it all the way home before the buckets up in the clouds overturned again. That didn't work, of course, and I was wet to the skin when I ran up the front steps. Eddie was in the front hall, sitting like an Egyptian cat statue, ready with a comment on the weather.

"Mrr!"

"Yeah, well, it's not like I ordered it." I bent down to unlace my shoes, dripping all over the front mat. "When I put in a request for rain, I always make sure to ask for it to fall in the middle of the night, so it inconveniences you as little as possible."

"Mrr."

"You're welcome." I climbed the stairs, leaving slightly damp footprints on the wood treads. Eddie trailed behind me, carefully stepping around my footsteps.

I hung my wet clothes over the shower rod and toweled off, and I was in the act of pulling on dry comfy clothes when my cell phone rang with Kristen's ringtone.

"Hey," I said. "How are the kids?"

"What? Oh. They're fine. We're all fine." She paused. "Well, except for the fact that my father-in-law is threatening to spend September here in Chilson."

"Trock can stand to be in one place that long?" The idea was ludicrous. "He hasn't spent that long in a single location since, what, high school?" Which might have been an exaggeration, but probably not by much.

"Doubt it'll happen," she said. "But he is getting

older, and he says he wants to be the best grand-papa in the history of grandpapas."

Sounded like Trock. "If you need someone to take him off your hands for an evening, Rafe and I can run interference for you. Um, what have you told him about the waffle cones?"

"Nothing," she said flatly. "And you're not going to tell him, either. That's what I wanted to talk to you about. The cone thing will work itself out one way or another. And now Remi Bayliss has been murdered, so the sheriff's office will be on it. You can stay out of the whole thing now."

"But—"

"But nothing," she interrupted, her voice rising. "The last thing I need right now is to worry about one more person, okay?"

"Sure, I get that. You don't need to worry, though. It's not like I'm doing anything dangerous. I'm just asking a few questions, that's all, and—"

"And I'm telling you to stay out of it!"

The phone went quiet. I stared at it, my mouth hanging open. Kristen had hung up on me.

Chapter 11

I told Rafe about Kristen's phone call that night over dinner. It had been my turn to cook, so it was heated-up frozen cheese ravioli—one of my all-time favorite college meals—accompanied by a very respectable salad of mixed greens, shaved carrots, grape tomatoes, and cauliflower bits. The healthy effect was somewhat diminished by the amount of salad dressing we drizzled on, not to mention the Parmesan cheese we strewed liberally over salad and pasta, but at least we were eating vegetables.

"Hang on," Rafe said, forking a pillow of ravioli into halves. "The Blond hung up on you?"

"In retrospect, it was more an abrupt end to the conversation than a true hang up, but at the time, yeah, that's what it felt like."

"Huh." Rafe chewed and swallowed. "That's weird."

It was indeed. Kristen had never been one to walk away from confrontation, even when it would be in her best interest. By nature, she was far more inclined to shout out whatever was on her mind than to keep her feelings buttoned up inside like a more traditional Midwesterner.

I'd been so happy the other day, when she'd seemed more like her old self, and now it was back to a Kristen I barely recognized.

"You've known her longer than you've known me," I said. "What should I do?"

"As far as what, and in what category?" he asked. "As a friend, as an amateur investigator, as someone interested in the future of Three Seasons, or as a fellow member of the human race?"

"Rafe, I'm serious," I said, putting my fork down. "I don't know how to deal with an unpredictable Kristen. And don't say she's always been like this, because it's not true and you know it."

He put his own fork down and reached across the dining table for my hand. "Light of my love. You're right. I'm sorry."

"What do I do?"

This time, my voice was soft and, if my ears were hearing correctly and I was hoping they weren't, a little bit trembly. The bedrock foundations in my life were my parents, Aunt Frances, Kristen, and now Rafe. The notion that one of those foundations might be shifting was more than disconcerting, like I was walking the tightrope of life and one corner of the net had broken loose.

Though I knew that someday I'd lose more of my net, as people didn't live forever, that was so far off over the horizon it wasn't even worth thinking about. But not now. And not in this way.

Rafe's thumb caressed the back of my hand. "The question is how to be a good friend, right?"

I nodded. "And is being a good friend doing what she says, or is it doing what I think is best for her?"

"Kristen doesn't take well to other people telling her what to do."

That was the understatement of the decade. It was one of the reasons she and her parents had barely spoken through her adolescence, it was one of the reasons she'd happily bailed on her fancy pharmaceutical career, and it was one of the big reasons she'd stayed single for so long.

"You know," I said, "maybe that's the thing. She and Scruffy never tell each other what to do. They talk things out, make decisions together. Now she has two tiny humans screaming at her all day and all night, and there's no room for negotiation. What they say goes."

Rafe made a noise that sounded suspiciously like a choked-back laugh. "The first time Kristen met someone she couldn't intimidate, she married him. Now she's outnumbered by people who won't listen to her. Infant people, but still. No wonder she's having a rough time."

The more I thought about it, the more I was sure I was right. Not that it got us anywhere, of course, because the question of the day still remained. What should I do next?

"Here's an idea." Rafe raised my hand, kissed my knuckles, and stood. "I'll do the dishes and you go for a walk. When I'm done in the kitchen, we'll do the texting thing and figure out what to do next."

"You're sending me out in the rain?" I stood and we gathered up the dishes. "Been there, done that already today and didn't like it much. What kind of fiancé are you, anyway?"

"Finest kind." He grinned. "What is it they say, there's no bad weather, just poor clothing choices? Besides, the little weather symbols on my phone show a tiny little sun poking out from behind a tiny little cloud starting now, so I bet you don't even need to take a raincoat."

"Your belief in a phone app's forecasting powers seems unreasonably strong."

"And what do you call that?"

With his chin, he gestured at the window. I took in the clouds opening up to blue skies and a sun starting its slide down to the horizon. There was only one answer to his question, and it was an obvious response.

"Luck," I said.

"Even a blind squirrel finds a nut once in a while." He kissed the top of my head. "Not that I'm calling you a nut or anything."

"Good story. You might want to stick to it." I slid my phone into my pocket. "I'm going to the marina. Maybe Louisa will be there."

I passed through the living room. Eddie was sleeping on the back of a couch cushion, doing his best to squash it out of shape. I gave the top of his head a pat, making it bob up and down, because it was just so much fun, and went out through the front door.

There, I pulled in a long deep breath of wet pavement, cut grass, and boat exhaust, the smells of summer. Hands in my shorts pockets, I wandered over to the marina. I lifted my foot to step onto Louisa's dock, then changed my mind. "Seventeen," I murmured, pulling the number of Harold Calkins's boat slip out of the back of my brain. Why said brain could manage to remember that but couldn't remember to buy milk on the way home instead of after I got home, I did not know. I only knew it was true.

I stepped up onto the dock that led back to number seventeen and craned my neck around. All boats looked to be present and accounted for, so I started planning the conversation as I walked to the end of the dock.

If Mr. Calkins was outside, it should be easy enough—gee, aren't you the owner of Seven Street? Gosh, what a coincidence. I'm a friend of Kristen Jurek's—and see what happened from there. I'd be perfectly safe, after all. I'd be on the dock, he'd be on the boat, and I was more than thirty years younger than he was if it came to a footrace.

I was drafting talking points as I walked and so managed to not hear the male voices until I was almost on top of them.

"What did you think?"

"There's a lot to consider."

"Agreed. And one of those things is which beer you're going to drink. I have No Rules from Perrin's, Widow Maker from Keweenaw Brewing, Bellaire Brown from Short's, and Two Hearted IPA from Bell's. Pick your poison."

It had to be Harold Calkins, he of the craft-beer preferences, who was talking. I stopped abruptly.

And, after a short internal debate about ethics and morality and the duties and limitations of friendship, I listened in.

"Nothing like a Two Hearted," the other man said, and there was a twin *pop!* of cans opening. "Cheers." A short pause, then: "Ah, that hits the spot."

"Everything tastes better from the deck of a boat," Harold said. "Especially when you have a view like this."

I stood on my tiptoes, looking over the top of the boat next door to him. The two men were sitting in chairs, facing the sunset, their backs to me. I inched closer.

"And here I always thought everything tasted better with beer," the other man said, and they both laughed. "But back to my question, Des. What do you think?"

"About your restaurant? Well, like I said, there's a lot to consider."

I tried to put myself back in time. Who was it that Eric Apney, my former boat neighbor, had said was looking at buying Seven Street? . . . Desmond Pyken. That was it. And this had to be him. Des. My foot brushed against a line coiled on the dock.

"Did you hear something?" Des Pyken turned, and I hunched down. If he'd heard me, he must have the hearing of a bat.

"Didn't hear a thing," Harold said. "But then I'm getting old. Anyway, I understand hesitating to buy a restaurant up here. The season is short, and there's lots of competition. Although with Three Seasons closed, that might change."

My eyes opened wide.

"For the better?" Des asked.

"Depends on your point of view." A chair creaked. "Not that I want anything bad to happen to Kristen, of course."

"Of course," Des murmured.

"And there's something to be said for a small tourist town having a variety of fine dining venues. Keeps people here longer, wanting to try them all."

"What do you think happened at Three Seasons?" Des asked. "And didn't I hear someone was killed at Angelique's? What's that all about?"

"Angelique's." Harold's head went back and forth in a slow shake. "That's a sad thing. My guess is an ex of some sort. But Kristen's gluten-free cones that weren't gluten-free, well, I just don't understand. You'd think the first person who tried one would have known something was wrong."

"You'd think," Des said. "But with a dessert like her 77, there are a lot of competing elements. Maybe it's not such a surprise."

"Competing?" Harold repeated. "Don't tell me you have the recipe."

There was a short pause, then Des said—and I would have sworn on a stack of first-edition Agatha Christies that he was smiling when he said the words—"You bet I do."

Back home, Rafe was sitting in the gazebo with a beer and the newspaper. When I told the story to him, though he put down the paper (but not the beer) and listened, he didn't clue in to its significance. "It's just a recipe," he said. "Why is this a big deal?"

"It's massive," I said, spreading my arms wide open to indicate the vastness of the deal's hugeness.

"Restaurants are known for specific things, signature dishes."

"You mean like the pizza at the Dearborn Italian Bakery where we have to eat every time we go down to see your parents?"

"And," I went on before he could come up with another example of me dragging him to restaurants outside his normal sphere, "like the burritos at Taco Boy, where we have to stop every time we're within half an hour of Grand Rapids."

"Point taken. Still, don't a lot of restaurants publish their recipes? Sell cookbooks full of the stuff they make?"

As this was a fact I'd pointed out to Kristen more than once as something that could be a revenue stream, I knew exactly what he was talking about. "Absolutely. But Kristen has always been insistent on keeping her recipes in-house."

"Secret Squirrel stuff?" Rafe asked, half grinning, half smirking.

"I'd call it proprietary, but whatever. The upshot is that no one other than Kristen, Misty, and Harvey should have the recipe for those gluten-free waffle cones."

Rafe put his beer down. "And Misty is on your list of suspects."

"There are other ways for someone to get hold of a recipe, other than someone handing it over," I said. Not that I could think of any, but there had to be at least one out there.

"Sure." Rafe nodded. "Plus, maybe this Des Pyken was lying. People do that, you know, especially when they're buying or selling something."

"Say it isn't so," I muttered, but he was right. I

didn't need to take Pyken at his overheard word. However, I also didn't want to make the mistake of latching on to that theory and following up on the possibilities of Misty as a suspect.

I sighed. It was all so much more complicated now that Remi Bayliss had been killed. It was a tragedy that her life had been cut short so abruptly. Waffle cones that had made people sick but not killed anyone was one thing, but outright murder put an entirely different slant on things.

Pushing away the thought that, of all my suspects, seeing Misty, a fellow chef, in Angelique's kitchen would be the least likely to raise any red flags, I left Rafe to the newspaper and went inside to do some Internet research.

It had been a day or two since I'd looked at any restaurant review sites, so when I pulled the first one up and typed in Three Seasons, I hit the Search button and closed my eyes, hoping that the waffle-cone comments had run their course, that people had moved on, that the storm had passed and that the focus could go back to satisfying the health department's requirements and reopening.

After sending up a small prayer, I opened my eyes.

Then immediately slapped the laptop shut.

"No," I said out loud. No to reading the horrendous reviews that were still coming in. No to the awful things people were writing about Three Seasons. No to what they were writing about Kristen.

And above all, no to Kristen's order to stop helping her.

I was going to rescue her restaurant whether she wanted me to or not.

* * *

Out on the bookmobile the next day, Hunter listened to my ramblings about Three Seasons, Angelique's, Remi Bayliss, and triticale. I almost slid into a discussion of the knife thing but pulled back from putting that much information out into the world, covering my fumble with a stuttering list of suspects.

"S-so," I said, "there are a few people I figure might have done it."

Hunter nodded. "Chef Misty, right? And what's-her-name who runs Angelique's. Cherise."

I held out two fingers and started to uncurl a third. "Harold Calkins, who's trying to sell Seven Street, and Des Pyken, who might be interested in buying it." I looked at my four fingers and stuck out my thumb. "And there's Parker McMurray, the guy who failed at the restaurant business and now thinks they should all be abolished as dens of iniquity."

"Which is your favorite?" Hunter asked, but then we pulled into our newest stop location and I was saved from answering.

This new spot was a long-shuttered miniature golf course that had already been closed when I was a kid. The parking lot was in decent shape because it had recently been used as a staging area for some road construction. When I'd approached the owner about using it, she'd smiled, revealing brilliantly white dentures, patted my hand, and said, "Honey, you're more than welcome. But you have to promise me one thing. I get to be the first one to borrow anything by Elle Cosimano."

It had been an easy promise to make—and to

keep—and today I had in my hot little hand a copy of the latest Finlay Donovan book. I knocked carefully on the door of the old farmhouse next to the former course, but despite my care, a few chips of white paint fell to the porch floor.

Petra Terlesky, however, didn't seem to mind. Her skinny arm pulled the door wide open, adding a few more paint chips to the pile, and she whooped as she yanked the book out of my hand and gave it a close once-over with rheumy eyes.

"Brand-new!" she crowed. "Brand-spanking-new." Her ear-to-ear grin was contagious and I felt myself smiling, too. "Got to hand it to you, missy," she chortled. "You deliver what you promise. You tell your momma that she raised you right."

I murmured that I'd let her know next time we talked.

"No, no." Petra shook her head. "Call her today and tell her. No time like the present, because there might not be a tomorrow. Speaking of which," she said, dropping her voice, "did you hear about that murder in Chilson? I worry about you in that big city."

The notion that anyone could consider a town of three thousand a big city just went to show that pretty much everything was relative. Then I got curious. "How did you find out about it?"

"Oh, the things I hear," Petra said, tucking a piece of long white hair behind her ear. "Cousins here, cousins there. Friends. They stop by and talk. People like to, you know."

Do tell. "You have a cousin in Chilson?"

"First, once removed. Sheila stops by once a week, brings me any extra eggs they have. They have this nice little backyard chicken coop. So handy. She lives next door to Parker McMurray, who had that nice little restaurant with all those adorable salt and pepper shakers displayed everywhere. Remember?" Her face was full with the excitement that can come with telling scandalous gossip.

I made a murmuring noise of agreement.

"Sheila heard about the murder from her son, who's an EMT for the city, so when she saw Parker mowing his lawn she went out to tell him." Petra's voice dropped to a raspy whisper. "Sheila said when she told him that Remi girl was dead, he keeled over. Fainted right then and there."

I wasn't sure how reliable Petra's information about McMurray might be, or how pertinent, but I tucked it away into the back of my head. If need be, I could probably track her down, because after all, how many Sheilas could there be in Chilson who had chickens in their backyards?

The city required a permit to keep backyard chickens—a fun fact I knew because a library patron who was researching building chicken coops had told me. It was also a fact I was never going to tell Rafe because he might just get interested enough in raising chickens to build one and that would not mesh well with Eddie's atavistic tendencies regarding the bird world.

No matter which way I went regarding sharing information with the love of my life, it probably wouldn't be that hard to walk down to city hall and chat with the zoning administrator long enough to get the information I was after. Permits were, after all, part of the public record. But was it worth my time and energy?

I also decided not to tell Hunter what Petra had said, as the idea of spreading that kind of gossip gave me a creepy-crawly feeling that made the skin on the middle of my back—the exact spot I couldn't reach—itch like crazy. Instead, I posed the question to Eddie.

"What do you think?" I asked quietly as I returned him to his carrier at the end of the stop. "Is this worth a follow-up? Fainting when hearing about Remi's murder might be evidence that Parker McMurray knew her, but does it prove anything else?"

Hunter was reshelving the picture books that a gaggle of kids had pulled out and left on the floor. I glanced back, saw that he was maybe half-done with the task, and returned to my one-sided conversation with a cat.

"Let's say Parker did kill Remi. If so, his reaction doesn't make any sense. Then again, if he didn't kill her, why would he have such a strong reaction?"

Eddie's mouth opened and closed in a silent "Mrr."

I sighed. There was no sense to a lot of things. I hardly ever knew why I reacted the way I did to any given circumstance; why should I think that anyone else's reaction should make sense? "You're right," I said, patting the top of the carrier. "You're always right."

This time his "Mrr" was not silent.

"You bothering the help up here?" Hunter asked, sliding into the driver's seat and starting the engine.

"Ask him." I nodded in Eddie's direction.

Hunter grinned. "Hey, buddy. Is she bothering you?"

"Mrr!"

"Cats," I muttered as Hunter laughed.

On the way back to Chilson, we discussed the low turnout at our new stop, but how the few people who did show up had vowed to text copies of the schedule to all their friends and relatives.

"We'll keep it on the schedule to the end of the year," I said, making the executive decision. "I'll decide before Thanksgiving whether or not it's going to be a keeper."

Hunter nodded and said, "Forgot to tell you. That mini-golf place that Mrs. Terlesky's husband built? My parents used to go there before they got married. Sounds like it was the place to go, back in the day."

We returned to Chilson. I got off, Julia got aboard, and I waved good-bye as they whirled away.

"The place to go, back in the day," I repeated softly, watching the bookmobile's back end turn a corner and vanish, and thinking about what to do next.

After a while, I realized that standing in the middle of the back parking lot, staring at nothing, wasn't going to accomplish anything other than making me look like someone who shouldn't be allowed out on their own.

My next step was obvious. It was lunchtime and I needed to eat, so why not combine that basic need with the need to learn more about each of my suspects?

I took one step toward the library, then stopped. Holly was working today. Holly was a good friend of Cherise Joffe. Holly almost certainly had some insider information about Cherise that might help, but there was no way I could in good conscience ask her questions with the aim of helping my friend Kristen and harming her friend.

Nope. Not happening. I had to get information some other way.

"The place to go," I murmured to myself as I walked downtown, because what Hunter had said was sticking in my head, and maybe, just maybe, it was sticking there for a reason. "Back in the day, the place to go."

These days, the place where everyone went was Hoppe's Brewing, but they'd only existed for a couple of years. The other places were Benton's General Store and the now-closed-but-soon-to-be-reopened Henika's Candy Emporium. Other than that . . .

Hang on. The Round Table. Of course! How could I not have thought about the Round Table?

I sped, in a fast-walking-but-not-running-because-that-would-be-silly sort of way, back behind the downtown blocks, then down a side street, and into the oldest restaurant in Chilson. The Round Table was a classic Up North kind of family restaurant. Booths up both sides of the main dining room, tables in the middle, with one large round table in back. This table was filled every morning with elderly men who'd known each other their entire lives, most of whom rarely set foot outside of Tonedagana County.

The pine paneling and faded acoustic-tile ceiling hadn't changed in decades. And, though their color indicated a birthdate long before I was born, neither had the vinyl seats in the booths.

At this point in my life, however, I'd now eaten

at the Round Table so many times that I didn't even notice the surroundings. Particularly today, when I was bent on talking to Sabrina, who'd been a waitress at the Round Table longer than there'd been a recipe for toast.

The woman herself eyed me as I slid into the booth at the back, the one everybody avoided because the upholstery was shot and it was next to the kitchen and the restrooms. Sabrina paused on her way past, her hands full of empty plates. "You don't have a book. Who are you meeting?"

I gave her a bright smile. "Just you."

"Like I'm going to believe that." She rolled her eyes and bumped her hip to open the kitchen door but was back soon enough, pulling a pencil out of her bun of silver hair and poising it over the pad she pulled out of her apron pocket. "Let me guess. Third-pound cheeseburger, mustard, ketchup, pickle, lettuce, light on the mayo. Fries and malt vinegar. Ice water and a cola."

It was my standard lunch order, and I was tempted, as always, to ask for something different. But I didn't want to give Sabrina a heart attack. Plus, I wanted to ask her a favor, and going off book for lunch wasn't the way to win her heart.

"Yes, please," I said meekly. "But . . . do you have a second?"

She finished writing and cast a quick, professional eye across the room. "For now. But soon as Cookie dings the bell, I need to pick up the food for table three."

"Sure. Thanks." I nodded. "You heard about Remi Bayliss, right? At Angelique's? Well, I'm the one who found her." That's when I saw something I never thought I'd see—Sabrina looking surprised.

"You're the one? Oh, Minnie, I'm so sorry. What a horrible thing." She glanced around and lowered her voice. "And I got to tell you, it has us worried. Carol and Hannah, anyway. They're spooked."

"Can't say I blame them."

"No, I suppose not, but"—another glance around—"I don't think they have anything to worry about. Word is they're about to make an arrest."

My eyebrows slid close together. "What do you mean?"

"Well, from what I hear, that manager over at Angelique's, you know the one with the attitude?"

"Cherise Joffe?"

"That's her. Well, I heard that Cherise and that poor Remi had a huge fight."

"Oh?" Everything inside me went still. "When was that?"

"The day before Remi was killed."

Chapter 12

I meandered back to the library, hands in my pockets, calm on the outside, all in a turmoil on the inside.

Was it true? Had Cherise really had a knockdown, drag-out argument with Remi less than twenty-four hours before the murder? Or had someone witnessed a minor tiff and it had blossomed into a full-blown slanderous rumor? Did Ash know about this? And who was it who had seen the fight in the first place? Sabrina had reluctantly said it was her friend Robert who'd told her about it, but he'd heard it from someone else, and no, she didn't know who it was, so stop bothering her and let her get back to work.

But there wasn't much choice, not if I wanted to be a good and upstanding citizen. So, yes, I needed to make sure Ash knew that Cherise and Remi might have had an argument. He'd ask all the normal questions, I wouldn't have any answers, he'd try to keep his eye roll to himself and would fail, I'd get irritated and walk out with my teeth gritted and go home to Rafe and complain about how his friend wouldn't listen to sense, Rafe would try to soothe me, Eddie would look at me like I was the stupidest person alive or dead, and after a massively huge bowl of popcorn—or maybe ice cream—I'd start to feel better.

Then again, if I used technology that had been available for years, I could skip most of that if I simply texted the information to Ash.

So I did, tossing Sabrina under the bus with careless abandon. Which meant I wouldn't want to go to the Round Table for a week or two, but I'd meant to stop eating out so much anyway.

With that settled, I slid my phone into my pants pocket and strode along the sidewalk, arms swinging, smiling up at the blue sky. It was a gorgeous August day, so it only made sense to enjoy it as much as possible. Summers were short in northern Michigan, and storing away the feel of the sun on my skin to help me through the long gray days of winter was a trick I longed to perfect.

Sure, I had no idea what was going to happen, long term, with Three Seasons, and knowing there was a killer running around loose in Chilson was more than a little disconcerting, but right then, right there, I felt certain that everything would work out. Though life wouldn't ever be all puppies, kittens, and cotton candy, given half a chance, things tended to turn out okay and—

My feet slowed, and I came to a complete stop. I'd been spending so much time on the bookmobile lately that I'd forgotten what was going on at the bricks-and-mortar library.

A white panel van was parked outside the side door, and two men were pulling out boxes of equipment. Gareth was standing there, talking with a third man, and all three of the strangers were wearing identical dark green polo shirts, a color that matched the writing emblazoned across the side of the van: VJD SECURITY.

It was the vandalism solution that no one had liked, but the one that everyone had eventually agreed was needed. Security camaras.

I reversed my earlier thought.

Everything was not okay.

The minute Eddie and I walked in the door that evening, I was told by my beloved that he and Ash had arranged for themselves and their significant others, Chelsea and myself, to meet up at Hoppe's Brewing for dinner. After a moment of irritation—because why on earth hadn't either of them communicated anything about the plans; they both had cell phones, and I was super sure they knew how to use them—I shrugged, let Eddie out of his carrier, turned around, and headed back out again.

"Thought you said you weren't mad about this," Rafe said a block later.

"Irritated isn't the same thing as mad."

"Maybe on the inside. From the outside, it sure looks the same. Furrowed brow, half-closed eyes, stiff shoulders."

I glanced at him. "If you say I have an upside-down smile, the wedding is off."

He grinned and took my hand. "Wouldn't dream of it."

The touch of his hand warmed me in a way that

nothing else ever had. "But to tell you the truth, I wasn't thinking about you at all."

"Huh. And here I thought I was the center of your life."

Rafe was the center of my life, my universe, my love, my heart. Always, always, always. But I couldn't say that in the middle of a public sidewalk. That would be weird. "You know you have to share space with Eddie."

"Right." He nodded. "Sorry. I wasn't thinking."

"Understood." I swung our hands high, back and forth. "What I was thinking about was Remi's murder. I had lunch at the Round Table and learned something that might be important." I told him what Sabrina had said, and that I'd texted Ash.

"Sounds like a very adult thing to do," he said. "And you're still thinking about this because?"

"Because Remi is also on the suspect list for getting at Kristen's waffle cones, remember? Ash and Hal will be focusing on solving the murder. Until that's done, they won't have time to work on the poisoning."

He squeezed my hand. "Didn't Kristen tell you, in no uncertain terms, to quit with the investigating thing?"

"And did you hear me agree to stop?"

"You know, now that I think about it, no. I didn't."

"Well, there you go." I grinned. "I can't break a promise I never made, now, can I?"

"Hmm." Rafe opened the door of Hoppe's Brewing, and the noise of a packed restaurant surged toward us. "Not sure Kristen is going to agree with you on that one. You know what she's like."

"I also know there's no reason for her to find out what I'm doing. No, don't look like that," I said, glancing up at him as I went inside. "She's not omnipotent."

"You're sure about that?"

"No one is. Not even Kristen. She's a force of nature, but she's not all-seeing and all-knowing."

Doubt was writ clearly on Rafe's face, but that was because he had no idea how to shift Kristen's momentum. I'd had far more practice than he had, and I knew the trick was pure diversion, and that was far easier since she'd had the twins.

Ash and Chelsea were already seated. "You might want to get your first round at the bar," Ash said over the noise of the crowd, which I'd learned was one of the sounds of an Up North summer. "They had a couple of people quit the last couple of days, so they're really short-staffed. Dinner might be a while."

Rafe shrugged. "We're in no hurry. Um, are we?" He looked at me belatedly.

I looked at Chelsea. "First he makes plans without telling me, then he expands those untold plans without asking. When I'm standing right here."

She laughed. "Paybacks, Minnie. It's all about paybacks."

"Hey, now." Rafe looked startled. "Let's not go there, okay?"

Smiling peacefully, I patted him on the shoulder. "Anything you say, sweetheart. Why don't you sit down while I fetch a nice cold beer for you."

He gave me a suspicious squint but sat in the chair I'd pulled out for him.

"Be back soon," I said, air-kissing him and giving Chelsea a huge wink, which got a laugh out of both Chelsea and Ash.

"Don't bring me one of those chocolate beers," Rafe said as I started walking away. "You know that's my least favorite."

"Chocolate, you say?" I called over my shoulder. "If that's what you want, that's what I'll get."

But what I wanted wasn't beer of any kind. What I wanted was to talk to Carol, the other forever waitress at the Round Table. I was pretty sure Carol and Remi Bayliss were about the same age, so maybe they'd been high school friends, maybe they were still friends, and maybe Carol, who was sitting at the bar with her husband, would be able to tell me . . . something.

The bartender took my order—one root beer for me, one non-chocolatey stout for Rafe—and while she was filling the pint glasses, I nodded at Carol. "Haven't seen you at the Round Table in a while. Everything okay?"

She nodded. "Our daughter had a baby. I've been helping out." Her cell phone had a photo of a tiny human.

I admired it dutifully, then said, "Horrible thing about Remi Bayliss. Did you know her?"

Carol's face flexed with warring emotions. Grief. Frustration. Anger. "Since kindergarten. We weren't best friends or anything, but . . . but we'd known each other more than forty years. Every time I saw her, she'd complain about Cherise Joffe. How she was so critical. How she wasn't near flexible enough when it came to employees. How she wasn't willing to change anything, no matter what."

"So she wasn't happy there?"

"She liked the money, and she liked everyone she worked with well enough. It was just that Cherise was awful. Remi kept saying Cherise would be moving on soon, restaurant managers don't stay in one place real long, so she'd just wait her out. And now . . ." She bit her lip and leaned into her husband's shoulder. He'd been talking with a guy on the other side of him, but when he felt Carol's head, without even looking he put his arm around her, pulling her tight.

I murmured a few words that were meant to be comforting, touched her shoulder, then picked up the drinks and headed back to the table, thinking.

Maybe Remi wasn't the only employee at Angelique's who was unhappy. Maybe other employees were, too. How that could be a factor in Remi's death, I had no idea, but it was something else that Ash needed to know.

Since for once I actually paid attention to where I was and what I was doing, almost every bit of our drinks was still inside the glasses when I returned to the table. "Because I love you so much," I said, sitting next to Rafe, "this beer is completely chocolate-free."

He gave me a solemn look. "You are too good for me."

"Got that right." Ash lifted his glass in a toast. "Here's to the women in our lives. May they tolerate us as long as we live."

Chelsea grinned and held up her own glass. "I'll drink to that."

We all did, but then I had a nasty feeling that, if we weren't careful, the evening's conversation would get mired in wedding minutia. Those two

were getting married in the spring, but our wedding
was hurtling toward us at a frightening speed. I
didn't in the least want to talk about the things I
should be doing but wasn't, and I certainly didn't
want to talk about the officiant we didn't have, so I
looked at Ash and said, "Up at the bar, I was
talking to Carol, from the Round Table."

Ash didn't look in Carol's direction, but he nodded. "Saw her when we came in."

Of course he had. In the few months we'd dated,
back in the pre-Chelsea and pre-Minnie-and-Rafe
days, I'd learned that one of the occupational haz-
ards of being a police officer was that whenever you
walked into a space, you did two things: checked for
alternate exits and scanned the room for potential
threats. Ash could do all that before my eyes even
adjusted to the light in a room.

I leaned closer and said quietly, "Carol told me
that Cherise Joffe was hard on the Angelique's
staff."

"Okay," he said. "Not sure why you're telling me
this."

"Because isn't that one of the things Hal Inwood
always says? That you never know what piece of
information might lead to the resolution of a crime?"

He snorted. "Far as I remember, and I have a
pretty good memory, I've never heard Hal say that."

"Really? Huh. I must have heard it somewhere
else." Some television show, most likely, though I
wasn't about to tell him that. "But it makes sense,
doesn't it?" Then I grasped the implications of the
expression on his face. The patient expression.
"Wait. You already know this, don't you? About

how Cherise manages Angelique's, how unhappy the staff is." And how unhappiness and discontent can lead to frayed tempers and acts of violence that can never be undone.

"Well, I am a trained law enforcement officer," he said solemnly.

"And a fine one, I'm sure." I hesitated. "Any chance you're going to tell me anything about the investigation, other than that it's coming along?"

"Nope."

"Even if I bat my eyelashes?"

"There would be even less of a chance."

Which was a good thing, because I wasn't sure eyelash batting was part of my repertoire. I was about to ask Chelsea if she knew how to do the eyelash thing when our waiter showed up, looking harried. She handed around menus, said she'd be back in a minute to take our orders, and to feel free to get a second round at the bar and add it to our table tab.

By this time, the beer in the glasses of the other three had reached a dangerously low level. Since I was feeling restless, I took their orders and got up.

Carol's seat was now empty, and her husband's had been taken by a man in his mid-forties with a graying Vandyke beard, dressed in the typical summer wear of flip-flops, shorts, and polo shirt. He was reading the extensive beer list and asking the busy bartender questions about the origin of particular ingredients.

Since I had nothing to do but wait for the bartender, I was more or less forced to listen to a conversation that bored me silly, so my mind immediately started to wander around restlessly. Weddings, security cameras, knives, ministers, cat hair, vandalism—

"There's a lot to consider."

My attention snapped back. I'd heard that voice, saying that same thing, and not long ago. I looked sideways at the guy, who was asking the bartender questions, and tried to place him. Library, bookmobile, Round Table? No, no, and no.

He pointed at the beer list. "There are a lot of competing elements in this one. Does it work?"

That's who it was, Des Pyken! I almost snapped my fingers. I'd heard him talking with Harold Calkins on Harold's boat but hadn't exactly seen either one of them. I sidled a bit closer and made a supreme effort to pay attention to what he was saying.

"Works for me," the bartender said cheerfully. "It's my new favorite."

Des smiled. "Do they pay you to say that?"

"Not enough."

He laughed. "Sorry for all the questions. It's a bad habit of mine. I have restaurants in Grand Rapids and I'm always looking for inspiration for new things."

"Yeah?" She put a pint glass underneath a tap and pulled the lever. "For beer? You own brew pubs?"

"Not yet," he said mildly. "But you never know. Right now I'm mostly working on food recipes. Takes a lot to get things right. The guy I trained under said one thing I could do to develop my own style would be to reproduce the signature dishes of successful restaurants."

The bartender gave him a hard look. "So you

develop your own menus by stealing someone else's recipes?"

"No, no." He laughed and held up his hands. "It's not like that. I'm not stealing anything. This is just a training exercise. Learn by doing, if you see what I mean."

She did, and so did I.

What I also saw was that this was a reasonable explanation for him having Kristen's recipe for gluten-free waffle cones.

The kitchen at Hoppe's was indeed slow that night. It took nearly an hour from the time our waiter took down our orders to when our food was slid onto our table.

"Sorry," she said, for approximately the millionth time. And for the million and first time, we assured her that we understood the situation, no worries, don't concern yourself about us, all good.

She flashed a tired smile. "Thanks. Tell you what, to save you some time, here's your tabs," she said, distributing the long pieces of paper. "If you want more drinks, that's great, I'll do a rerun, but this will get you out the door if you have somewhere to go."

Other than home and bed, we did not. However, all of us had jobs to get to in the morning, so we paid our bills and wove our way through the crowd. By the time we reached the door, our table had been cleared and another group was already settling into our seats.

I felt a tiny childish pang of outrage—something along the lines of "Hey! Those are our chairs!"— but squashed it immediately and also decided to never ever tell anyone I'd had such a ridiculous thought.

"Penny for them?" Rafe asked, catching hold of my hand after we'd waved good-bye to Chelsea and Ash and started our way home in the deepening twilight.

"Um." *No, no, no, don't tell him! He doesn't need to know!* But then I did, and sighed, steeling myself for his response.

"You know," he said thoughtfully, "I think I get what you mean. For two hours, those were our chairs and ours alone. That we've left them behind to the mercies of strangers unknown is a betrayal of sorts."

I stared at him. "So you understand what I'm talking about?"

He gave my hand a comforting squeeze. "No. You're nuts. But you're my nut, and I love you."

Which had been the reaction I'd been expecting. I gave a contented sigh. "And you're my stick-in-the-mud and I love you."

"If we were writing our own wedding vows, we could work all that in."

"One more reason not to do that, then, isn't it?"

Early on, we'd made the mutual decision to opt out of personalized vows. I was hesitant to bare my soul like that in front of 150 people, and Rafe said the writing would be too much stress for him, although since the man had never felt stressed in his life, I suspected it was more laziness than anything else.

I felt a buzz in my pocket, slid out my phone, and showed it to Rafe. It was Kristen.

"If The Blond One calls," he said, "you must answer."

"She'll be glad to hear that." By this time we were walking up our porch steps, so I dropped into the cushioned wicker love seat and answered the phone. "Hey. What's up?"

"Have I ever told you that you're the best friend anyone could ever have?"

Smiling, I kicked off my shoes and tucked my feet up onto the cushion, crossing my legs. "Not today."

"I should have. I'm a mess these days, thanks to those darn kids and the fuss with the restaurant. I haven't wanted to admit it, but I am now. I'm a wreck and I need to make time to talk to you more often."

"About time," I fake grumbled. "Thought I was going to have to do some kind of intervention."

"No need. What I do need is help."

"What kind? You know all you have to do is ask."

"Not sure yet. But I'll let you know as soon as I figure it out." She paused, then said softly, "You're the rock in my life and I wanted to make sure you knew it."

"Any particular kind of rock?" I asked lightly, but my heart was warm with relief. Kristen was going to be okay. She'd asked for help, and she'd be okay. Maybe not right away, but she'd get there. "A gemstone would be nice. Nothing over-the-top, though. Semiprecious would be fine."

She blew out a sigh. "Give the woman a compliment, and she wants more. Let it go, Hamilton. Let it go. Time is wasting away, the girl and the boy are asleep at the same time, so I need to take advantage of this moment and do the matron-of-honor thing, which means bugging you about a replacement for the skateboarding minister. What's the scoop?"

"No scoop. Not even of ice cream." Which suddenly sounded like just what I needed. Mint chip in an adorable little sundae glass, with a spritz of whipped cream, chocolate sprinkles, and—

"What do you mean?" Kristen demanded. "I thought you and Frances had it under control."

"Yeah, well. About that." I went through the short list, and the whys behind them.

"Huh." Kristen gusted a heavy sigh. "Now what are we going to do?"

"We are going to do nothing. This is not your problem. Aunt Frances and I will figure it out."

"But—"

"No buts. What you just said about needing help? This is me helping you by not letting you help."

"What about my guilt level? I feel horrible that I can't rush to your rescue."

"You can rescue me from something else. No feeling guilty about this. Aunt Frances and I will figure something out. There's plenty of time."

Kristen snorted. "Have you looked at the calendar?"

"Weeks away," I said airily. Then I counted the weeks on my fingers, and was startled to barely need two hands. Five full fingers and down to the knuckles of a sixth. "Well, anyway, I'm sure something will work out. Speaking of which, do you know a Des Pyken?"

She couldn't place the name, so I filled her in on

his status as a potential buyer of Seven Street. Then I gave her the more important information point that he'd busied himself with re-creating her waffle-cone recipe.

Kristen laughed. "What is it? Imitation is the sincerest form of flattery? If this Des dude is copying me, I must be doing something right."

"You don't think it's weird?"

"I used to do the same thing. Still do, to some extent."

The restaurant business was something I would never understand. "So you don't think it's suspicious that Des Pyken knows how to make the cones that ended up poisoned."

"Minerva Joy Hamilton," my best friend said in a dangerous tone. "Did I or did I not tell you to stop poking around into this?"

"Sure, but—"

"And didn't I tell you that we have law enforcement officers for a reason? Officers who are trained to investigate crimes?"

"Not those exact words, but—"

"And didn't . . ." An infant's wail pierced my eardrums and I took the phone away from my ear. When it subsided slightly, I hesitantly put the phone close to my head. "There, there, little one," Kristen was saying. "Momma's here, Momma's here."

The wails diminished in decibel level, but not in intensity. "Um," I said, "maybe we should catch up some other time."

"Good idea," she said, still in that soothing tone. "Yes, little one, good idea for Momma to talk to Auntie Minnie later. Say bye-bye to Auntie Minnie. Bye-bye."

The phone went quiet.

I sat there, legs still crossed underneath me, looking across the lights of the marina, at the darkness that was Janay Lake, thinking about Kristen, about her babies, about her restaurant, and about our friendship.

Much later, long after my feet turned numb, I slid off the chair and went into the house.

Still thinking.

Chapter 13

I had a hard time sleeping that night. Whenever I shut my eyes, I'd start seeing the blue handle of a big knife. Then I'd open my eyes and be wide awake. Then I'd reach for my e-reader and read until I fell asleep and it dropped to the floor, the noise of which would wake me up. Then I'd take a long, calming breath and consciously try to relax every muscle in my body, starting with my toes. When I got to my eyes, I'd shut them. Then I'd see the handle of that knife and the cycle would start all over again.

My phone's alarm didn't wake me as much as it alerted me that my purgatory was over. With a fatigued sense of relief, I showered and dressed, and it was when I was staring at my oatmeal, eyes bleary and mind fuzzy, that the real reason for my poor sleep occurred to me.

"I'm worried," I said out loud. Rafe had already left the house, so I was talking to Eddie, but he had the capacity to be a better listener than my fiancé, who tended to get distracted by anything shiny, including, but not limited to, sports, the laughter of other people, the noise of power tools, or the smell of hamburgers on the grill.

Then again, that same list—outside of the sports item—was equally distracting for my cat. Eddie, however, was currently fitting himself onto the kitchen windowsill that overlooked the backyard. It was a windowsill that wasn't big enough for an Eddie-size cat, and parts of him overflowed, but he happily spent hours there, so he couldn't have been too uncomfortable.

He also looked as if his attention was completely on the robin that was hopping around the lawn, so I cleared my throat loudly.

"Like I said, I'm worried. That's probably why I didn't sleep for beans last night after talking with Kristen. I'm worried about her. And Sabrina. And Carol. And Reva and Isabella and Misty and Corey and the guys at Fat Boys and everywhere else in town. What if some nutjob really is targeting Chilson's restaurant workers?"

Said out loud, it sounded ridiculous, so I was glad Rafe was gone. Eddie might criticize me about many things, but his cat brain wasn't interested in the abstract questions I posed when thinking out loud about criminal theories.

"Mrr," Eddie said, looking at me with steady yellow eyes.

"Yes, I know it sounds stupid, but my dreams came from somewhere. Manifestations of whatever is on your mind, right?" I paused. What did cats dream about? I was pretty sure they did dream, because I'd seen Eddie when he was snoring the snore of the just, his feet moving through the air as if he was in a super-slow-motion run.

"Anyway." I got up and put my spoon and bowl into the dishwasher. "I'm worried about Kristen and all the others. Maybe worrying about a mass targeting of restaurant workers is dumb, but people do dumb things all the time. So I'm not going to stop investigating, no matter what Kristen says."

"Mrr!"

"Glad you agree."

The next step, of course, was to continue investigating. I thought about what that should look like as I walked through the quiet streets of downtown, nodding early morning greetings at passersby, at this point mostly summer visitors being towed by dogs of various shapes and sizes.

What shape should my investigation take next? I'd discovered a few things, and found out a few more things thanks to a willingness to eavesdrop, but I needed to get more proactive if I was going to—

"Minnie!"

I jumped at the sound of my name. On the other side of the street, Rafe was climbing out of his truck.

Frowning, I stood on the edge of the curb. As he came near, I asked, "What's the matter?" Because for him to abandon his carefully laid back-to-school plans had to mean something dire had happened. "What happened? What's the matter?"

He took my hand. "Everyone's fine," he said, and led me to a quiet bench tucked into a narrow alleyway. "Let's sit a minute, okay?"

I sat. He sat next to me.

Silence ensued.

"Um," I said hesitantly, "at some point you're going to tell me something, right?"

"Right."

More silence.

"And this is going to happen sometime soon, yes?" I asked.

"Yeah. Any second now."

Time ticked its way forward, one second at a time. Possibilities ran through my head one by one, each version more frightening than the one before, starting with a fender bender and ending with the news that even though I'd left home barely ten minutes ago and hadn't seen a fire truck or heard a single siren, our house had burned into a heap of ashes and no one knew if Eddie had escaped.

"Rafe," I finally said. "Whatever it is, tell me. I'm imagining all sorts of things, and I'm getting scared. If you want to call off the wedding, just say so. If you want to—"

"Other way around," he said tightly, leaning forward to put his elbows on his knees and his chin in his hands. "You're the one who's going to want to call things off."

That didn't make any sense. "Rafe," I pleaded. "Just tell me."

He pulled in a deep breath and let it out in one big gusting puff. "All right. It's Chris. And Skeeter."

I fought an urge to laugh. In all the worst-case scenarios I'd dreamed up in the last five minutes, I'd never once thought about anything involving the marina rats. Then again, a mention of Chris and Skeeter this early in the day couldn't be good.

"Does this have anything to do with the wedding?" I asked, suddenly suspicious.

"Well, they know we don't have anyone to marry us."

Not a huge surprise. I was pretty sure the entire town knew. "And?"

"They called me this morning with the answer to the problem."

Sure they did. "And that is?"

"You're not going to like it," he murmured. "I mean, you're really not going to like it. But they were so excited, and I didn't know how to tell them no, and—"

"Just tell me."

"Right." He nodded. Nodded again. "Well, it turns out that Skeeter knows a guy with a ship captain's license. And you know how captains can marry people? Well, Skeeter says this guy will be in Chilson the week of our wedding. He's contacting him right now to see if he'll have time to officiate."

"A ship's captain?" I blinked.

"I know, I know. It won't work. There can't be room for a hundred and fifty people on whatever boat this is, for one thing. And Kristen doesn't do boats, and our moms . . . well, let's not go there." He sighed again. "I'll tell them . . . something. They were geeked about it, is all, so I said I'd talk to you as soon as I could."

"It'll be okay," I said, putting my arms around his waist and giving him a hug. "Truly."

With a sigh, he put his head against mine. "I want to fix everything for you," he murmured, "not make things worse."

Tears stung at my eyes. I swallowed and cleared my throat. "Funny you should say that, because I think the rear brakes on my car need work."

"They'd better not," he said, but the tremor he might have had in his voice was gone. "Darren re-did those last spring, remember? Might be the front brakes."

It wasn't the brakes at all. He knew that and I knew that. We also knew that public displays of emotion were not our thing, and that we both had to get to work. "I love you," I said, lightly tapping my head against his. "Thanks for telling me about this in person. We'll figure something out, wedding-wise."

"You're not so bad," he said, "for a librarian."

"And you're not the worst middle school princi-pal in the world."

We sat there for a moment longer, wrapped in each other, then we got up and went our separate ways. After I waved at his truck as he went back up the hill toward the school, my feet took me not to the library but to Cookie Tom's. This was now a morning that required baked goods.

Inside, there were two people in front of me, which worked out well as it gave me time to make my choices, and to remember something. When Tom and I had been out on the sidewalk the other day watching Parker McMurray exercise his right to free speech, what he'd said had made it seem as if he knew Parker on a personal basis. Clearly the universe was trying to tell me something.

Or maybe not. Either way I'd get a custard-filled chocolate Long John out of it, so no matter what, I'd win.

When I got to the front of the line, Tom crossed

his arms and gave me a long look. "Thought we had a deal."

I grinned. We did indeed. Not only did Tom sell me bookmobile-bound cookies for a discounted price, he also let me sneak in the back door so I could avoid the lines. "Not a bookmobile day," I said. "How about a dozen assorted? And I have a couple of questions for you."

He'd started folding a box but paused. "Not hard ones, I hope."

I glanced around. There were a couple of people who'd come in behind me, but they were being attended to by Tom's assistant. The ones in front of me were seated at one of the small marble-topped tables, busy getting their fingers gooey with sticky-bun stickiness. "No," I said. "It's about Parker McMurray. Do, um, you know him well?"

Tom shook his head. "Yes, but no. And 'friend' was the wrong term. He's my wife's cousin. Second? First, once removed? Twice? Anyway, something like that. We see him at the big family get-togethers and that's more than enough."

"Understood," I said, nodding. "Doesn't everyone have a cousin like that?"

Tom pointed at the custard Long Johns. I held up three fingers. "I spend a lot of time before dinner," he said, "making sure I'm at the other end of the table from Parker. He's one of those guys who thinks he knows everything when most of the time he doesn't have any idea what he's talking about."

I murmured something soothing and held up two fingers when he pointed at the cinnamon twists.

"And this year I'll have to work even harder to not talk to him," Tom said.

"Oh? Why's that?" I asked, nodding at the inclusion of a bear claw.

"My wife told me he's been saying since May that he was going to bring his girlfriend to Thanksgiving dinner. He's never done that before. Then a couple of weeks ago, I hear that she dumped him. And now . . ." He shrugged.

"Now what?" I asked, pointing at the cider doughnuts with two fingers.

"You don't know?" Tom's surprised glance flicked up at me. "Parker was dating Remi Bayliss."

How the knowledge of Remi Bayliss and Parker McMurray being a former couple had escaped me, I wasn't sure. It certainly seemed like something I should have heard from someone in the last few days.

Remi's murder was the biggest topic of conversation in the county, so why wasn't there a rumor running around that Parker was a suspect? Wasn't it general knowledge that people are most often killed by the people closest to them? Didn't everyone always point their collective fingers at the ex?

I puzzled about it off and on all day. After an internal debate with myself on the ethics of creating and perhaps even spreading a rumor, I pulled Holly into my office, shut the door, and asked her if she knew anything about Parker and Remi's romance.

"Not sure I'd call it a 'romance,'" Holly said, putting air quotes around the word. "Not from what I heard, anyway."

"Oh?" I leaned against my desk. "If it wasn't a romance, what was it?"

"Parker McMurray being a desperate bachelor?" She shrugged. "Yeah, I know I should feel sorry for the guy, following his dream and sinking all his money into that restaurant, then losing everything but the clothes he was wearing, but he's such an idiot. If he'd listened to anyone who knew anything about the business, he wouldn't have opened the place to begin with, not in that location. But, oh no, he's going to be different. His restaurant is going to be *so* special that people will find him down a narrow, dark, short side street where no one except the city's park staff ever goes," she said, rolling her eyes.

This was going in a different direction than I'd expected. I tried to pull her back to my intended topic. "If Parker and Remi weren't really dating, what was it?"

"From what Cherise said, and she didn't tell me a lot, because I don't think there was much to say, it was a handful of dates. Parker would text Remi and ask about going to dinner, or to a movie, or something. Sometimes she'd go, because she didn't have anything else going on, and I guess he's not the ugliest guy around."

"Not the romance of the century, then?"

She frowned. "Is that what he's saying? It wasn't even close. If that's the story he's telling now, he's just looking to be the center of attention, now that Remi was murdered."

"What I heard is that he's upset about her death."

Holly sighed. "Fair enough. He's not a horrible person. Just dumb. And a little weird."

There was one more thing I wanted to ask. "It sounds like Cherise and Remi had a close relationship."

"They did," she said, her voice dropping low. "Not friends, exactly, because Cherise was the boss, but Remi had been at Angelique's forever. Cherise leaned on her. I'm not sure what she's going to do without her. And now she's having to deal with being a murder suspect?" Holly shot me a glance loaded with meaning.

"Don't ask me," I said. "Ash isn't telling me anything. That active investigation thing."

Holly made a rude noise. "Is this a guy thing or a cop thing? Seems to me they'd move along a lot faster in their investigations if they talked to more people about the investigations."

It was an excellent point, and I made a mental note to pass it along to Ash. Which probably wouldn't do any good, or change anything at all other than increase his irritation level with me by a degree, but I figured it couldn't hurt to plant the seed.

I told Holly that unless she wanted to talk to Ash herself, I'd tell him about the non-relationship between Parker and Remi.

"All yours," she said with a grin, opening my office door. "Far as I'm concerned, the less time I spend in the sheriff's office, the better."

Until not that long ago, I'd felt the same way. Now I was on a first-name basis with the sheriff, her command staff, the front office employees, and a good share of the deputies. Corrections and dispatch weren't all that familiar to me, but you never knew what might be around the corner.

That thought stayed with me the rest of the day and into the evening, when Rafe and I went to Aunt Frances and Otto's house for a cookout in their backyard. "Cookout" being a loose term, because they'd just had an outdoor pizza oven installed, and we were their first pizza guests.

We were seated at their glass-topped patio table, enjoying the light breeze and the slanting light of the sun, when my aunt slammed the oven door shut and stalked our way, her hands full of a pizza tray. "We can order out," she said grimly.

The pizza was nearly black on the left, just barely cooked on the right. Otto tipped his head to one side. "This is just the way I like it. How did you know?"

Aunt Frances's glare should have melted his back fillings, but he just smiled up at her. Though she tried to keep a straight face, she couldn't hold it. "There's another in the oven," she said, laughing. "I just need to rotate it in five minutes."

Rotate it she did, and pizza number two was outstanding. I slowed down after eating two pieces, as did my aunt. Otto and Rafe were both well into their third when I said, oh so casually, "By the way, Chris Ballou and Skeeter have a solution to the wedding-officiant problem."

My aunt, who'd picked up the bottle of white wine, thumped it back down. "Those two? I can't wait to hear this."

Rafe said, around a mouthful of pizza, "Ship's captain."

"That won't work," my aunt said. "Change the venue at this late date? Are they serious? What am I supposed to do now?" she asked, exasperated.

Otto reached for the wine bottle. "This won't be a problem," he said, pouring all around.

"Easy for you to say," my aunt muttered.

"Well, there's still a problem of a missing offici-ant, but the ship captain won't be a factor. It's a myth that ship captains can marry people."

Rafe, Aunt Frances, and I looked at each other, then simultaneously reached for our phones and started typing.

"You're right," I said happily, scrolling through official-looking website after official-looking web-site. "It's a total and complete myth!"

"Silly me for not checking." Rafe bumped my arm with his elbow. "Could have saved a whole bunch of trouble."

"Chris and Skeeter are the ones who should have checked," Aunt Frances said darkly. "Thank you, Otto, for your knowledge on the subject. How did you happen to know that, anyway?"

"My mind is a collection of typically useless facts. Glad something in there was of service this time." He held up his glass. "Cheers."

An hour later, pizza gone, dishes done, and marina rats texted, Rafe and I walked downtown to the Wood Shed. Little more than a dive bar from Sep-tember through May, the place burst at the seams all summer long. I didn't get the attraction, as I didn't care for the smell of stale beer or places so packed with people you could hardly hear what the person next to you was saying even though that per-son was six inches away from you, but it was proba-bly good for me to get out of my comfort zone every so often. Or so Rafe told me.

He opened the scarred wooden door and a wave of noise swelled out. "Hope they found a table,"

Rafe said, holding the door for me. I smiled, tacitly agreeing, and ventured into the din.

Tank and Kerry, his latest girlfriend, were at a table near the door, both of them draped across empty stools, one for Rafe and one for me. "Thanks," I said loudly, sitting.

Kerry grinned. "No problem. I just told the boss that if he didn't let me reserve this table he'd be looking for a new bartender."

Right. I'd forgotten. Kerry worked in a dentist's office year-round, but she tended bar here in summer. "Hard to find good help these days?" I asked.

"Hard to find any help," she said, "good, bad, or indifferent. I help out the boss with interviewing, and I tell you, it's not getting better. Even if you find someone, you never know if they're going to show up, and even if they show up, you don't know how long they'll stay before they get poached away by someone else."

"Poached?" I frowned. "That's a regular practice?"

She laughed. "Been going on as long as restaurants have existed, my guess. It's all part of the game, you know? Some people, they'll stay in one place forever because they have friends working there. Others? They'll leave a place in a heartbeat if they get an offer of a dime more an hour."

On an intellectual level, I knew all that was true, or at least I'd heard enough people talk about it to grasp the reality. But what I hadn't thought about was if employee poaching could be part of what was behind the waffle-cone poisoning.

Or Remi's murder.

Chapter 14

I talked the idea over with Eddie the next morning as I ate my cold cereal. Rafe was already up and gone, out early on a Saturday to help a buddy install an irrigation system. It was possible one of them knew something about irrigation, but it was also possible neither one of them had a clue and would be attending the University of Google to figure it out. Either way, I had the entire day ahead free to do whatever I felt like doing, as long as that included pulling weeds, doing a load of laundry, and working out what to make for dinner.

"What do you think?" I asked my furry friend. "Is there a connection between all the employee poaching that's going on and Kristen's situation? And/or Remi's death?"

Eddie, who was sitting in the middle of the floor in a shape that bore a striking resemblance to a meat loaf, gave me a long, unblinking look. He then heaved a huge sigh and closed his eyes.

"No, hang on," I said. "You barely even consid-

ered the idea. There could be merit to it." Though
he opened one eye, I could tell his attention wasn't
going to last long, so I hurried ahead with spinning
the theory out. "Okay, my suspects are Parker,
Cherise, Harold, Des, and Misty. Harold could be
trying to hire away other employees to staff up
Seven Street before he sells, along with destroying
the competition of Three Seasons through the poison, and he killed Remi because . . . because he was
trying to convince her to come work for him, it
turned into an argument, and in the heat of the moment, he killed her . . . with the knife he, um, always
carried because . . . because . . ."

"Mrr," Eddie said, yawning.

"Yeah." I slid off the kitchen stool. "It's not
working, is it?" And that was the best idea I'd had.
The employee poaching tie-in for all the other suspects was even more tenuous. So much for the confidence I'd felt at two in the morning that I'd hit on
a concept that would explain everything and lead
directly to the bad guys.

"Bad guys," I murmured, noting the plural I'd
unintentionally used. What if more than one person had been involved with the crimes? What if—

Eddie leapt to his feet, galloped around the
kitchen island twice, then glared up at me. "Mrr!!"
he said, then ran off in the direction of the dining
room.

I watched him go. "The volume of the voices in
your head get turned up?" I called.

"Mrr!" he called back.

"Let me know if I can help you with that," I murmured, wondering for the zillionth time if all cats
were as weird as mine, or if he was a special case.

I started the first load of laundry, decided the weeds were too wet with dew to do any weeding, and chose dinner by the simple means of opening the freezer, closing my eyes, rummaging around, and pulling something out.

Pot stickers? Excellent. We'd made a big batch a couple of months ago, frozen the rest, and I'd totally forgotten about them. All I'd have to do for dinner was make a dipping sauce, and by sheer coincidence, my favorite sauce had only three ingredients. Heat up some frozen edamame, and we'd have an outstanding dinner.

With that settled, I decided to wander downtown to Corner Coffee. Sure, I could finish drinking the coffee Rafe had made and poured into the carafe to keep warm, but there was more morning left than there was coffee remaining, and it was easier to keep the coffee-morning ratio correct by getting something from Corner Coffee than to make another pot.

"Rationalization, thy name is Minnie," I said, stepping outside and shutting the front door behind me. It was a beautiful mid-August morning. Light blue skies, wispy clouds, seagulls squawking, songbirds singing. Janay Lake was already dotted with fishing boats, and in a few hours it would be crowded with speedboats, pontoon boats, and personal watercraft buzzing around in small annoying circles. It was the sound of summer in northern Michigan, but in a few weeks they'd all be gone.

"Just a few weeks," I muttered to myself, as I found myself standing in a six-person-deep line for a simple cup of coffee. "Just a few more weeks and we'll get our town back."

Corner Coffee was full up with tourists; there

wasn't a single chair or stool open anywhere, so I topped my large order with a lid and went back into the fresh air.

I stood there for a moment, sipping, regretting the sip because the coffee was still too hot for human consumption, and considering my next move.

A movement in a store across the street caught at the corner of my eye, and I frowned. It wasn't even nine o'clock. The retail shops didn't open until ten; why was anyone already inside Gennell Books & Goods?

I crossed the street and peered inside. Blythe was standing next to a metal cart filled with books, transferring them one by one to the store's shelves. She saw me standing there, smiled, and came to the front door.

"Morning, Minnie. You're out and about early."

"But I'm only out for coffee." I hoisted my cup. "You're working, and it looks like you've been here for some time."

She glanced back at her cart. "Turns out that if you want to sell books, someone has to open boxes, unpack them, scan them into the computer, and put them on bookshelves."

"And to order them in the first place," I said.

"That, too."

She smiled, but I heard the underlying sigh. "Still not able to find employees?"

"Not anyone who will work for the wages I can afford to pay. I did find a high schooler to take some afternoon hours after school starts, though, so there's that at least."

"I'll ask Rafe," I said. "My fiancé. He's the middle school principal. He might know someone."

"Oh, Minnie, that would be fantastic. Because right now I have two choices. Run this place by myself or put the Closed sign on the door."

Neither one of those sounded like a recipe for success. I said I'd be in touch, let her get back to work, and made my way down the block. If anyone had been paying attention to me, it would have looked like a very aimless kind of meander, which was probably true, but only because I was paying more attention to what was going on in my head than to what was going on under my feet.

To date, none of my amateur investigating had moved me a single step closer to my goal of clearing the reputation of Three Seasons and getting it reopened.

My steps slowed, then came to a stop. I pulled out my phone.

Minnie: *Did the Health Department give you the all clear to reopen the restaurant?*

Kristen (after a short pause): *Late yesterday. Sorry, meant to tell you, but . . . babies. Misty, Isabella, and Harvey are there now, trying to figure out a menu.*

Minnie: *That's great!!*

Kristen: *Guess so. Just not sure how many people will walk in the door, given the waffle cone thing. We can't afford this too much longer.*

Minnie: *It'll work out. I'm sure it will.*

Kristen (after a pause): *Hey, you're not poking around into anything you shouldn't be, are you? Told you to stop, remember? There's a killer out there, you numbskull.*

Minnie: *Just walking down the street, drinking coffee in the sunshine.*

Kristen: *Any progress on a wedding officiant?*

Minnie (after a pause): *Getting closer and closer. Give the kids a kiss for me!*

I turned the phone off and slid it back into my pocket, out of sight and out of mind. What Kristen didn't know wouldn't hurt her, and besides, she wasn't the boss of me. Eddie was.

No, what I needed to do now was get my thoughts into some semblance of order. I'd let myself get distracted—library vandalism, summer sunshine, upcoming wedding, all that—and it was time to think about the crimes in a logical way. Or at least in a way that was logical to me.

So. I had my suspects.

Misty Overbaugh, Three Seasons chef, reported to be opening her own restaurant, and who'd left the Three Seasons door unlocked the night before the poisoning.

Harold Calkins, current owner and seller of Seven Street.

Des Pyken, potential owner and buyer of Seven Street.

Parker McMurray, failed restaurateur who had a one-sided love interest in the murder victim.

Cherise Joffe, manager of Angelique's, who had a deep and abiding hatred for Kristen and who'd reportedly had an argument with the murder victim not long before she was killed.

It seemed to me that Cherise was the most likely suspect. She had the most skin in the game, so to speak. As a restaurant worker, she had the know-how to mess with waffle cones. And not that I was trying to find a killer, but Cherise seemed volatile, and if Sabrina's tale of a fight between her and Remi soon before the murder was true, well . . .

"Well," I said out loud. That meant my next step should be to find out more about Cherise. I couldn't ask Holly, so who could I ask? Who else knew her?

"You are so stupid," I said. Sabrina had said she'd heard about the fight from a guy named Robert, who'd been working at Shomin's Deli that summer. He was career coast guard, just retired from twenty-five years of sailing around the Great Lakes. There could be more than one Robert doing restaurant work in Chilson, but wouldn't most of them go by Rob or Bob? Yes, they would. And wouldn't it be reasonable for me to make sure this was the right Robert if I wanted to confirm this story for Ash? Yes, it would.

Sure, I'd already texted Ash about the incident, but I hadn't mentioned Robert's likely place of work, so to save Ash time and trouble, I should stop by Shomin's, see if Robert was there, and confirm whether or not I had the right Robert.

Yep, I was a good friend. So considerate.

I walked down to the waterfront, sat on a sunny bench, and leisurely finished my coffee. By that time it was past nine o'clock, the earliest I thought someone might be at Shomin's. After I knocked on the glass door a few times, a frowning Reva popped her head out of the back. When she saw me waving, she smiled and came up front.

"Hey, Minnie. What's up?" She ushered me inside and locked the door behind me.

"I have a weird question. Is Robert here?"

Her frown returned. "No. He's not on the schedule until Tuesday. Is something wrong?"

"Oh. No, nothing like that." I hesitated. "Well, you know I'm the one who found Remi Bayliss, right?"

"Yes, I'd heard." Her face softened into sadness. "That must have been awful."

"Worse for Remi, but yeah. I'm still getting nightmares."

"Do you want to talk to David about them?"

I blinked, then remembered her husband was a psychologist. "You know, that's a good idea, but that's not why I'm here." I saw her expression turn toward puzzlement, so I went on. "The police are working the case, I know they are, and I'm sure they'll find the killer soon. Then again, it might help them solve it faster if we pass along anything that might be pertinent."

"And you think Robert knows something?"

Reva was no slouch in the brains department. "I heard from someone else that Robert heard Cherise and Remi having a huge fight the day before the murder, so I wanted to . . . what's the matter?"

She was staring at me with wide-open eyes. "Oh, wow. I never once thought about it."

"About . . . ?"

She shook her head. "Sorry. It wasn't just Robert. It was also me and Corey and Marlow and everyone who was getting a late lunch that day. Cherise and Remi were right here." She pointed at the floor. "Remi was in line to order, and Cherise charged in, that long hair of hers flying all over, and started yelling at her."

"About what?"

"Cherise asked what was she doing taking a lunch break when there was so much to do? That the desserts hadn't even been started yet and how did she think everything was going to get done? That the last thing she should be doing was wandering off, and who did she think she was, going off without permission? Remi shrugged, said a girl's got to eat, and that she'd be back in fifteen minutes."

I felt a pang. Why hadn't I known Remi? "What did Cherise say?"

Reva smiled. "That if she wasn't back in ten minutes, she'd be fired. Then she stomped out."

"And what did Remi do after that?" I asked, fascinated.

"She looked around, saw that everyone in the store was staring at her, said something like, 'Glad I don't have my bad days in public,' and everyone laughed." Reva bit her lip. "I'm going to miss her so much. I was always trying to get her to work here, but she made a lot of money at Angelique's. It's hard to walk away from that, you know?"

I thanked her for her time and headed out, thinking. Since my best thinking was often done when I was in motion, I kept walking through the streets of downtown. It was still relatively quiet, and would be for another hour or so, although dogs and their walkers were out in full force.

Since I wanted to keep on thinking, I pretended to be a nonlocal city person, keeping my head down and not making eye contact with anyone, not even the dogs.

What had I learned?

That Cherise didn't see any problem with berating an employee in front of strangers. That she liked to keep close tabs on her employees. That she was feeling the stress that came with running a high-end restaurant.

All interesting, but to me it added up to one thing, that none of that would lead to murder. It might lead to Cherise firing Remi, or Remi getting tired of Cherise's attitude and quitting, but murder? I just didn't see it.

Then again, there was always the heat-of-anger thing that could pop up in pretty much anyone, given the exact wrong set of circumstances. Sure, Cherise would have to be incredibly stupid to commit a murder in her own restaurant in broad daylight, and then just let me wander in after her . . . though maybe that was a ruse. Maybe she had indeed killed Remi in the midst of a rush of white-hot anger and used my serendipitous presence as a way to look innocent.

I thought about that for a moment. It could be true. Though Cherise had looked shocked and scared that day in the kitchen, that reaction could all be attributed to having killed Remi in the first place.

I blew out a huge sigh. This was getting me a total of absolutely nowhere. If I was going to help Kristen, and maybe in a sideways sort of way help figure out who killed Remi, I needed hard facts, not speculation, and speculation was all I had right now.

Sure, I'd learned a few things, but none of them were giving me the feeling that I was making any progress. All I was doing was spinning theories, and that wasn't helpful to anyone, not to Kristen, not to Ash, and certainly not to Detective Inwood, who, though I resisted admitting it, was the one I most needed to convince about the guilt of any given suspect.

"This is hard," I muttered, sounding like a whiny ten-year-old told to clean her room. Embarrassed at myself, and more than a little ashamed, I looked around. My feet had taken me up a side street, and there wasn't a soul to be seen, a small favor that had me breathe a sigh of relief.

Then I realized where I was. Across the street from Angelique's.

I stopped and sat down on the front step of an insurance agency, the concrete chilly underneath me as the sun hadn't moved around to this side of the street and everything was in the shade.

Huddling with my knees pulled up to my chin and my arms around my legs, I studied the front of the restaurant. The police tape that had closed off the front door on Tuesday afternoon was already gone and the restaurant's white clapboard siding, blue trim, and geranium-filled flower boxes were revealing nothing of what had happened inside only a few days earlier.

There were, however, a number of bouquets of flowers laid on the sidewalk, propped up against the building. I wondered whom they were from. Co-workers, I supposed. And friends. Relatives. People who'd heard about the murder and wanted to do something to help.

I sat there, holding myself tight, mourning a woman I wished I'd known, when a stocky man of about fifty walked up to Angelique's, a huge bouquet of red roses in his hands.

Parker McMurray kneeled on the sidewalk and tenderly placed the flowers against the building.

"These are for you, Remi," he whispered, just loud enough for me to hear. "I wish things had been different. I wish *I* was different. I wish you'd loved me the way I loved you. But mostly . . ." His voice broke. "Mostly I wish you were still alive."

He caressed the velvety petals of the roses, then heaved himself to his feet and walked away, his shoulders bent with sorrow.

Chapter 15

I withdrew from the shadows of the insurance office's doorway. Unintentionally watching a man's grief was not something I wanted to do. And I was also more than a little ashamed that I was already picking apart what he'd said, parsing out his words as potential proof, of either innocence or guilt.

He'd said he wanted things to be different. That he wished she'd loved him. And that he wished she was still alive.

Those sounded like something an innocent person would say. But even if he'd killed her, he could wish those things, especially if he'd killed her in the heat of the moment.

So what had I actually learned? That Parker McMurray loved Remi and was mourning her death. All so very sad, but not useful in terms of finding a killer. Or a poisoner.

No progress. I was getting nowhere and could feel an irritated panic start to creep up on me. What if we never caught who had poisoned Kristen's waffle cones and killed Remi? What if the reopened Three Seasons failed to thrive and went out of business? What if Angelique's went out of business? What if Chilson got a reputation for being dangerous, what if the tourists left and never came back, what if the town's economy slid into a downward spiral from which it might never recover?

I shook my head. What I needed was something to ward off the pending sense of failure. Something to perk me up and give me momentum.

"Got it." I snapped my fingers. I'd told Blythe I'd talk to Rafe about potential employees for her. Which I would do, as soon as we were both in the same space at the same time, but before that I could go up to the library and ask my coworkers. Surely one of them might know someone who was looking for some work.

Because somehow it wasn't quite ten o'clock yet, I went to the side door and used my key to get inside. The first thing I saw was Gareth up on a ladder, his cell phone in one hand and his other hand on the front end of a blocky metal object about the size of an elongated shoebox.

"How about now?" he said into the phone.

Josh's voice came through loud and clear. "What I saw was Minnie coming in. Good to know it can pick up someone that short."

I stuck my tongue out at the security camera as Gareth turned around.

"Morning, Minnie. You working today?"

"Nope. I'm helping a friend, Blythe Gennell. She has the new bookstore downtown and she's looking for part-time help. You know anyone who might be interested?"

Gareth climbed down the ladder. "What is she paying?"

"Working in a bookstore is a great job for anyone who likes books. Happy customers, you see all the newest releases, and you get a discount on anything you buy."

He gave me a sardonic look. "So the pay is low?"

Of course it was. I gave him the number and he shook his head. "Going to be hard for her to find anyone at that rate."

"But if you think of anyone?"

"Will send them over there, sure. So what do you think?" he asked gesturing at the camera. "Full coverage outside, and all the entrances from the inside."

"Do I have to like it?"

Gareth laughed. "You look like you just ate a lemon. But I get it. Having to install security cameras means there's a need to install security cameras. Not nice to think that our little town needs something like this, yeah?"

I had a thought. "Um, I don't suppose there's any chance of them going away once the vandals are caught, is there?"

He gave my shoulder a pat. "Always nice to talk to you, Minnie," he said, collapsing the stepladder. "Get outside in the sunshine and think about something else."

It was good advice, and as soon as I talked to Donna, I'd follow it. I wandered up front and found our seventy-something part-time clerk singing Taylor Swift's "Shake It Off" as she sorted through the books from the returns bin.

Donna was an excellent example of what a

seventy-three-year-old female was capable of doing. She worked at the library in order to fund her hobbies of marathon running, skiing, and snowshoeing, and for years I'd held her as a role model of who I wanted to be like when I grew up. That, however, was starting to shift, as I wasn't sure I had her energy now, let alone in another forty years, something that was confirmed as I saw her making up book-involved dance moves.

She did a quick spin, slid the books along the counter toward the computer, and looked up, smiling. "Morning, Minnie. What's up?"

I repeated my quest for finding bookstore help.

"Hmm." Donna folded her arms on top of the counter. "I assume Blythe can't pay much more than minimum wage, right? No, I didn't think so. Let me think about that. My grandkids are already busy with sports practice, but I'll ask around."

"Thanks," I said. "Blythe is wearing herself to a frazzle. If she doesn't get help soon, she's going to burn out, and I would hate to lose her." Not to mention her store.

"Agreed." Donna gave a sharp nod. "I'll do what I can."

I thanked her again, started to leave, then stopped. "What do you think about the security cameras?"

"Long past time," she said promptly. "Back when all the plans were being made for this renovation"— she waved her arms at the building around us—"I told Stephen security should be included, but he didn't want to spend the money." She snorted at the decision made by our former boss.

"You don't think they're intrusive?" I asked.

"Of course I do. But everything is a balance, and

in the name of safety and peace of mind, the good of having them in place outweighs the bad."

I nodded slowly and headed home to my chores, thinking about good and bad and how to find the line that marked the difference.

Back home, I flipped washed clothes into the dryer, started another load in the washer, went out to pull weeds, went back inside to wash up, folded clothes, and flipped the newly washed clothes over.

"And now," I said to Eddie, dusting my hands together for no reason other than it was fun to do, "there's almost an hour before those clothes are ready to fold. Should I go back outside to pull more weeds, a Sisyphean task if there ever was one, or should I do something that doesn't get me so dirty before I have to touch clean clothes?"

Eddie, who was sitting in a square of sunshine by the front door, blinked at me and yawned.

"Nice. You do realize the roof of your mouth is one of your least attractive features, right? That spot is honestly a little creepy."

He opened and closed his mouth in a silent "Mrr."

At least he hadn't opened his mouth far enough for me to see the weird dark gray spot again. I'd been worried about that spot early on, because it sure looked like something that didn't belong there, but Dr. Joe had said it was just part of his coloring and nothing to be concerned about.

"And it's not even a solid color," I said. "Kind of mottled. An inconsistent gray." The description pleased me so much that I decided to repeat myself. "That's exactly it. An inconsistent gray. Inconsistency is consistent with your character, so—"

Without a single glance my way, Eddie jumped to his feet, galloped upstairs, took a hard left turn at the top, and disappeared from view.

"Love you, too!" I called, then grabbed my cell phone and headed out the front door to pursue the next step in my self-appointed task to make sure Three Seasons came back to life. I'd texted Kristen that morning, asking how things went at the restaurant the night before, but still hadn't heard back, which could mean something or nothing. I considered texting Harvey or Misty but didn't want to go behind Kristen's back. So the next best way to find out would be to talk to the female half of my houseboat-renting couple and ask some gentle prodding questions. And if, at the same time, I ran across Harold Calkins, well, that was all to the good, wasn't it?

It was a solid plan, and I felt positive about it on the short walk to the marina. Plus, the sun was out, the late morning air was turning downright warm, and my chores for the day were mostly done. Those were all good reasons to feel as if things were going to work out, and though I wanted to believe that, I was having a hard time shaking a vague sense of unease.

As I stepped onto the dock, I made a valiant effort to push it away to the back of my brain.

"Morning, Minnie!" Isabella was out on the houseboat's front deck, shaking a throw rug over the railing. "What's up?"

"Avoidance behavior," I said. "It's either this or pull weeds."

She laughed. Her long, silky dark hair was tied up in a tight braid and coiled at the nape of her neck, the way she always put it up for working at Three Seasons. "One great thing about living on a boat, no yard work."

"Speaking of work," I said, leaning against a dock piling. "How did things go last night? I texted Kristen but haven't heard anything."

"Yeah." Isabella made a face. "Can't say I blame her. Let's just say the four waiters she'd scheduled were three too many."

My unease popped up, fresh and shiny. "Well," I said uncomfortably. "It was just the first day. Things are sure to pick up tonight, right?"

She shrugged and gave the rug one last whipping shake. "Hope so. Got to say, though, everyone's on edge these days. With what happened to us, and what happened at Angelique's? People talk, you know?"

I did indeed. "But you and Corey are okay, aren't you? You're still planning to manage the candy store?"

"Oh, sure." Isabella flashed a wide smile. "We plan to reopen Henika's after Labor Day. We'd hoped to do it sooner, but it's so hard to find staff right now."

My tentative plan to ask her about potential bookstore workers faded away. "Well, I'm glad you're still going ahead."

"Absolutely. Yeah, a lot of work, but fun work, if you know what I mean?"

I did know, and understood. Though my wages at the library were on salary, I routinely worked far more hours than my position description stated. Graydon had, on occasion, shooed me out the door and told me to go outside and play.

"You and Rafe coming tonight?" Isabella asked.

"Um . . ."

She smiled. "I thought for sure Rafe was in on that conversation. He didn't tell you, did he? Corey and Skeeter and Chris and Eric decided we needed to have a party tonight."

"Wasn't there one yesterday?" Every Friday that I'd lived at the marina there'd been an unofficial Bring Your Own at the picnic area.

"This is different. They're hauling in grills, the marina is buying the meat, people are bringing food and drinks. Basically everyone has said they'll show up. Should be fun, but I have to work, so I'm hoping for leftovers." She grinned. "And that it runs late."

"We'll be there," I said, instantly changing my plan. It would be far easier to strike up a conversation with Harold Calkins at a party than over the gunwale of his boat. "But now I have to go home and make something to bring to the party."

"Deviled eggs." Isabella nodded. "You can never have too many."

She was probably right, but that would involve so many steps. Cooking hard-boiled eggs, peeling them, slicing them, mashing up the yolks, mixing them with mayonnaise and other bits, spooning them back into the cooked egg halves, finding the right tray so they didn't slide all over on the walk to the marina . . . no, it was too much.

My cooking skills—and even more important, my innate disinclination to cook—meant I chose recipes based on the number of ingredients and the number of steps. Five ingredients was my top end, and the number of steps about the same. This, of course, created a very limited repertoire of things I could cook, but there was more than one benefit to marrying Rafe.

Luckily, guacamole was one of the two things I could make without a recipe (the other being a breakfast of cold cereal) and all it took was a short trip to the grocery store, fifteen minutes of chopping and mixing, and our social obligations were done.

I spent the rest of the morning finishing up the laundry and deciding that the thawed potstickers would be just fine for a meal on Sunday. In a burst of energy, after a lunch of grilled cheese and an apple, I spent enough time in the front flower bed so that the daylilies and the border of snapdragon annuals outnumbered the weeds.

"And that's that," I told Eddie, washing the dirt off my hands in the cold water of the outside faucet.

My cat, who'd been watching my efforts with a critical gaze, closed his eyes, rolled over, and stretched himself into the longest Eddie ever seen.

"Right," I said, climbing the steps and scooping him up. "And now I'm officially done with chores. What do you think should be next on the schedule?"

"Mrr," he said snuggling into my arms.

Clearly, naptime for Eddie was coming up soon. He'd had a hard day so far, of course, doing all that Minnie supervising.

So Eddie and I spent the afternoon in the gazebo Rafe and I had nearly finished, Eddie curled up on the ottoman's cushion, while I was partly re-reading Angela Thirkell's *August Folly* and partly looking out over the waters of Janay Lake, thinking about Remi, Kristen, and all the restaurants and restaurant workers in Chilson.

Rafe, encrusted with dirt from head to toe, got home late in the afternoon. Though I tried to berate him for not remembering to tell me about the marina potluck, that stuck about as well as I expected. He did, however, say he'd make it up to me by cooking my favorite breakfast the next morning, then went upstairs to shower and change.

On the short walk over to the marina, I told him about my intention to talk to Harold Calkins.

"About what?" he asked, shifting his grip on the cooler that held the guacamole, bottled water, and beer.

"To learn more," I said, "about him, about Seven Street, about him selling it."

Rafe gave me a sideways look. "You want me to be okay with that?"

I grinned and switched the bag I was carrying of tortilla chips, big bowl, and big spoon to the other hand so I could tuck my hand inside his elbow. "Yup."

He was quiet for a moment, then nodded. "Seems harmless enough."

"One of the side effects of being efficiently sized," I said, "is people never think I might be a threat."

Rafe laughed. "Only someone who doesn't know you could think that."

I wasn't sure if that was a compliment or not, but since we were walking into the already crowded picnic area, I decided not to think too hard about it.

"Yo. Niswander!" Chris Ballou called out, brandishing a set of the biggest grilling tongs I'd ever seen. "Get over here. Need your help, dude."

Since half our potluck contribution was in the cooler that Rafe carried, I went with him over to the cooking zone. The marina had two permanent grills for people to charcoal grill, but for the party Chris had hauled in three propane grills from somewhere, and all five were going full bore.

Half a dozen men were already huddled by the biggest grill. Chris, Skeeter, Ted Axford, Eric Apney, Corey Moncada, and an older man who looked familiar but whom I couldn't place.

"Medium well," Eric said, popping a beer.

"With you on that one." Rafe gave him a fist bump.

Corey grinned. "Give me rare."

"Every time." Ted nodded agreement.

Skeeter shrugged. "Hard to go wrong with medium rare."

"Medium-rare guy," Chris said, poking at his own chest. "Ladies and gentlemen, we're now in a three-way tie for the best way to cook steak. Harold, how about you? Give us the tiebreaking vote."

I blinked and suddenly started paying attention to the inane conversation. That's who the older man was—Harold Calkins. I inched closer.

He laughed. "Sorry, my friends. My steaks are always well done. Nothing like it to toughen up your jaw muscles. Plus, the more you cook, the more flavor you get."

My mouth dropped open. That wasn't how it worked. Even I knew that. But I'd been in the restaurant kitchen more than once and listened to Kristen—or Misty or Harvey—rant about people who ordered well-done steak, moaning about the waste of a fine piece of meat, and I'd learned that no real restaurateur would condone well-done steak, let alone tout its virtues.

I took the cooler from Rafe's grasp and headed to the biggest picnic table, where food of all shapes and sizes was being laid out on the marina's classic tablecloth of an old sail.

"Quite a spread," I said to Louisa Axford as I put the cooler on the table's bench seat.

She smiled, tossing her long white hair over one shoulder. "Mine is the broccoli salad. Say nice things about it in Ted's hearing, if you would. He wanted me to do baked beans, but that's what Eric made."

"Promise," I said, and put the guacamole bowl on the table. "What did the new guy bring?"

"Harold?" Louisa laughed. "Harold brought plates, utensils, and napkins. Here we were all hoping for something fancy from the guy who owns Seven Street, but he says he's the worst cook ever. Owns the restaurant because he likes going out to eat, not because he can cook."

I looked across the lawn to the men at the grills.

Harold couldn't cook.

Huh. Now wasn't *that* interesting?

Chapter 16

D on't you think that's interesting?" I asked Eddie.

It was Sunday morning, and the rain that had pounded us half the night had blown off and the sun was out. My cat, who was sitting on the edge of the bathtub watching me try to tame my stupidly curly hair into some semblance of order, stared at me with his unblinking yellow eyes.

"Stop that," I said. "You're getting creepy."

He gave a little kitty sigh, adjusted his feet, and continued to stare.

Though I kind of wanted to punish him for not doing what he was told, on some level I understood that explaining that to anyone would have sounded childish (as in "He's *looking* at me and I want it to stop!"), so I turned my back to him and kept talking.

"If Harold can't cook, it doesn't seem likely that he would have known how to make waffle cones. By itself, that fact doesn't clear him of murder, but since we know"—I heard myself say the word and corrected myself—"since we very, very strongly believe that the Lee knives mean Remi's death and the poisoning were done by the same person, Harold's lack of cooking ability is a point of proof that he's not a killer. Or a poisoner."

I looked at my hair in the mirror. Still an unmanageable mess. I tried to take comfort in the fact that at least I'd tried.

"What do you think?" I asked Eddie, twisting a tie around my hair to turn it into a bulky ponytail. "And FYI, I'm not talking about my hair, I'm talking about my Harold's Not a Good Suspect Theory, and don't ask your dad for help on this," I said. Rafe was already gone, having returned to his buddy's house to tweak the irrigation system they'd laid the day before. He'd said it wouldn't take long, but I was already assuming I'd be making the sauce for the potstickers by myself.

"Which I can do," I said to Eddie, "because there are fewer ingredients than I have fingers on one hand. Easy, right?"

There was no response from my cat. I looked over, but he was gone. I traipsed around the house, looking for him, and eventually found his tail sticking out from underneath the couch.

It was new, purchased earlier that summer during a long-weekend trip to Grand Rapids. We'd met up with friends of mine from college, had dinner, and gone to a concert at the Van Andel Arena. The next day, when Rafe and I had walked around downtown, we'd come across a furniture gallery and made a huge impulse buy. It was on sale and was the nicest thing we owned. Most of our furniture was still garage sale purchases and hand-me-downs from relatives, along with a few things picked up at auctions. This lovely long leather couch was the first thing either one of us had bought at a real grown-up furniture store, and I still got a rush of pleasure every time I slowed down enough to really look at it. Rafe claimed that the six-foot stepladder we'd picked up during the same trip could also be considered furniture, but he was wrong.

"What are you doing under there?" I asked.

The tail flicked back and forth.

"Okay," I said. "Don't tell me. And since I'm a grown-up human and not a cat, I'll tell you what I'm doing. I'm going out."

The tail flicked again, only faster.

"Good talk," I said. "See you later, buddy."

I closed the front door on a muffled "Mrr!" and shook my head about the contrariness of cats as I headed down the porch steps. *Now* was when he wanted to tell me something? Seriously?

My goal for the morning, other than get out of bed at a time that wasn't embarrassing (check!), was to talk to Ash. I'd asked Rafe to let me know whether or not he'd seen Ash's vehicle on his way past the sheriff's office. Subsequently, he'd texted me emojis of a tiny SUV and a tiny law enforcement officer, because apparently it was too much work to text "Saw Ash's car in the lot."

Either way, communication had been achieved, so I walked to the low brick building and stood at the glass door, texting.

Minnie: *Would like to talk to you. I'm up front.*

Ash (after a short pause): *Right now?*

Minnie: *Yep.*

Ash: *You going to keep bugging me until I listen to what you have to say?*

Minnie: *Yep.*

Ash (after a longer pause than before, during which it didn't take much imagination to get a visual of his heavy sigh): *Be right out.*

He gave me a baleful look as he pushed the locked door open. "You know the reason I'm here on a Sunday morning is to get some quiet time to write reports, right?"

"Next time," I said, "you might want to hide your SUV."

He grunted and checked the door to make sure it was locked behind me. "This isn't going to take long, is it?"

"Fifteen minutes. Tops."

"Believe it when I see it," he said, but he led me back to his shared office, with a short detour for the both of us to get coffee from the pot he'd already made. He settled into his chair and made a Go Ahead gesture with his mug.

"It's about Harold Calkins." I perched on the front edge of the guest chair, doing my best to project a vibe that I wasn't going to stay long.

"Guy who owns Seven Street?"

"For now." I told him what I'd heard about the potential sale, and how he could have a motive to destroy the reputations of other restaurants, another reason—outside of the Lee knives—to connect the two crimes. "But that's not why I wanted to talk to you," I said. "What you should know is that Harold has the cooking ability of a Minnie Hamilton."

"Whoa." Ash fake dropped his jaw. "Didn't know that was possible."

"Funny, not funny. So I would say he's cleared of poisoning people but not of Remi's murder."

"Wait, now you're saying that the two crimes are not connected?" He did the one-eyebrow thing.

The man clearly had a hearing problem. "I'm saying it's unlikely that Harold Calkins doctored the waffle cones himself. Although I suppose," I said slowly, thinking out loud, "he could have had someone else do it."

"I've heard of hired assassins, but a hired poisoner?" Ash laughed.

"And I'm out," I said, standing. "Thanks for your time, Deputy Wolverson."

"Anytime, but please never again on a Sunday morning, Assistant Library Director Hamilton, soon to be Niswander."

Huh. He was right.

I opened my mouth to say something funny. Closed it, because I couldn't come up with anything. "See you later," I said lamely, and left.

I scooted out of the building before Ash came after me with something else I struggled to respond to. Once was bad enough, but if he did it twice in one conversation, I might have to seriously reconsider our friendship level.

The front door closed behind me and I headed out into the morning's sunshine without a clue as to what the rest of the day might look like. Though what I really wanted to do was to find the killer/poisoner, restore the reputation of Three Seasons, comfort all those grieving Remi, solve the employment problem, and cure the common cold if there was any time left in the morning, I also had no concrete idea how to go about doing any of it.

"What would Aunt Frances do?" I asked, mostly to myself, because she was one of the people I most wanted to be like when I grew up. Tabitha Inwood, Hal's wife, was another one, along with Carolyn Mathews, the library board's newest member, my friend Barb McCade, the Queens Elizabeth, and the fearless Amelia Earhart.

The next step in my investigation suddenly became obvious. What I needed to do was go to Gennell Books and take a look at the newest biographies. If that didn't bring me any closer to solving anything, well, at least I'd have scanned some new books, maybe noted a few for library purchase, and, ideally, learned a few fun facts about someone.

I was mulling over the suspects—Harold, Cherise, Parker, Des, and Misty—when I popped into the bookstore. "Am I first?" I asked Blythe.

She smiled but gave me a blank look. "First what?"

"In the store for the day. You just opened, right? Do I get a prize?"

Blythe's face cleared and she laughed. "Sure. You get the prize of knowing you're the first one in the store today."

I wound around the book displays and approached the front desk. From the front door, Blythe had looked as she always did, bright and cheerful. Up closer and more personal, I saw fatigue cutting grooves in her face and weighing down her shoulders.

Alarm bells sounded in the back of my head.

Someone needed to do something for this poor woman before she collapsed from sheer fatigue. I took a small breath.

"You need a break," I said gently, but firmly. "It's a beautiful morning. Do you have any printed directions on running the register? Great. I worked in a bookstore during college . . . yeah, this all looks familiar to me. Go out, get a cup of coffee, sit in the sunshine, and don't come back for at least an hour."

"I can't," Blythe said, glancing around at her store, at the cart laden with books. "There's so much to do."

"What, shelving?" I rolled my short sleeves up two inches and did my best to project confidence and competence. "You know to whom you speak, yes? Yes. Anything that's obvious, I can do, file, shelve, or put away. Anything that's not, I'll hide so you can't ever find it. And look, you can still laugh! Good to know. Now, go."

I shooed her out the door and immediately locked it, which made her laugh again, so even if I didn't accomplish anything else the rest of the day, I could call it a success.

But I did plan to get more things done, and one of them was to work on an investigation plan. I was usually great with plans—drafting, developing, refining, amending, all that—so I wasn't sure why I was so off track. Maybe the wedding was distracting me? Or maybe it was because Kristen had told me to stop? Then again, maybe there was some other reason I wasn't considering.

Sighing, I unlocked the door and started working on the cartful of books. General fiction, gardening, mysteries, young adult; all easy enough to categorize and shelve appropriately. I picked up a new book I hadn't yet seen, *A Pictorial History of Chilson*, and couldn't resist flipping through the pages.

Most of the buildings in the black-and-white photos were long gone, lost to fire or demolition or renovated beyond recognition, but a few looked the same as when they'd been built, decades ago.

An idea stirred in the back of my brain.

I poked at the notion a bit, wondering how stupid it would sound if I said it out loud, then shrugged and pulled out my phone. I hesitated—it was Sunday morning, after all—but shrugged again. If Bianca Koyne didn't want to answer, all she had to do was ignore me.

"Morning, Minnie. How are you this fine morning?"

"Sorry to bother you on a Sunday, but I have a quick question."

She laughed. "Real estate agents are always on call. Have to be if we want to earn a living. What's up?"

"Remember we were talking about Harold Calkins selling Seven Street? I heard that Desmond Pyken might be buying it. Is that true?"

"Might be," she said cheerfully. "Negotiations are ongoing. Why, do you want to put in an offer yourself?"

Just as much as I wanted to be run over by a truck. "It's more I'm wondering about Des Pyken. Can you tell me anything about him? I'm, um, I'm wondering if the Friends of the Library should contact him about joining. Or maybe he's willing to sponsor one of the library's fund-raising events?" Yep. Sounded just as stupid out loud as it had in my head.

"Wow, good questions," Bianca said. "But I hardly know the man. He's from downstate, has a couple of restaurants in the Grand Rapids area, and he's wanted to buy Seven Street since the first time he came to Chilson."

That wasn't anything more than I'd already known. "Do you know when that was?" I asked, more to ask any question than because I was actually interested. "The first time he came to Chilson, I mean?"

"Oh, wow, I don't really know. But from some of the things he said, it had to be soon after he opened his first restaurant downstate."

"If he buys Seven Street, is he going to keep the name, or is he going to change things?"

Bianca laughed again. "That's what we're negotiating. Des wants to call it Pyken's, just like his other places, but Harold wants it to stay Seven Street. He's insisting on it, says it's his legacy. Hey, I have to go, okay? I'm showing a house and the client just got here. Catch you later!"

She clicked off, but I kept my phone open to do a little Internet research and quickly learned there were three Pyken's restaurants in the greater Grand Rapids area. One on 28th Street, one on Alpine, and one in Rockford.

I opened the "About" page on the Pyken's website and learned something else. The first Pyken's restaurant had opened almost fifteen years earlier.

The door opened, a troop of customers came in,

and I slid my phone back into my pocket. I'd have to think about what I'd learned later; it was time to turn into a bookseller.

While Blythe didn't take a full sixty minutes away from the store, she was gone for well over half an hour. When she returned, she got mental bonus points from me for flattening her face and hands up against the glass door.

Putting on a fake frown, I opened the door. "Young lady, now I'm going to have to wash this window. Would you have done that if you owned this store?"

"You bet," she said promptly. "What's one more washing?"

I laughed, let her inside, and started to show her what I'd done in her absence. "Hope I didn't mess up anything," I said, suddenly uncertain that I'd done the right thing by barging into her store and kicking her out.

She gave me a swift, hard hug without even glancing at what I'd done. "A little break was exactly what I needed. Thank you so much. I'm good to go now."

"No problem," I said. "Happy to help. It was fun." And it had been. Plus, I'd learned a little more about Des Pyken, knowledge that might or might not be useful, but any information had to be good information at this point. Time was ticking away, and the longer the crimes went unsolved, the worse it was going to be for Three Seasons and for Remi's family and friends.

How, though, could the ability Des had for long-range planning be part of any of this? Lots of people made plans. So what if Des had an exceptional capacity?

My thoughts tumbled into a downward spiral.

What if no one ever figured out what happened at Three Seasons? What if business slowed to the point where Kristen closed it for good? Parker's restaurant failure had wounded him deeply. What would the same thing do to Kristen? Far worse, what if Remi's murder was never solved? What ripple effects would there be? It was a tragedy to lose a loved one to murder, but to know the killer was still out there, free and unpunished . . .

"Stop," I said out loud. Enough of that. Time to move on to the next item on my short mental investigative to-do list, an item I'd just put on, because I'd just remembered something. I put my hands in the pockets of my shorts and wandered down to the waterfront.

The wide sidewalk, now that it was nearing noon, was filling up. Stroller-pushing parents, gaggles of teens, solo runners, people of all shapes and sizes walking dogs; it was a typical summer day. Smiling faces were everywhere, including mine.

I then stepped off the sidewalk and onto the park grass. Last week I'd spotted Misty just about here. Most people—and I was no exception—operated in a very rut-like way. If Misty was like most humans, if she showed up here, she'd probably locate herself in roughly the same spot.

There were more people in the park now than last week, and I picked my way around families with picnic baskets, couples with foam clamshells filled with take-out food, and others just sitting in the sun, enjoying life. Misty was not in the same place; she was all of ten feet away. I was about to call out and joke with her about it, but then I clued in to her body language.

She was sitting on a beach towel, arms wrapped around her drawn-up legs, staring out at the water. She was also making frequent rubs at her face with the back of her wrist. It was a gesture used only by people who were drying tears, and it stopped me in my tracks. Should I leave? Make a noise to let her know I was standing there?

My indecisiveness must have been loud, because she looked up. "Minnie. Hey. What's up?" Her attempt at a smile was an epic fail.

"Not much. How about you?"

She shrugged her narrow shoulders and used her fingertips to wipe her eyes. "Same. How's the wedding planning coming along?"

I hesitated. "Misty, are you okay? Because if you want to talk, I'm happy to listen. If you'd rather I went away, I can do that, too, and understand completely that you'd rather be alone. No harm, no foul."

"Oh. Um . . ." She heaved in a huge breath, then let it go. "It's just . . . I feel awful about Remi Bayliss. I liked her about as much as Kristen likes Cherise, you know? But I didn't want her dead."

I murmured vague platitudes of the John Donne variety, that everyone is a part of everyone else, that every death is a loss for us all.

Misty nodded, sighing. "Yeah, I know. But I'm a mess mostly because, um, you know I'm starting my own restaurant, right? Yeah, everyone seems to, even though I haven't told anybody," she said, almost smiling. "But the closer it gets, the more it scares me. What was I thinking to even think about going out on my own?"

It wasn't a question I'd ever thought about on a personal basis. If you didn't count Little Free Libraries, opening your own library wasn't really a thing. I edged closer. "Don't say anything, but Kristen said basically the same things before she opened Three Seasons."

"Really? Somehow that makes it worse." She wiped her eyes again. "Kristen and Harvey and everyone there, they're like family. How can I leave them?"

Since there was no way I could walk away from someone who was crying, I sat down next to her.

And listened.

After a few minutes, Misty's tears slowed; she stopped gulping her words, took a few deep breaths, and eased back into the Misty I'd known for years, the Misty who was a solid, calm, highly professional chef.

"Sorry about that," she said, rubbing her whole face with her palms.

"No worries. I get it. Change is scary. Anyone who isn't scared about big changes in their life isn't thinking through all the possibilities."

She slid me a sideways glance that held a hint of a smile. "Says the person who's getting married in a few weeks."

"Um . . . uh . . ." I stopped trying to talk. Was that what this was all about? Was my recent and uncharacteristic lack of to-do lists an offshoot of wedding jitters? I hadn't thought I was nervous about the event in the least, but . . . maybe?

My knee-jerk reaction of denial wisped away

into the sunshiny air. "You could be right," I said. "And opening your own restaurant is on a different level, but just as frightening. Goes against the run, hide, or fight options. It's more like"—I searched for an analogy—"marching into the lion's den."

She gave me a speculative look. "You and me against a lion. Who's going to come out the winner?"

"We are," I said firmly. "Two smart and strong-minded women versus a pesky lion who doesn't know what he's up against? No contest."

Misty laughed, then said, "Thanks for listening, Minnie. There's something about you that always makes me feel better."

I gave her shoulder a pat. "Now you're embarrassing me. That's my signal to go."

She thanked me again as I stood. I mumbled an awkward "You're welcome" and was thankful to hear my phone make the *ping!* of an incoming text message.

I moved off a few steps and pulled out my phone. It was Gareth in a group text to me, Graydon, and Josh. On a Sunday. This could not be good news.

Gareth: *Can one or all of you come over to the library?*

Josh: *Right now?*

Gareth: *Yes.*

Minnie: *If I walk fast, I can be there in 10 minutes.*

Graydon: *Fifteen for me.*

Josh: *Same.*

Gareth: *Thanks. I'll be in the back parking lot.*

My heart rate, which had already increased, soared into high exercise level. The back parking lot was where we parked the bookmobile. I half walked, half jogged up to the library, making it there in less than my estimated time. Skirting the library building itself, I zipped around to the back.

From a distance, I could see that the bookmobile was still there. That eased my biggest worry, that it had been stolen, but then I started worrying about vehicular destruction. Someone backed into it. Someone sprayed graffiti over it. Someone broke its windows. Someone—

And then I got close enough to see what had happened.

I slowed to a walk and came up next to Gareth, who was standing in the driveway to the gravel parking lot, hands on hips. The two of us were still standing there when Josh and then Graydon arrived.

"Well," Graydon finally said. "This was unexpected."

The scene the four of us were surveying was one of mild, but widespread, destruction. Yesterday, the parking lot had been relatively smooth and tidy. Today it was a pockmarked mass of holes interspersed with heaps of dirt.

"Who would do this?" I looked at the closest hole. Not only had last night's rain filled all the holes, but it had also eradicated any tracks that might have been left.

"No idea," Gareth said grimly.

Graydon looked at the mess, sighed, then looked at Josh. "We need to review the security video. I haven't set it up on my cell yet."

"Got it, boss." Josh whipped out his phone and started tapping buttons. "The roof camera covers this parking lot. Give me a second and . . . uh-oh." He held up his phone. "There's no video."

The three of us stared daggers at the IT guy.

"Hey," Josh said. "I'm the IT guy, not the security video guy. Let me go inside and see if I can work out what happened."

What happened next was that we all traipsed into Josh's office and hovered over his shoulder as he fiddled with the security software, fussing with files and controls and all sorts of things I didn't understand. And at the end of it all, he shook his head and reached for his phone.

"I can't find any video from that camera. I'll call the camera guys; they're supposed to be available twenty-four seven, right?"

Graydon muttered something I couldn't quite hear. Then again, I was pretty sure I didn't need to hear it, either.

Josh's call was answered, but at the end of the long conversation, the result was the same.

We still didn't know who was vandalizing the library grounds.

Chapter 17

When I arrived home, Rafe was sitting on the gazebo steps, throwing sticks for Eddie to fetch. I could tell that was what he was doing because he'd throw a stick, look at Eddie, say "Fetch," then point at the stick.

"What are you doing?" I asked, sitting next to him. It was a tight fit for two people, but we made it work.

"What do you think it looks like?"

I squinted at Eddie, who was lying in his classic meat-loaf shape in the middle of the lawn. He was glaring at Rafe and had one ear flattened against his head. "Like you're wasting your time and annoying the cat."

Rafe put his arm around me and gave me a quick squeezing hug. "You are the smartest person on the left side of this step. What have you been up to today?"

"Lots," I said, and proceeded to tell him about my stop at the sheriff's office, my short volunteer stint at the bookstore, about talking with Misty, and about what Gareth had discovered up at the library. Rafe's reaction was predictable.

"Hang on. What you were worried about most was that someone might have stolen the bookmobile?" The love of my life laughed. "Who did you think was going to steal it? A rogue librarian? Or is there a lucrative black market out there for bookmobiles? Tell me you haven't been asking the dark web about this."

I increased the distance between us from no inches to as many as I could manage without falling off the step. "It's not like I can help my reaction, you know."

"Sure." He gently pulled me back toward him, and I let him do it. "But you also knew I was going to laugh at you."

Of course I did. Rafe wouldn't be Rafe if he didn't make fun of me on a regular basis. Which was fine, because I did the same thing to him.

I put my head on his shoulder. "After talking with Misty, I think I can cross her off the suspect list. Not only does she consider Kristen and Harvey family, but she's too much of a professional to intentionally poison anyone."

"You don't think she had anything to do with Remi's murder?"

What I thought was that I liked Misty very much and didn't want her to be involved with anything criminal, bad, or even mean. But there was one thing, and I couldn't ignore it. "She has a temper."

"Long way from that to killing someone." Rafe threw another stick. Eddie gave it a long look, sighed, and closed his eyes.

"She's nowhere near Kristen's level, temper-wise, but a couple of times I've heard her rip into kitchen staff. For uneven squares of cilantro, or poor plating, that kind of thing. But . . ."

But it was still a huge jump from a kitchen rant to outright murder.

"Next step," I said, "is to keep going with learning more about the suspects."

"Who's on the list again?" This time Rafe threw a balled-up leaf he'd picked from an adjacent lilac bush. It fell short of Eddie's nose by five feet. He reached out with one white paw, grasped that his paw wasn't anywhere near long enough to touch the leaf, then closed both eyes, still in the one-paw-out position. Cats were so weird.

"Parker McMurray," I said. "Cherise Joffe. Des Pyken. Plus Harold Calkins and Misty, although right now they're at the bottom of the list."

"Have you worked out alibis for anyone?"

"No," I said, and wondered why I hadn't done that yet. Alibis were a basic part of crime investigations. What was wrong with me?

"Then that's something to work on, right?" he asked. "Of the three toward the top of the list, who do you think is most likely to be the killer?"

I thought about his question and realized the answer was easy. "Tie between Cherise and Des."

"Okay. To me it looks like there's a choice here, alibi-wise. Find alibis for Harold and Misty so you can eliminate them altogether, or concentrate on working out what Cherise and Des were doing the day of the poisoning and the murder. Either way, you'll narrow down the list."

I pulled back and eyed him. "Look at you, being

logical. Who are you and what have you done with my fiancé?"

"I'm a work in progress," he said. "Thought you knew. Come on." He stood and held out a hand to pull me to my feet. "I have an idea."

"Does it include him?" I nodded at Eddie, still in the middle of the lawn with one paw out.

Rafe scooped him up. "Not this time, pal. But we'll be right back."

Seconds later, Eddie was inside with his nose pressed up against the window, and Rafe and I were on our way to the marina. At least that's what I had to assume given our direction, because my beloved hadn't provided any indication of what was happening.

"What are we doing?" I asked.

"Going to talk to Harold Calkins."

"Oh? About what? And I didn't realize we were on such friendly terms with him that we could just march up to his boat and start questioning him."

"Watch and learn, my little dandelion."

I rolled my eyes but let myself be led down the sidewalk and over to the marina's picnic area, where Harold was sitting by himself, eating a sub sandwich from Fat Boys Pizza.

"Afternoon, Harold," Rafe said easily. "Want company?"

The older man nodded. "Sure. I hate eating alone. Was hoping someone would come along." He pushed the bag of potato chips across the table. "Rafe and Minnie, right? From the potluck the other night."

We exchanged opinions on who had brought the best food and agreed on anything Louisa Axford made.

"That woman can cook," Harold said, nodding. "People assume I can because I own a fancy restaurant, but half the reason I went into the business was to avoid cooking myself."

"You know, I never thought of it that way," I said speculatively. "Say, Rafe, do you think—"

"No," he said. "Not a chance."

I laughed, then said, "Harold, I hear you're selling Seven Street. Does the new owner feel the same about cooking as you do?"

"Nothing's settled yet," Harold said. "The sale is probably months away. But I might have a serious buyer interested. He has some restaurants down around Grand Rapids. He's a cooking guy himself, but after what happened at Angelique's, the deal might be off."

Rafe and I exchanged glances. "You mean the murder of Remi Bayliss?" I asked.

"Des had lunch there that same day," Harold said.

I blinked. "He . . . did?"

"Enough to put anyone off, I suppose." Harold rearranged the meat that was starting to slide out of his sandwich. "Des said he needs to think things through. Makes sense, but my accountant says it would be best to sell my place before the end of the year."

Rafe and Harold went on to talk about the upcoming college football season, but I did not, because I was thinking one thing and one thing only.

That Des Pyken had been at Angelique's the day of the murder.

On our way back to the house, I looked at Rafe. "What was it I was supposed to learn from that?"

"No idea."

I squinted at him. "You said, and I'm quoting directly, to 'watch and learn, my little dandelion.'"

"Yeah, not sure where the dandelion part came from. What do you think of it as a new term of endearment?"

"Calling me by the name of one of the most annoying weeds ever is not going to win you any points. And at the risk of repeating myself, I'm going to repeat myself. What was your intent as far as me learning something? I mean, I did learn that Des was at the murder scene, but there was no way for you to know we'd learn anything, let alone something important."

He put his arm around my shoulders. "That doing something is better than not doing anything, even if you don't know what you're doing."

While I liked the feel of his arm around me, it made walking difficult. I went with it for a few steps, then shrugged it off and took hold of his hand. "Not much of a learning moment when it's something I already knew. I know how to eat an elephant."

"One bite at a time." Rafe grinned. "So what's the next bite?"

It was a good question, and I kept thinking about it the rest of the way home, as we puttered about the rest of the afternoon, as we ate dinner, and when we went for a walk down the waterfront as the sun was making its final fast slide down to the horizon.

"I'm not sure what the next bite should be," I said, sighing. "There's so much going on right now. Everything is changing. Creepy vandalism at the library, our wedding, restaurants being sold, people leaving jobs, Kristen being . . . not Kristen. It's a lot."

"Okay." Rafe took my hand. "But why is that translating to not knowing what to do next? Usually you have more ideas than you have time."

"Maybe . . ." I swallowed. Being completely honest with myself was making my throat tight. "Maybe I'm hiding a little. It's one of the three primal reactions to danger, right? Hide, fight, flight. Change is scary, so maybe not taking the next step is like hiding."

My fiancé gave me a long sideways look. "You're scared to marry me?"

"What?" My eyes flew open so wide that my contacts were in danger of popping out. "No! That's not what I meant!"

"So what's scary?"

"Like I said, the wedding. You know I don't like to be the center of attention, and I will be, all day long."

He gave my hand a squeeze. "Not to worry, my yellow buttercup. Once we meet up at the front, I'll stick to your side like glue. If anyone dares to look at you without your permission, I'll fling myself in front of you to take the hit."

I was pretty sure yellow buttercup was redundant, but my wildflower knowledge wouldn't withstand the slightest bit of scrutiny, so I let it go. "Appreciated. Good to know I can rely on you."

"Always," he said.

The low tone he'd used made my heart go mushy. Since we were on a public sidewalk with dozens of people in sight, I didn't throw my arms around him and hug him as tight as I could. Instead, I lifted his hand and gave his fingers a light kiss. "Back at you," I whispered.

And then I thought of something. Tone. It wasn't just about voices; it was also a writing thing. Sentence structure, word usage, all that. Some people had such a distinctive writing tone, or writing voice, that their work was like a signature.

Back a few days ago, Josh had said he couldn't tell the real names of the people who were posting the bad restaurant reviews. But what if . . .

I smiled. "Got that next bite figured out," I said to Rafe.

"That didn't take long."

"No. Can we go home?" I asked, stopping and tugging at his hand. "I suddenly have a lot of work to do."

Rafe let me redirect our path—partly because he remembered there was a Tigers baseball game playing and partly because if we turned around right then he could casually avoid a group of middle school parents walking our way—and soon he and Eddie were sitting in front of the television and I was sitting at the dining table with my laptop and a pad of paper.

My intent was to copy and paste text from all the negative Chilson-area restaurant reviews I could find into a spreadsheet. I'd track the date and time posted, reviewer's screen name, the review rating, contents of the review, and anything else that seemed pertinent.

Maybe I'd learn something and maybe I wouldn't, but at least I'd be doing something, and according to Rafe, that was way better than sitting around fussing that I didn't know what to do. Or words to that effect.

I looked at the most popular review sites and used search engines to find less popular ones. Copied. Pasted. Made notes. Then copied and pasted and made more notes.

For hours.

When Rafe tapped me on the shoulder, I bolted upright from the slouch I'd fallen into. "What's the matter?"

"It's past your bedtime, sleepy pants," he said. "Do you need help getting out of that chair? You haven't moved in forever."

"Oh. Thanks. Um, I'm good. I'll be up in a minute." My attention drifted back to my laptop.

"No, you don't." Rafe flipped my laptop closed. "I know what you're like when you don't get enough sleep. Can this wait until tomorrow? Yes, it can. Go to bed."

I made a token protest because I didn't want him to get in the habit of telling me when I should go to bed, but he was right. Besides, I'd finished pulling out the bad reviews.

There were a lot of them. So many that it was a little frightening. Sleeping on it all and coming back to it fresh in the morning might be just the ticket.

The sun must have stayed up too late the night before and the next day chose not to get out of bed. I knew this because on Sunday the tiny little pictures on my phone's weather app had sworn it would be a bright, sunshiny Monday morning, yet what we got was an overcast haze that foretold a day full of heat and humidity.

"What do you think?" I asked Eddie.

"Mrr."

"Exactly. How is it that weather forecasters can be wrong so often yet still keep their jobs? Here I thought accountability was a thing for everyone. Why do they get to be exempt?"

"Mrr!"

His second response was closer than the first one had been. Much closer.

With some hesitation I looked up from my laptop, over the top of my cereal bowl, and into the face of my fuzzy friend. "You do know that if your dad sees you up there he'll turn your fur into a pair of mittens, right?"

"Mrr," he said quietly.

"Lucky for you he's already gone." I gave him a hard look. "But you knew that already, didn't you?"

Eddie studied his front paws, which were just out of my reach. Also out of my reach was the newspaper Rafe had left behind for me to read, but instead I was reviewing last night's spreadsheets.

"Do you have something to tell me, or are you just taking advantage of Rafe's absence?"

The paw introspection continued.

"Well, normally I'd yell at you, pick you up, and drop you on the floor, but since it's going to be hot and humid today, I'll forgive you this one time." Why I was suddenly equating Eddie Discipline with the weather I wasn't sure, but being hyper-aware of my own motivations was not one of my strong suits.

I took another bite of cereal. "You never said. Do you have something to tell me?"

"Mrr!"

"Yeah, well, sadly that doesn't help." I sometimes wondered what it would be like if Eddie spoke English. Did he ever have something important to say? A translation of the Voynich manuscript? The answer to why fried food tastes so much better than almost all vegetables? Then reason would kick in, because I was pretty sure that ninety-nine percent of what he was trying to communicate was to either let him outside or to let him inside.

"Mrr." He gave me a glaring look, then walked to the edge of the island, put out his paw, and pushed the newspaper to the floor.

"Is this your hint that I should pay more attention to current events? If so, you should know that the *Chilson Gazette* is more chamber of commerce events than investigative journalism." The newspaper editor, my friend Camille Pomeranz, did her best, but there was only so much to write about in a small town.

Eddie walked off into the dining room, flicking his tail from side to side.

I clambered off the stool and retrieved the paper. Front page, above the fold, was a photo spread of a recent boat fire out on Lake Michigan. No one was hurt, but the black smoke had been spectacular. Below the fold was a summary of the Tonedagana County Board of Commissioners meeting and budgeting concerns.

"This was what you wanted me to read?" I called out. "Really?"

"Mrr!"

Cats.

I turned the page. Upcoming events around the county, movie listings, a piece from the conservation district about fire danger, and . . . I put the paper down on the counter. Camille had written about the investigation into Remi's murder in an article titled INVESTIGATION CONTINUES. I scanned it quickly, then went back and read again, more carefully.

"Well." I sat back. All in all, there wasn't much that I didn't already know. The one thing I hadn't realized was that Chilson's mayor was concerned about the murder. "We hope that this will be resolved quickly," she'd said. "An unsolved murder could have a chilling effect on our town's economy."

I felt stupid. Of course that was a concern. If negative reviews impacted restaurant business, news of an unsolved murder might be just as damaging to Chilson's overall reputation, if not more so. How could I not have thought about that? Life as a library employee insulated me from a fair amount of local politics, but I should have been aware of what the general public was thinking and saying. Especially on social media.

Sighing, I refolded the newspaper and went back to the last soggy bits of my cereal and my laptop. The computer screen looked the same as it had a couple of minutes ago. My spreadsheet tally from last night was still telling me the same information, most of it bad.

By percentage, Chilson restaurants were getting more bad reviews than restaurants in other cities in the region. And a majority of the worst reviews had a sentence structure, a rhythm, that told me one important thing.

They were all written by the same person.

Chapter 18

You know this how, exactly?" Blythe asked.

I hadn't been able to contain my excitement at what I'd learned, so when I dropped into Gennell Books & Goods I blurted out my findings. Now, of course, I had to backtrack and clarify. "Do you happen to be related to a Detective Inwood? Never mind. Okay, I don't *know* know, but it's the only explanation that fits all the facts."

Doubt remained on Blythe's face. "And the facts are what?"

"Look at this." I tapped open my phone. Because I'd created the spreadsheet on my cloud drive, I could access it from all our devices. I used my thumb and forefinger to enlarge the information I'd tallied at the bottom.

"See?" I pointed. "That's the number of zero- and one-star restaurant reviews in Chilson the last two months. And that"—I thumbed the image sideways a little—"is the percentage of zero- and one-star restaurant reviews that have the same type of complex sentence structure, and also use a vocabulary that fits an eleventh-grade reading level."

"Almost ninety percent." Blythe made a *hmm* sort of noise. "Seems unusual, but I don't see that as proof."

I almost asked a second time if she was related to Hal Inwood. "No, but look at this. That's the number of two- to five-star Chilson restaurant reviews for the same time period. And that," I said, pointing again, "is the percentage with that same combination of complex sentence structure and reading level."

Blythe took the phone from me and peered at the screen. "That's basically zero."

"And that's why I think all those horrible reviews were written by the same person. That's why I think—"

My voice came to a screeching halt. Involving Blythe in my theories about who might have killed Remi wasn't anything I'd planned to do. She didn't need to hear about this. And she probably didn't want to.

"That's why I think," I said, shifting mental gears, "that I need to talk to my friend at the sheriff's office. Maybe it will help them figure out who killed Remi."

"Good idea." Blythe handed my phone back to me. "And now I have to ask why you're here first thing on a Monday morning."

"Here to help," I said promptly. "Monday mornings are classic errand time. Running to the bank, to the grocery store to get coffee, to the hardware store to find a replacement for that one shelving unit clip. I don't have to be at the library until after lunch, so I'd be happy to spend a couple of hours with your books." I grinned and rubbed my hands together, then stopped. "Unless, um . . . unless I screwed up the register. Did I? If I did I'm so sorry, your directions were great, it was me and—"

"Stop already, will you?" Blythe laughed. "You did fine. I just don't want to take advantage, that's all. Asking you to work for free is just wrong."

"And you're not. I'm volunteering, see?"

It took a little more work, but I eventually convinced her to grab her purse and go. "And don't come back for at least two hours," I called. I shut the front door behind her and looked around for a job to do that would be helpful but not interfering. But the bookshelves were all tidy, the window and door glass was clean, and the wrapping paper station was fully stocked. As far as I could tell, everything was shipshape.

Since I didn't know what else to do with myself, I decided to get more familiar with the point-of-sale software. I went behind the counter, brought the computer that also served as a cash register to life, and pulled out Blythe's sheets of instructions.

Once I'd satisfied myself that I could do all the basic functions, I started mousing around, poking around into the program's more complicated features. How to run a percentage-off sale. How to do a cash refund. How to do a credit refund. How to give store credit. How to add someone's e-mail address to the store's newsletter list. How to add a name to the membership list of the buyers' club. How to—

I stopped and went back one link. The store had a club? Did I know that? If I did, why hadn't I joined?

Tsking at myself, I entered my contact info and became the newest addition to the Gennell Books & Goods frequent buyers' club. If I bought one hundred dollars' worth of items, I would get ten percent off my next purchase. How cool!

A thought popped into my head. For half a second, I hesitated. Then I squared my shoulders. "In the name of crime fighting," I murmured. In the search box for last name, I typed Pyken. Zero results. Same with Overbaugh and Joffe. There was a McMurray, but the first name was Robert. I typed in Calkins . . . and there was Harold.

Hmm.

I leaned forward. The screen showed the date Harold's membership began, showed a code and cost for each item he bought, and tallied the total amount spent. He was almost to his second hundred, which I mentally applauded. Idly, I clicked on the first code. It popped up with all sorts of information. Title of the book he'd bought, its author, publisher, ISBN, the date it was scanned into the store's inventory, date and time it was sold, sales price—hang on. Date and time?

Clicking quickly, I worked through Harold's purchases. I learned that he was a fan of travel books, Patrick O'Brian novels, and nonfiction about World War II. He tended to buy books around lunchtime, and he tended to buy them during the week. He'd purchased *Desolation Island* the previous Tuesday, at the exact time Remi was murdered.

If this entry was right, and I had no reason to think it wasn't, he couldn't have killed Remi.

Harold was innocent.

I checked and rechecked the club listing, but the other suspect names stubbornly refused to materialize for my convenience.

But if I found an alibi for Harold, maybe I'd be able to find one for Misty. And maybe even for Parker.

I suddenly realized what I was doing. "Stop that," I murmured. It wasn't right to want to take people off the list of suspects just because I happened to like them, any more than it was right to be okay with certain people being at the top of the list because I didn't particularly like them. Bias, thy name is Minnie Hamilton, and I needed to be aware of and combat my unconscious assumptions.

Easier said than done, of course, but I figured awareness had to be a step in the right direction, and surely it was a good thing that I'd started the journey, even if it was a baby step.

Customers trickled in, and I spent an enjoyable hour handselling books from *Pat the Bunny* to *The Historian*.

"Don't bother putting that in a bag," a gray-haired man said. "I spotted a bench a block away that looks perfect for reading until my wife finishes buying vacation presents for the grandkids."

I put one of Blythe's bookmarks inside his new copy of *Murder Your Employer* and slid the hardcover book across the counter. "If you start this, you might need to send her back out to shop for their birthday presents, too."

"You've read it?" He tucked it under his arm.

"Stayed up way too late reading a few months ago, and it was worth every minute of lost sleep."

He grinned and twenty years vanished from his face. "Thanks for the heads-up."

"All part of the service here at Gennell Books & Goods," I said, smiling. As he walked out, he held the door for an entering Blythe.

"Minnie, you're the best," she said. "What can I possibly do to thank you?"

I smiled and edged out from behind the counter. "Um, stop saying thank-you, probably. And now it's time for me to get going. Lunch to grab, errands of my own. See you later, okay?" I scooted out before she could go emotional on me. Gratitude was nice and all, but I preferred it from a distance.

Outside, the reality of the muggy day came back full force. My walking speed, which had been brisk, dropped suddenly down to a slow stroll, because it wouldn't do to show up at the library all hot and sweaty.

I made my way down the sidewalk to Shomin's Deli, thinking about what to do next, investigation-wise, because a sense of urgency was starting to gather inside my skin. Though this feeling usually meant I was getting closer to finding an answer to a problem, I was pretty sure that wasn't the case this time around. This time all I had was a list of five suspects with one crossed out. Maybe what the rising urgency meant was I had to start working harder.

So. I needed to do something. Finding one alibi hadn't been that hard, once I'd leveraged the opportunity that had presented itself. What I needed to do was find more. Tomorrow was a bookmobile day, so I could talk to Julia and any patrons about the murder and the suspects. Sliding that into a conversation would be easy enough, given the mayor's quote in the paper, and you never knew what might turn up from a casual chat.

But what about today? What about right now?

Sighing, I pulled my attention out of my head and tried to focus on the sights and sounds around me. The first thing that caught my attention was a tall blond head exiting the toy store.

Kristen. Who had zero problem being the center of attention.

If she saw me, she'd stand there in the middle of the sidewalk, hands on hips, and yell at me for not responding to her numerous text messages demanding that I stop trying to find out who messed with her waffle cones.

In a cowardly yet instinctive reaction, I made a rapid turn and ducked into the nearest store. It wasn't until I got all the way inside that I realized I was inside Oliver's, a place I'd never entered because I'd never been in the market for clothing items that cost more than my first car.

The first thing I noticed was the softly natural lighting, which must have cost a fortune. The second thing I noticed was how few clothes were on display. The third thing was a sixtyish couple standing next to an artful collection of polo shirts, Russell and Barb McCade. He was examining a salmon-colored shirt, and she was looking as bored as I did when waiting for Rafe to finish a school board meeting.

They looked up as I approached and their instantaneous smiles warmed my heart. We exchanged hugs, and I said, "Haven't seen you all summer. What have you been up to?"

Russell, more commonly known as Cade, was an internationally famous painter of landscapes that were panned by critics but loved by basically everyone else, gave a huge sigh and polished his knuckles on his shirtfront. "It's a burden being so popular."

His loving wife rolled her eyes and pushed back a strand of her graying brown hair. "As if. What's popular with our son and daughter-in-law is having parents with time to help out with an infant who never seems to sleep."

I asked about grandchild photos, they obliged, and when I was done admiring, Cade gave me a measured look. "Tell me, Minnie Hamilton. What are you doing in Oliver's? And no prevaricating."

"The letter of the day is 'P'?" A few years ago, the McCades and I had bonded over the use of words starting with "D," and we'd carried the odd tradition forward every chance we got.

"Precisely," Barb said, gaining herself another point.

I laughed. These two were some of my most favorite people on the planet. So I explained, starting with the allergic reactions to the waffle cones, why I got involved, told them about Remi's murder, and ended with why—and how—I was avoiding my best friend.

"You live a full life," Cade said thoughtfully. "Are you ever going to let me paint your portrait?"

"Nope." But I smiled sweetly to take the edge off. Then I had an idea. The McCades moved in vastly different social circles than I did. If I'd been smart, I would have contacted them way earlier about this, but better late than not at all. "Do you know Harold Calkins? Or Desmond Pyken?"

"Harold? Sure," Barb said. "Des, not so much."

"Did you know Harold is selling his restaurant?"

"He told us the other night," Cade said, nodding. "Got all misty-eyed about it."

Barb made a rude noise. "You call it misty-eyed, I call it getting greedy. All last summer he talked about selling, now he has a solid offer, and he's going to make Des wait until after the holidays to take over? My guess is he's hoping to get a higher offer from Des."

Cade shrugged. "Things shift."

After we'd done a little more catching up, I peered through the window. The sidewalk looked Kristen-free, so I headed out, thinking.

Though Des Pyken had the opportunity to kill Remi, since he'd been at Angelique's right before the murder, why would he? And why would he run around adding triticale to Kristen's waffle cones? A restaurant sale almost four months in the future felt like more than a stretch.

I took a mental look at my suspects. Des was still on there, but I slid him all the way down to the bottom.

The next day was a bookmobile day. The heat and humidity we'd woken up to the morning before was blessedly gone, a fact that was lost on my furry friend.

Eddie normally took note of the change in my routine when I was bound for a day on the road. Super-comfortable shoes, pants that wouldn't show the dirt, a peanut butter and jelly lunch, and car keys in my hands; all were signs that he was going to be included. But instead of his usual prancing around and getting into his carrier early in hopes of making bookmobile time arrive faster, he'd curled himself into a tight Eddie ball on the new couch.

"You feeling okay?" I sat next to him. His breathing seemed normal, his eyes and nose were clear and not ooky, and he didn't flinch when I petted him. "It's not hot and sticky today. It's low humidity and a high in the mid-seventies. Perfect Eddie weather."

"Mrr."

He squinched himself tighter into the couch's corner, up against one of the pillows we'd bought at the furniture store, getting cat hair on something that had, up until that point, been cat-hair-free. The hair transfer was inevitable, of course, but I'd held out a ridiculous hope that at least one of our possessions would escape the fate.

"Did you stay up all night again?" I asked. A week or two ago his antics with a tissue box had destroyed my sleep patterns. The box hadn't turned out well, either. "If so, I'll understand if you'd rather stay home and not go out on the bookmobile. Julia will be disappointed, but I'm sure she'll understand if you're not up to—"

In one sudden motion, Eddie swooped himself off the couch and galloped through the dining room and into the kitchen, where I heard him do a body slam into the carrier.

I stood and headed his way. "You didn't hurt yourself, did you? Speak to me, pal."

"Mrr!"

In Eddie parlance, that could only mean "I'm fine, what are you waiting for? My adoring public awaits!" so I did all the commuting things and in short order we were in the bookmobile, pulling out of the parking lot and headed to the southwest part of the county.

"Um," Julia said, swiveling her head to look at the damage in the parking lot. "What's going on out there? Looks like an army of giant gophers took on the library grounds and won."

"Don't want to talk about it," I muttered.

"Too bad." She settled back into the passenger's seat and tapped her toes on top of Eddie's strapped-down carrier. "Eddie and I both want to hear and we won't rest until you tell us."

"Mrr!"

I slid him a look. "Nice. Even my cat takes your side. Life is so not fair."

"Never has been, never will be," Julia said cheerfully. "Now, spill."

Accepting the inevitable, I told her the little I knew. "Yesterday," I said, "the security camera people told Josh and Graydon there'd been a software patch they hadn't installed."

"So you think the camera guys are in league with the gophers?" Julia asked.

I didn't look over because I was turning us through Chilson's back streets to get to the main road, but I knew what her face looked like. "Quit with that smirk. This is serious."

"Oh, sure," she said. "Which is why you're dealing with this and not me. I think it's hilarious. I mean, honestly, at the end of the day, what's been the ultimate damage? Nothing."

I wasn't sure Gareth would agree, but I did see what she meant. For vandalism, it could have been much worse. No spray paint, no broken windows. "Anyway, the cameras are working now and Josh is triple-testing them. If the vandals come back, we'll know who they are."

"Maybe," Julia said. "But how are you going to tell them apart? To me, one giant gopher looks a lot like every other giant gopher."

"Mrr!"

It figured that Eddie agreed with her about rodent identification. Then again, he tended to agree with everything Julia said, so why should this be any different?

I spent the rest of the drive to the first stop thinking about the vandalism, the cameras, Remi, Kristen, the ice cream cones, and my suspects. Though I'd eliminated one from the list and done some prioritizing, what I needed to do was determine alibis. Eliminate two, and I'd halve the list. Eliminate three, and the job would be done!

However, I was super sure it wouldn't be that easy. But if I could eliminate even one suspect, I'd be ahead.

The day's first stop was a relatively new one, a small township park overlooking the south shore of Janay Lake. I parked in the shade of a cluster of white birch trees and we quickly went through the steps to set up shop for the next hour.

As soon as we were ready, I sat in the driver's seat—now rotated completely around to face the flipped-down countertop that now held a laptop computer—and started typing.

If I was going to try to determine alibis, a good

thing to know was where the suspects lived. I already knew that Misty lived north of Chilson, and thus on the other side of the county from where we were today, and I wasn't sure Des Pyken even had a place here yet, but what about Parker McMurray and Cherise Joffe?

Thanks to a complete lack of privacy in the world, a few targeted Internet searches later, I was able to learn that Cherise owned a house outside of Peebles, which was a tiny town in the southeast part of the county and nowhere near where we were going today. I also learned that Parker McMurray lived in Wicklow Township.

"Huh," I murmured.

Then I smiled, because for the first time in what felt like forever, I knew exactly what I was going to do next.

Chapter 19

I parked the bookmobile on the far side of the smooth new asphalt parking lot of the Wicklow Township Hall, in the shade of a massive maple tree. It was just after lunch and we were about to start the third stop of the day.

As soon as we were set up and ready to go—rear chair detached from its bungee cord, Eddie released from his carrier, computers fired up, rooftop vent popped by the person in the bookmobile who could reach it unaided, and the front door opened to invite everyone inside—I poked my head outside. Other than the small SUV next to the building, there wasn't a car, truck, bicycle, or pedestrian to be seen.

Perfect.

I looked at Julia. "If it's okay with you, I'm going over to the township hall a minute."

"Of course it's okay." She sat on the carpeted step that ran underneath the bookshelves and served both as seating and as stepstool for those of us who were vertically efficient, feet and knees together, her shoulders back and head up, every inch of her portraying alertness. "Edward and I will wait for your return," she said in a low, grave voice. "We will not let you down, ma'am."

I wasn't sure if she was playing a real part or one she'd just made up. With Julia's vast repertoire up against my minimal one, it was hard for me to tell, but I did my best to play along. "At ease, Corporal."

"Yes, ma'am!" She snapped off a sharp salute.

One of the best things about working with Julia was that it was never dull. Smiling, I headed down the stairs and across the pavement to the fieldstone building. Inside, the hall looked the same as it had the last time I'd been in there, about a year and a half ago. Of course, neither the interior nor the exterior looked as if it had changed much since its construction. Wood floor, wood paneling, wood ceiling; all had been installed during the boom lumber years when the cheapest building material was the stuff in the closest woodlot.

Just left of the front door was a bulletin board tacked with meeting announcements, and an office with a sliding glass window. The window was open, and the township clerk was smiling at me. "Good to see you, Minnie!"

It was easy to return her smile. In her early sixties, with solidly blond hair, Charlotte was one of those people who went through life always seeing the bright side of things, and I hoped to be more like her when I finally grew up.

"Hey, Charlotte." We spent a couple of minutes catching up, then I said, "I have an odd question for you."

She laughed. "Honey, that's my favorite kind. Lay it on me."

I took a deep breath. "A friend of mine is thinking about starting a restaurant. I'm trying to connect her with people who can give her the good, the bad, and the ugly. I hear Parker McMurray lives out here. Do you know him? Do you think he's a good person to talk to about restaurants? It didn't turn out well, I get that, but it was a while back so maybe he'd be willing to talk to my friend, do you think?"

Charlotte, who'd endured my babbling with a patient grace, turned to look at a wall calendar. "It's Tuesday, isn't it?" she said, quietly. Then, sighing, she faced me.

I didn't know Charlotte all that well, but I did know I'd never seen her with such a serious expression. And it was more than serious. She looked sad.

"Park," she said, "is some sort of cousin to my husband. Second, once removed? Something like that. Park's a nice person, he just has . . . problems, if you know what I mean."

"Um, sort of," I said, making it a kind of question. Because, sure, everyone had issues and baggage, but I got the distinct sense that she wasn't talking about something in general. She was talking about something in particular, and I had no clue what it was.

My frown of puzzlement must have communicated that I wasn't picking up what she was putting down. Charlotte half smiled and said, "There are some things I can talk about, and some things I can't. Does your route go past Valley Church? Good. Can you be there about three this afternoon?"

I nodded, and she nodded back, as if that was the end of the conversation.

Which it was. Her office phone rang, she gave me a cheery wave, and she slid the glass window shut. "Wicklow Township Hall," she answered. "How can I help you?"

Still puzzled, I walked back across the parking lot to the bookmobile, where Julia was entertaining two families with small children by reading *Goodnight Moon* in a Swedish accent, with Eddie directing the event from the console. It was just another day on the bookmobile, and I smiled at it all, thinking once again that I had the best job ever, even if interactions with local township officials left me mystified.

But I also figured Charlotte wouldn't send me or the bookmobile on a snipe hunt, so I timed our departure from the township hall to coincide with a three-o'clock arrival at the church. The building was in the middle of a small unnamed hamlet and was made of that blond brick common to schools built in the sixties, but not built anywhere ever since then.

I parked us across the street, next to a gas station and convenience store. We'd stopped here before, in the same exact spot, for snacks and to use the restroom, so our presence shouldn't raise any eyebrows.

"Need to pop across the street," I said casually. "Should only be a minute."

"Wait, what?" Julia gave the church a startled look.

"I'll explain when I get back. Promise." I hadn't said anything to her about what Charlotte had said because I'd been too busy working through possibilities about what I'd find. That, plus I didn't want her to talk me out of anything.

I trotted across the road. The church's parking lot was occupied by maybe ten vehicles, ranging from a pickup truck that had more rust than paint to a shiny Mercedes convertible that looked as if it had never driven down a gravel road in its life. SUVs and sedans were the other lot occupants, and I didn't recognize any of them. Not that I'd truly expected to, but you never knew.

The glass front door opened smoothly. I slipped inside and the door shut without a sound. In front of me a hallway ran the length of the building, ending in a stained-glass window. To the left was a half wall topped with glass with a swinging door open to the empty and dark sanctuary. Immediately to the right were restrooms. Past that were two doors that led to what I assumed were office spaces, meeting rooms, or both. One of the doors was slightly open, and from it came a murmur of voices.

I approached slowly, my feet silent and ears wide open. Charlotte had sent me here for a reason, but disrupting a meeting of church deacons was not anywhere on my bucket list.

As I drew closer, the tone of the voices started to sort themselves out into female and male, old and young. Then someone who sounded forty-something said, "Okay, it's time to get started. Who wants to go first? Great, thanks. Go ahead."

A chair squeaked. "Um, my name is Parker, and I'm an alcoholic."

I froze.

This was a meeting of Alcoholics Anonymous. A very private meeting. I absolutely shouldn't be here. No wonder Charlotte had been uncomfortable giving me this information.

Slowly, I inched backward as the other voices said hello to Parker.

"Remember last week, when I talked about my ex-girlfriend?" He took a huge breath, then let it out. "She's the waiter at Angelique's, the one who was murdered."

Shocked noises and words of sympathy.

"Thanks," he muttered. "It's been hard. Really hard. So far I haven't had a drink. Had a bottle in my hand last night, though."

I backed out of earshot, away from the raw emotion that I shouldn't have heard. But I had heard it, and my brain ticked through a mental calendar.

Remi was killed one week ago today, at almost exactly this time. If Parker had been here at an AA meeting, he couldn't have been thirty miles away in Chilson. Parker McMurray had a rock-solid alibi for Remi's death.

He was innocent.

That night, I talked the whole thing over with my feline friend. Rafe would have been my preferred choice as a sounding board, but he'd gone back to work to deal with a major emergency of two new teachers who seemed to be changing their minds about coming to teach at the Chilson Middle School.

The notion had boggled my mind—how could anyone not want to work for Rafe, how could anyone not want to live in this flat-out gorgeous part of the world, and how could anyone give their pending boss this news just two weeks before school started?—but Rafe had explained.

"They want to come here," he'd said as he'd shoveled a hamburger and potato into himself. "But they can't find anywhere to live that's even close to affordable."

I'd straightened up. "Give them Celeste's phone number. She's changing over the boardinghouse to be year-round, remember? There might be a couple of rooms left. Wouldn't be good for a family, but if they're single, then it might work."

"You're the smartest person I know." He'd given me a smacking kiss that tasted slightly of salt. "Later, my lemon butter fern."

His terms of endearment had been trending toward the flora side of the spectrum, so I'd been preparing a mental list of fauna versions. "See you when you get home, my duck-billed platypus!"

"So, what do you think?" I asked Eddie as I put the last dish in the dishwasher. "Not about the fern-versus-platypus thing, I clearly won that round even though it's not a contest. About the Parker McMurray thing. He couldn't have killed Remi, and since I still think the Lee knives connect the murder and the dessert, he didn't do either one."

My cat, who'd once again squeezed himself onto a windowsill that wasn't wide enough for him, visibly sighed as he looked across the backyard.

Almost certainly he was trying to guilt me into letting him outside and wasn't actually paying attention to what I was saying, but saying what I thought out loud often helped me think about things in a relatively logical fashion, so I kept going.

"Plus, we're going to eliminate Harold Calkins. That's two suspects down, with three left. Cherise, Des, and Misty." I put them in alphabetical order not only because I was a librarian, but also because then I didn't favor one over the others.

"I really don't want it to be Misty," I said to Eddie, "but I don't have any information that eliminates her, so—what are you doing?"

The question had to be asked because my cat was now standing on his hind legs, whapping at the top corner of the window with one front paw. I couldn't see anything, so either he was batting at something too small for me to see, or he was batting at something invisible. Either one was possible.

"That's quite the reach, pal," I said mildly. "Watch yourself, okay?"

He flicked me a quick glare over his shoulder.

"Yes, I know you're a skilled acrobat and not inclined to fall, but even you can have a bad day."

He thumped to the floor and stalked off, giving me another glare as he went past.

"Love you too, buddy," I said.

His tail flicked from side to side, then he vanished into the dining room.

I rolled my eyes and went back to thinking about my three suspects. Cherise, Des, Misty. A while back, I'd slid Des to the bottom of the list when I was mentally listing them in order of likelihood. That put Cherise at the top and Misty in the middle. What I wanted, though, was to eliminate Misty as a suspect altogether.

After a little more thought, I made a decision. If what I wanted was to find an alibi for Misty, I should prepare myself for hearing something I didn't want to hear, and go talk to her.

I sent Rafe a text about where I was going, pulled my bicycle out of the garage, and took a leisurely ride over to Three Seasons, taking a route that avoided some tourist traffic, but not all of it, because that would require a much longer bike ride than I wanted to take. When I rolled in, Misty herself was sitting outside the kitchen on an upturned milk crate, poking at her phone.

"Hey," I said, braking to a stop in front of her.

She looked up. "Hey, Minnie. What's up?" she asked, but there was no life in her voice.

"I was out for a ride and decided to stop by to see how things are going." I looked out over the parking lot, which was mostly empty. "Did, um, most people eat early tonight?"

"No idea." She shrugged. "Most people ate somewhere else."

"Still dealing with fallout from the dessert thing?"

"Guess so," she said.

Her listless tone worried me. Of all the things that could run Three Seasons into the ground, I'd never once thought it would be a staffing issue. Kristen was beyond loyal to her employees, and in return they were loyal to her. If Misty was losing heart, things had to be bad.

"Things are getting better, though, right?" I asked.

Misty sighed and turned her phone off. "We've doubled the number of customers from the day we reopened, which sounds great, but not when you realize that on the reopener we served ten people. Ten," she repeated, staring at her fists.

I swallowed. "Kind of makes you wonder about going into the business?"

"Sure does." Misty blew out a breath. "Then again, on the plus side, I'm not opening my place until next year." She gave me a half grin. "That'll give me plenty of time to forget all this, right?"

Hang on. Next year? That meant—

The kitchen door opened and Harvey poked his head out. "Misty, are you— Hey, Minnie. How you doing? Heard anything from Kristen lately?"

I decided not to mention that though I'd seen her not long ago, I'd fled so I wouldn't have to talk to her. "Not really. Have you?"

He shook his head. "We call and text her but hardly ever hear back. You think the twins are doing okay?"

"If they weren't, we'd know," I said, projecting as much confidence as I could, but it didn't feel sincere, because his obvious concern was oozing into me. "But I'll reach out tonight. I'll let you two know the minute I hear anything."

They thanked me and headed back to the kitchen, discussing the best entree to do a social media post about in hopes of drawing people back to the restaurant. The door shut on a good-natured spat that primarily involved each other's photo-taking capacity—"Harvey, every picture you take of food looks like something that hit its best-by date a month ago," followed by "At least I know better than to post photos of people chewing"— which amused me so much that I actually smiled.

When I got home, I rolled my bike into the garage, then wandered over to the gazebo to do some serious texting with my best friend. I'd turned on my phone and opened the messaging app when an odd *thump thump* noise pulled my attention away from what I was doing and up to the kitchen window, where Eddie was headbutting the glass over and over again.

Cats were so weird.

I went up the deck stairs and opened the back door. "Okay, you can—never mind. You're out already." Belatedly, I questioned the wisdom of letting a cat outside when it was starting to get dark. But since the deed was done, I mentally shrugged and returned to the gazebo.

The chair squeaked as I sat. I hooked my foot around the other chair and pulled it close so I could prop up my legs.

"Mrr!" Eddie jumped onto chair number two and immediately settled into the spot that I'd reserved for my feet.

I gave him a look. "Good to know that I won't have to hunt you down to get you inside tonight."

He, of course, didn't respond, so I wedged my feet next to him. "Don't worry," I said. "You don't have to move. I'll contort myself so you can stay comfortable."

Though there was no comment from Mr. Ed, I did start to feel a gentle vibration in my left anklebone. Smiling, I started texting Kirsten.

Minnie: *Hey. Haven't heard from you lately. Anything up?*

Minnie (five minutes later): *Marco*

Minnie (another five minutes later): *You're supposed to answer "Polo."*

Minnie (after yet another five minutes): *Marco Polo is a stupid game to play solitaire.*

Between text messages, I ticked time away by checking e-mail and looking at projected weather forecasts. When it had been half an hour since the first text, I closed the text app and called her. Five rings in, just when I was starting to formulate the message I was going to leave, she answered.

"Sorry," she said breathlessly. "Is this important?"

"On a scale of one to ten, it's maybe a seven."

"Then it can wait."

In the background, I could hear two high-pitched wails and one male voice, a voice usually calm and measured, but now sounding harried and raw.

"Um, how are the twins? I stopped by the restaurant tonight, and Misty and Harvey are a little worried that they haven't heard from you."

"They're running fevers," she said. "Not high. Enough to make them cranky, though. Doctor says it has to run its course, but it's not running near fast enough."

"What can I do to help?"

She gave a short laugh. "Make sure my restaurant doesn't burn down, okay? Because that would be the absolute last straw." An infant's wail swelled to such epic proportions that I could hardly hear her say, all in a rush, "Gotta go. Love ya."

The phone went quiet.

Before I forgot, I texted Misty and Harvey an update. They both said thanks and that they'd be sure to watch for fires. I shut down the phone and gave Eddie a nudge with my foot. "Did you hear that?" I asked. "Kristen said something about Three Seasons that means she hasn't completely detached from it."

His purr faltered.

"Okay, maybe it's a stretch from not wanting it to burn down to going back to the hands-on ownership in the days of yore, but it's more than she's indicated so far, right?"

The purr started rumbling again.

"Glad you think so. And now that I know Misty isn't planning on opening her own place until next year, I'm moving her to the bottom of the list, underneath Des Pyken." I wondered how much Kristen knew about Misty's plans. She might know everything, but then again, she might not. If Kristen didn't mention it to me soon, I'd have to give Misty a nudge. And if that didn't work, I'd have to tell Kristen myself.

"Which won't be any fun," I muttered. "At all."

Eddie shifted around, a long sequence that ended up with his chin propped up by my right instep.

"Comfy?" I asked. "Because it's possible that your actions are resulting in a loss of blood flow to my feet. If I end up with gangrene, I want the record to state that it's your fault."

"Mrr," he said lazily.

I leaned forward and gave him a long pet. There were times when I really did think he understood what I was saying. "Okay. Two suspects down, three to go. Sort of. Do I really think Misty had anything to do with Remi's murder or the ice cream thing? No, I do not. But just because I like her and want her to be innocent doesn't mean I shouldn't be following up. Alibis," I said, trying for a posh English accent, but sounding mostly like the college roommate I'd had for a summer semester who'd hailed from Boston. "That's what I need, my young fellow. Alibis. If I can find one for—"

My phone chimed with an incoming call. I

picked it up, assuming it was Kristen, but I wasn't even close. "Graydon?" I asked. Far as I could remember, my boss had never once called me at night. "What's up?"

"It's hard to explain." He paused. "Are you busy? Is there any chance you can come up to the library?"

For some reason I looked around the backyard. The sun had been down for almost an hour, and it was full dark. "You mean right now?"

"Yes."

There was only one good answer. "Be there in five minutes."

Chapter 20

My unexpected trip to the library had been eventful, and the next morning Graydon and I gathered everyone in the boardroom for an emergency staff meeting. Between a few called-in favors and the promise of Cookie Tom's doughnuts, we'd managed to get everyone present and accounted for, one way or another, even those who weren't scheduled to work.

Though most everyone was sitting in the big leather chairs, a few faces looked down at us from the big video screen the board used. I was pretty sure Donna's background of shelves laden with leather-bound books was fictional; same with Kelsey's, which was nothing but giant coffee beans.

Graydon sat at the far end of the long table. "Thanks to all of you for coming in this morning," he said in a grave and serious voice.

At the opposite end of the table, I took a deep breath, studied my folded hands, and didn't dare look at either my boss or Gareth, who was halfway down the table.

The three of us were the only ones who had a clue about what was coming. If the group reaction was anything close to mine of the night before, I wasn't sure the building would stay standing. Sure, it was almost a hundred years old and had endured floods, blizzards, straight-line winds, and economic upheavals galore, but it had never seen anything like what was about to come.

Graydon picked up the remote that ran the screen. "What you're about to see," he said quietly, "will shock and surprise you. There is no audio to the video, but to ameliorate its disturbing impact, we've added a sound track."

A what?

My gaze flicked up to Graydon. Last night there'd been no discussion of adding music. Not even a hint of a whisper. I narrowed my eyes at him and got a stone stare in return. This resulted in an internal vow to never play cards with him. And in a heightened interest in what was about to happen.

"There's no way to truly prepare you for this," he said gravely. Since everyone's attention was on him, I felt free to roll my eyes and made a Move this along gesture with my index finger.

He gave me a regal nod. "And now," he said in a stentorian voice, "behold the identity of our library vandals." He flourished the remote and in a slow, dramatic fashion that he could have learned from Julia, he pressed the Play button.

Nothing changed on the screen, not at first, but there was a faint sound of drumming, followed by what I thought was a flute, then a clarinet.

One side of my mouth quirked up. Graydon was playing Ravel's "Bolero."

As more and more instruments added on, the screen finally sprang to life. It was the back parking lot again, and the date-time stamp showed it as last night, just after sunset. Only this time, a figure was squeezing through the shrubs at the back and coming into view. It was clear that it wasn't human, but it wasn't immediately obvious what it was other than four-footed. And big. Because even at a distance, you could tell by the way the animal moved that it had size, girth, and weight.

"What is that?" Josh asked.

"Bear," Holly said, but there was a question mark at the end.

Graydon waved them to silence. The video continued, and the music continued to increase in complexity and in volume.

The animal made its way into the lot, then stopped and turned. A second figure burst through the bushes, followed quickly by a third, and after a pause, a fourth but smaller one came through.

As a quartet, they gamboled and cavorted, ran around the bookmobile, and hurtled themselves from one end of the parking lot to the other. The smallest one made a sharp turn and headed for one of the many large granite rocks that lined the parking area. Its front paws dug away at the rock's base, and even in the dim light we could see the dirt piling up behind it.

"Our vandals are . . . dogs?" Donna asked.

Graydon smiled but didn't say anything, and we watched as the dogs made a ring around the rock and started excavating in earnest.

The music was now so loud it would have been hard to hear anyone say anything, and its tempo came close to matching exactly the speed of the digging. Then the strings soared, cymbals crashed, and brass flared, at the exact same time that the rock tumbled on its side. The dogs scrambled away as the music dropped to a close. They ran flat out, squeezed out through the bushes ten times faster than they'd squeezed in, and disappeared from view.

"Good heavens," Donna said. "Were those Saint Bernards?"

"Our best guess is they're a breed called Boerboel." Graydon used the remote to bring up a website with photos of the breed, one that I'd never heard of until the night before. "A type of mastiff from South Africa. Fully grown males can get up to two hundred pounds."

Holly let out a long, low whistle. "Wouldn't want to feed one of those, let alone four."

"Who owns them?"

"Not sure yet," I said. "I've talked to the city police, sheriff's office, and animal control, but so far no one knows. I left a message for Dr. Joe, to give me a call if he knows anything."

"He might not if they're up here with summer people," Kelsey pointed out.

Graydon smiled. "Exactly. Which is why I'm asking all of you to keep an eye out. If you see even one of those dogs, contact me or Minnie and we'll take it from there."

"Dogs," Josh said, sounding disgusted. "All that energy we wasted on being scared was for a bunch of dogs. I can't tell this story to anyone; it would be downright embarrassing."

Gareth nodded. "Know what you mean," he said gloomily. "I was so sure it was kids messing around."

We sat there, looking at each other. Then Josh nodded. "It was just dogs," he said.

Holly smiled. "Just dogs."

Through the speakers came the sound of a faint wolf howl. It was Donna. "O-oooooo!" she called. "O-ooooo!"

All at once, the entire group burst into a long round of laughter. It had an immediate cleansing effect, washing us clear of the doubt, worry, concern, and anxiety that had been nipping at our heels. It felt good to laugh, and even better to be free of the negativity that had been . . . well . . . dogging us.

I was tempted to say that out loud but shied from starting a round of puns. Something like that would inevitably escalate into a contest, and that never ended well.

When the laughter started fading, Graydon said, "Thank you for coming in early this morning. Watching the group reaction was worth the overtime I'll have to pay. And now," he said, waving good-bye to our virtual attendees and thumbing off the video equipment, "it's time to get to work. Thanks again, everyone."

We filed out, with me coming last to not-quite-obsessively straighten the chairs to be perfectly square to the table and turn off the lights. Graydon went into his second-floor office, and the rest of us traipsed down the wide switchback stairs.

Holly was just ahead of me, and I hurried a bit to catch up with her. "Hey," I said. "Seems like forever since I've talked to you."

"Really? I guess it has been a minute. Summer, you know. Getting the kids ready to go back to school, all that. Brian has been home, so that's both help and hindrance, if you know what I mean," she said, laughing.

Holly's husband worked in the mining industry. From what I understood, he pulled down serious bank, but his job had one monstrous drawback. It was a couple of thousand miles away, in Wyoming. He was gone for weeks at a time, then was home for weeks. It wasn't a life I would have wanted, but they made it work.

"Um," I said. "How's Cherise doing? Finding a friend like that, it couldn't have been easy. I'm still having nightmares and I didn't even know Remi."

"Well, I've been wanting to talk to you about that," she said, sliding me a glance. "Cherise isn't dealing with it very well. At all. I know the two of you weren't exactly getting along that day, but I was wondering if you'd mind stopping in. If she could talk to someone who really understood, maybe that would help."

The cynical part of me thought that maybe Cherise wasn't dealing well with Remi's death because she'd been the one who killed her, but I kept that thought inside my head where it belonged. "No problem," I said, pushing open the door at the bottom of the stairwell. "I don't mind a bit. I can stop by Angelique's tonight, if that works on her end."

Rafe had scheduled himself to tour some homes with Bianca Koyne and a prospective teacher candidate in hopes that he could help with house sale negotiations and thus complete his fall teacher roster, so I was flying solo for the evening.

"Hang on. I'll find out." Holly pulled out her phone and started tapping. She hit the Send button and within a few seconds it dinged with a return message. Holly scanned the text. "Tonight, she'll be there until close, so about ten."

"Would it be okay if I stop by about nine?" I asked.

Holly tapped some more, waited, then nodded. "Thanks, Minnie," she said. "You're a nice person, no matter what Josh says."

I laughed. "Pretty sure that if Josh said anything nice about anyone other than his wife it would be a sure sign that the world was ending, so I'm good."

It was also good to know that I had a non-sneaky way to talk to Cherise. Sure, I'd be using the opportunity for additional investigative work, but Holly had essentially initiated it, and if Cherise was innocent, I absolutely wanted to help her.

So it was with a (mostly) clean conscience that I got to work, starting with reading e-mails, which had apparently spontaneously generated the entire time I was out on the bookmobile.

Lunch came and went, along with my scheduled departure time. When I stretched and did a final pushback from the computer, it was just past seven o'clock. Going home, then coming back to Angelique's at nine didn't feel like the best use of my time, so I fired up my phone and ordered a veggie sub from Fat Boys Pizza.

"Hey, Minnie," the night manager said as we exchanged food for cash over the counter.

"Thanks, Brendan. How's the employee retention going?"

He blew out a breath. "Let's just say I'll be glad when the summer's over and things slow down. Then maybe I cut my hours to eighty."

"Every two weeks, like a normal person? Good for you!"

But he was shaking his head. "Eighty hours a week will be way less than I've been working since Remi was killed. I've been losing people left and right. And now the high school kids are back doing sports?" He sighed. "It's great that kids are active, but losing them before Labor Day is pushing me to the limit. So, like I said. I'll be glad when things slow down."

I hesitated. "Um, but haven't people been saying the shoulder seasons are lasting longer than ever? The last couple of years, hasn't September been almost as busy as August? And didn't the new guy from the chamber say that October is the new September?"

Brendan suddenly looked a decade older than the forty-something that he was. "Yeah," he said. "After Labor Day, we'll have to go to reduced hours. Maybe close on Mondays. I can't keep this up much longer."

"Then," I said, holding up my long white sandwich bag in toasting position, "here's to Labor Day."

He smiled and gave me a limp thumbs-up. "Thanks, Minnie, I—" The phone on the wall next to him rang shrilly. Mechanically, he picked it up and turned to the computer. "Fat Boys Pizza. What can I do for you?"

I left him to it. Brendan often looked worn-out

by the end of the summer, but I'd never seen him looking like this. Not just worn-out, but worn down. And worse than that, he seemed discouraged. In the best of times, finding seasonal help was always a struggle Up North, and these were far from the best of times. If Remi's murder was making things even worse, could that be a tipping point for Fat Boys? For Three Seasons? For Shomin's? For Hoppe's, Corner Coffee, and all the other restaurants in town?

The concept was past frightening. No way. No possible way would that happen. And absolutely no way would I let even a fraction of a brain cell consider the faint possibility of Cookie Tom's and the Round Table fading out of existence.

If they did, what would be left? What would Chilson be like without all our informal gathering places, our third spaces, as the planners called them. Sure, the city would survive in some way, shape, or form, but would it thrive? Would it be a happy place?

I found a vacant bench in an alley's pocket park and sat down to eat my dinner. My view was the brick side of a fudge shop. Its owner, along with the downtown development authority and the historical society, had commissioned a painting that was an aerial view of Chilson circa 1900. The basic street layout was the same, along with a handful of buildings, but I wasn't sure that if I'd been whirled back 120 years into this same exact spot, I'd even grasp that I was in my own town.

"Why did I think that?" I muttered as I took the last bite, which I'd miscalculated and so ended up with far more bread than filling. "Why?"

But I had lots of questions right now. Though why I routinely came up with thoughts that creeped me out was certainly one of them, the priority of finding an answer for it was way low on the priority list.

I swallowed my last, slightly disappointing, bite of sandwich, balled up the wrapper, and tossed it into a nearby garbage can. If I walked at a grandpa pace and took the long way around, I'd show up at Angelique's right at nine o'clock.

The streets and sidewalks of downtown Chilson were, on this warm Wednesday night, busy with summer traffic. Hoppe's had a line of people out the door, and many retail stores still had their front doors open wide, welcoming people inside. Gennell's was one of them.

I stopped and peered inside, hoping that Blythe was open because she'd finally been able to hire some help. But no. Inside, my friend was smiling at a customer and ringing up a small stack of paperbacks. Even from this distance I could see that the size of the bags under her eyes rivaled the size of the bag she was filling.

The woman needed help. I had a thought or two about how to do that, but I needed a little more time to put it into play. Since it wasn't a done deal, I didn't want to say anything to Blythe, and since I was a horrible liar, I needed to avoid talking to her, at least for a couple more days.

I moved on down the sidewalk, out of sight of Blythe, and strolled the streets of downtown, soaking in the soft sounds of the summer night until it was time to head up to Angelique's to talk to Cherise.

My plan was to express my sorrow about the

tragedy of Remi's murder, ask her some general questions about how she was feeling, and watch carefully for signs of lies, evasion, or anything that might provide a clue.

The back door was pushed open to let in the cooling evening air, something that was understandable, but curious in light of the fact that an employee had been killed there just over a week ago.

I climbed the concrete steps. Inside the kitchen, Cherise was sitting on a stool, staring at a computer tablet, propping up her head with a hand, her long dark ponytail a thin straggle down her back. One employee had his arms deep in a sink of sudsy water; another was plating two desserts: a piece of cheesecake and a thick, gooey brownie. Restaurant kitchens were normally noisy places, but this one had a pall of silence so thick I could almost see it.

Knocking on the metal doorframe, I gently called her name. "Cherise? Do you have a minute?"

She looked at me blankly, then recognition dawned. "Hey, Minnie. Holly said you might stop by. How are you doing?"

"Okay, but not great," I said. "You?"

Her mouth twisted in a way that meant one of two things. Either she'd just eaten a lemon, or she was trying not to cry. "Same. Holly said this has happened to you before. You know, finding a murder victim. How do you deal with it?"

"Not very well," I said, with complete and utter honesty. "And it's really hard when you know the person. How long did you know Remi?"

Cherise shook her head. "Since Angelique's opened. So a couple of years. Did you? Know her?"

"Um . . ." I stumbled over my own tongue for a

couple of beats. "No. Sorry, I didn't. Say, do you know if Remi knew a guy called Des Pyken?"

"Who?" Cherise stared at me. "I have no idea. Why? Who's he?"

"Um, some restaurant guy from downstate," I said lamely. "Sorry. It's been hard to focus lately, if you know what I mean."

She sighed. "Yeah. I do. I keep thinking it'll get better, but it hasn't. My momma says give it time, it hasn't been that long." She sighed. "Momma knows best, I suppose. What advice did your mom give?"

As I hadn't told my mother about the incident, I gave a noncommittal and vague response. Cherise murmured agreement, and she began to talk about Remi's family and how they were planning a memorial service in the fall.

I tried to pay attention to what she was saying, but I was still unfocused, and not because of the emotional trauma of finding Remi's body. Instead, I'd been distracted by something else entirely.

Not ten feet away from me, at the end of a long stainless-steel shelf, was a five-pound plastic tub of triticale.

Chapter 21

The next morning, I was still mentally sorting through everything I'd recently learned. To help me think, I'd left the normal distractions—newspaper, laptop, and phone—in the kitchen and come out to the front porch to eat my cereal and finish my first cup of coffee.

I always felt that thinking out loud helped me sort things out—mostly because once I heard my ideas out loud I realized how stupid most of them actually were—and since Rafe had already left, I'd brought Eddie outside with me.

"Cherise really seems to be having a hard time with Remi's death," I said. "Yeah, I know, I'm well aware that her reaction could be guilt for having killed her."

Eddie, who'd draped himself over the porch railing, gave me a one-eyed look. It could have meant "Grief is unpredictable and takes many forms" but most likely meant "Why aren't you done with your cereal? Because I'm ready for the milk that's left in the bottom of the bowl."

"And," I went on, flourishing my cereal-laden spoon at him in demonstration that I was still eating and that it wasn't his turn yet, "there was that bucket of triticale. How many restaurants have any of that stuff in their kitchen, let alone in amounts like that?"

From what Kristen had said, it had sounded like hardly any. But how much did she really know about the inner workings of other restaurant kitchens? Sure, she'd worked in her fair share, back when she was learning the trade, but that was years ago. And no matter what, it was still a small sampling.

I wondered how I could learn more without alerting anyone to what I was doing. The University of Google was always an option, but I wasn't sure that entering "How many Chilson area restaurants typically have huge buckets of ground triticale on hand?" would be very useful.

Still, nothing ventured, nothing gained, so I put my cereal bowl on the porch floor, went inside for my phone, and came back to see Eddie's pink tongue lapping up the last molecule of milk.

"Glad I could make you happy," I said, returning to my seat.

He licked his kitty lips, giving me a look that was clearly "That's all I get? Seriously?"

It was a look I could easily ignore, so I did as I typed my triticale question into my phone. The top response was Wikipedia, with an entry about triticale in general. The second was an entry for a bi-monthly magazine titled *Growing Hay and Silage*, proving once and for all that there was a trade magazine for everything.

Back issues were available online, so I spent a few minutes scanning articles. Topics ranged from harvest timing to in-depth farmer bios to possible long-term implications of plastic net wrap.

It was a fascinating peek into a completely different way of life, but it wasn't teaching me anything about the use of triticale in restaurants.

I poked around on the magazine's website and quickly found the editor's e-mail address. Going once again with the nothing ventured, nothing gained thing, I came up with a message that didn't sound too stupid and sent it off.

"What do you think?" I asked Eddie. "Fifty-fifty chance of hearing back?"

"Mrr," he said, but his attention wasn't on me. It was on my phone, which was jumping with incoming text messages. With trepidation, I picked it up.

Mom: *It is exactly one month until the wedding.*

Aunt Frances: *Yes, isn't it exciting?*

Mom: *Less so if there is no officiant.*

Aunt Frances: *Working on that right now.*

Mom: *And?*

Aunt Frances: *Minnie's coming over this morning. We're going to finalize the details. I just put the coffee on.*

Interesting. Up until that moment, I hadn't realized my morning was going to include my aunt, but with the promise of her stovetop-brewed coffee in the near future, I found it remarkably easy to stop asking questions and, instead, wondered if Otto would be there. If so, there was also a very good chance we'd be offered slabs of his coffee cake.

I was hoping for the version that included toasted walnut pieces when I knocked and walked in the front door.

"We're out back," Aunt Frances called. "Pick a mug on your way."

Otto and my aunt were at the patio table with a coffee-urn centerpiece. No coffee cake, but there was a pile of steaming biscuits, along with butter and honey.

"Dig in," Otto said, pushing plates across the table.

My aunt looked at me, regret in every line of her face. "I can't find anyone to officiate your wedding. Other obligations, health issues, on vacation, you wouldn't believe the excuses. I've failed and I am so, so sorry."

The silence was deafening.

"Well," Otto finally said, pasting on the fakest smile I'd ever seen on him. "How about a biscuit?"

The flaky, tangy biscuits helped the dour mood, but they were not a cure-all. "It's time," I announced as I took my second one. "We're going to elope."

"You're not eloping." Aunt Frances was looking off into the vast reaches of space. "That would cause more problems than it would solve, and you know it."

"But do we?" I asked. "Do we really? Let's count the reasons to zip over to the courthouse and get married tomorrow. We never did decide on our wedding dance song, so there's a ton of time and energy saved right there. Plus Rafe can't dance for beans. He's already afraid seeing him dance in public might end our marriage before it gets started."

My aunt's attention drifted to me. "Just think," she said severely, "about your parents. What do you think they'll do if you run off and get married without them?"

I glanced at Otto. "They'd forgive us."

"But would they?" Aunt Frances asked, spinning off my earlier question. "Would they really? And even if they did, how long would that forgiveness take? And do you think there would be any family gathering in the next twenty years where someone wouldn't make some snarky reference to it?"

Mom would. Dad would. My brother wouldn't, but my sister-in-law might. And my niece absolutely would. Then there was the money my parents had volunteered to pay for Kristen's costs, and I knew she'd already paid half up front to a lot of vendors to ensure delivery. Rick and Lois would be polite to me, but I was pretty sure Rafe would get some grief when he was alone with his parents.

And then we'd have to deal with the reaction of greater Chilson, from Mitchell to Pam Fazio to my coworkers to Rafe's teachers to everyone at the marina.

"It's not worth it, is it?" I asked, sighing.

"Of course not." Aunt Frances rolled her eyes. "And you're not serious about eloping."

I wasn't so sure about that, but whatever.

"Wait," she said. "Did you ever contact the district court?"

Asking the court administrator about the possibility of the district court judge marrying us had been on my list. "Not yet. I was so sure you'd come up with someone that I hadn't bothered." I pulled out my phone. "It's after eight thirty. I'll call right now."

In short order I was connected with the administrator for Tonedagana County's District Court, a woman named Kelli. After introducing myself, I asked the big question.

"Weddings?" she asked, and you could hear her smile. "The judge loves doing weddings! When is it?"

"Um, it's a Saturday wedding, here in town. Does she do those?"

Kelli laughed. "Not often. But she loves the bookmobile, so I bet she'd be happy to marry you. What's the date?"

I told her, and then the conversation fell apart. "Oh, I'm so sorry. The judge is out of town that entire week. I don't suppose you could change the date?"

We could not. I thanked her for her time and hung up fast, cutting off what was sure to be an apology so she wouldn't hear the catch in my voice. "I'm going to end up being married by a man named Tank," I said, burying my face in the coffee mug.

"You are not," Aunt Frances said. "What about Kristen? Doesn't she have any contacts?"

Of course she did. "Kristen has too much on her plate. I'm not asking for her help on this."

My aunt made a rude noise and brought her phone to life. "I'm calling her."

I made a half-hearted swipe, but Aunt Frances dodged. "Morning, Kristen. Minnie and I have just struck out on wedding officiants. If you don't have any ideas, Tank what's-his-name is going to marry them." She listened, then nodded, turned the phone to speaker, and put it on the table.

"Kristen wants to know who we've contacted," Aunt Frances said.

She rattled off close to a dozen names, and I added a few more. "Plus I just talked to the district court administrator, and she said the judge will be out of town that week."

"The judge is?" Kristen said. "For an entire week?"

I thought back to what Kelli had said. "Think so."

"Hmm. Once upon a time, I dated a family court judge. Court conferences never seem to last an entire week."

I squinted at the phone, then at my aunt and Otto, who looked as puzzled as I felt. "What does that have to do with—"

"Everything," Kristen said confidently. "This will work out. Leave it to me. And don't you have indentured servitude obligations to fulfill? Off you go."

So I did, arriving at the library only forty-five minutes late for being an hour and a half early.

At lunchtime I decided that, thanks to the biscuits, I could skip eating a meal. By two o'clock, however, my empty stomach was starting to give me a headache and I knew I had to do something more than eat a stale vending machine protein bar or I'd be risking a hunger-induced migraine.

"Back in half an hour," I said to Holly as I passed the front desk, figuring that was the amount of time it would take to walk to Shomin's for a prewrapped sandwich and to take a circuitous route back. When I was almost there, a couple in a convertible pulled out of a curbside parking spot. A large sedan veered over, put its blinker on, and performed the fastest, smoothest parallel parking job I'd ever seen.

A man in his mid-forties with a graying Vandyke beard got out of the driver's seat, whistling, and headed my way.

Des Pyken.

The nothing ventured, nothing gained attitude was still with me, so I walked toward him. "Nice job with the parking."

He grinned. "Just a little skill I've picked up."

"By the way," I said, "we almost met at Hoppe's the other night." I held out my hand and gave him my name. His large hand enveloped mine as he introduced himself. "Des Pyken," I said, working for a trying-to-remember tone. "Sounds familiar. Are you from around here?"

"Grand Rapids," he said. "Ever hear of the Pyken restaurant chain? No?" He fished in his shirt pocket for a business card. "Here's a ten percent off card for next time you're downstate. But I'm considering buying Seven Street from Harold Calkins, if we can work things out for me to buy it in late December. You're a local. What's your take on the place?"

I laughed. "I've been there all of once, and that was when someone else paid. Librarians can't afford to eat at high-end restaurants like that more than once in a blue moon."

"Okay, I get that. But if you did want to go somewhere for a special occasion. Birthday. Anniversary. Whatever. Would you go to Seven Street? Or would you go somewhere else?"

I suddenly saw how to push the conversation

where I wanted it to go. "There are lots of good restaurants in Chilson," I said. "It would depend on the occasion and who I was with. How about you? Have you been to Three Seasons? Or Angelique's?"

"Not yet," he said. "Reading reviews is as far as I've gone. And I have to say, there are a lot of bad ones out there. Doesn't look good for Chilson's restaurants right now, from diners up to fine dining. With all that bad press and how hard it is to find help, I'm not sure about buying Seven Street. It's not looking like the investment it was made out to be."

"No?" I blinked. "Oh. Well, that's too bad. But maybe things will turn around. The restaurant business is a fickle one, isn't that what they say?"

"They say a lot of things," Des said, smiling, and I caught a whiff of mansplaining. "Half of them true, half of them not. The trick is to sort out fact from fiction."

Which was true, but was also something I'd known since I was seven years old.

Both of us murmured "nice to meet you" type words, and we parted ways.

The rest of the way to Shomin's, I barely knew what I was doing or where I was going, because my brain was shrieking one thing, and one thing only.

Des Pyken had lied about Angelique's.

I pushed away thoughts of Des Pyken so I could shift from doing three things at once to only two: walking while eating my egg salad sandwich. Earlier, over a cup of grimace-inducing Kelsey coffee, Donna had told me that her running goal for the year was to get a personal-best marathon time, so she was fine-tuning her ability to run while eating and drinking. "It's all in the timing," she'd told me. "You need to swallow at the right point in your stride."

The time it took to develop that particular skill was yet another reason I was never going to take up serious running. The main reason was, of course, that I wasn't interested in it, but I also had little to no ability to drink while walking. Eating was as much as I could manage, and even that was limited.

"One foot in front of the other," I said as I turned the sandwich to avoid getting a bite of all crust. "Pay attention to what you're doing. Be more like Donna."

It was because of Donna that I was headed in a particular direction. The employee meeting had ended with suggestions for tracking down the dog vandals, and Donna had said there was a park not far from the library. It wasn't a dog park, per se, but rather a small neighborhood park with trees on the outside, a large grassy space in the middle, and nothing else, and the most frequent users were people with dogs.

I took a hard left at the next intersection, finished my sandwich, stuffed the wrapper in my pocket, and texted Holly that I was going to be a few more minutes.

The odds of seeing the dogs there were slim to none, of course. But it wasn't outside the realm of reality to talk to a dog owner who might recognize our miscreants. They couldn't live too far from the library, and the library was a five-minute walk from the park, so chances were high that the dogs spent at least some time there.

That was my reasoning, which had felt sound when I'd come up with it, though it felt less reasonable when I stood in the middle of the park, talking to the two people walking their pets—one golden retriever, one Jack Russell terrier—and heard nothing but denials.

"Sorry," said the golden's owner. "My husband and I are in a short-term rental. We've only been here a few days."

It was the same story with the terrier's dad. "Wish I could help," he said, his arm stretched out long trying to hold back his dog's bouncing energy. "But my husband and I just got here yesterday. Say, do you have any restaurant recommendations?"

One more short-term-rental dog owner later, I had an idea, and instead of heading back to the library, I took a detour and walked to the office of the city of Chilson.

The fiftyish woman at the front desk looked up and smiled. "Well, if it isn't our friendly neighborhood bookmobile driver! It's been too long since you stopped in."

I smiled back, something that was easy to do. Cathy was the city clerk, and if there were awards given for Clerks You'd Most Like to Have As Your Sister, she would get my vote every time. "How has your summer been?"

Cathy picked up a lock of her black hair and looked at it cross-eyed. "Not white yet. We'll see what happens tomorrow."

Laughing, I asked, "It's been that bad?"

"Oh, not really." She leaned back in her chair. "Typical summer stuff. People complaining about parking. People complaining about the heat. People complaining about the wind. People complaining about having to smell their neighbor's grilling. And did I mention the parking complaints?" She smiled, but there was a distinct rueful flavor to it.

"You," I said solemnly and sincerely, "are the personification of all that is good and true in the world. Your work here is important, undervalued, and underappreciated, and at the next city council meeting I will make a public comment saying so."

"Don't you dare," Cathy said, smiling, and this time it felt real. "And thanks for the kind words, even if you were just trying to make me laugh."

Though I had been trying to lighten her spirits, I'd also meant everything I'd said. "It's always good to see you," I said, "but I did stop by for a reason. The city licenses short-term rentals, right?"

"If they're in residential districts, you bet. We don't track the ones in commercial districts."

"So the licensed addresses are part of the public record?"

Cathy gave me a penetrating look. "Why don't you tell me what you're really looking for, and I'll tell you if I can legally provide you with the information. And depending on what you want, you might have to file a Freedom of Information Act request."

"Be happy to." I nodded. "What I'm wondering is how many short-term rentals might be within a six-block radius of the library."

She sat up and reached for her keyboard. "I can tell you that pretty easy. The city contracts with a software company that keeps track of all that. Let me pull up a map and I'll show you. Any particular reason you're looking?"

"Dogs," I said succinctly, and explained.

Cathy's mouth twitched. "There are so many possible jokes, I don't even know where to start. But I do know this. I don't need a map to tell you where those dogs have been staying."

I looked at the Notes app on my phone. Yep, the address Cathy had given me matched the address of the house in front of me. The house had classic white clapboard siding and large double-hung windows. Its deep porch, which wrapped around on two sides, had an aqua blue ceiling, warm gray floorboards, and cushioned rattan furniture that longed for someone to sit in it, sip iced tea, and play board games for hours and hours.

The house also sported a fenced-in backyard and four large brown puppies who were staring at me and barking as if today was the last day they'd ever be able to bark and they had to get in a lifetime of barking before dinnertime.

"Paul!" a man shouted. "George! Ringo! John! Be quiet!"

As there was no discernable difference in the noise level, I began to understand the reason behind the many complaints Cathy had taken about this particular house in the last couple of weeks. "They're nice people," she'd said, "but the wife is the only one who can control those dogs, and she's been down in Traverse City half the time, working on some development project. They pay no attention to him or the kids. The only way I've been able to talk the neighbors off the ledge is their stay is over tomorrow."

"Don't the police take those nuisance calls?" I'd

asked. Graydon had talked to the city police, and they'd told him no one had reported anything about a roaming pack of overgrown puppies.

She'd shrugged. "Sometimes. But it gets complicated with the short-term rentals. I issue the licenses, so I get the complaints."

I stepped onto the front porch and the dogs went berserk.

"OoooOOoo! OooOOO!" "Woof! WOOF!" "OooOOO!"

The front door opened. A woman a few years older than me appeared, rubbing her shoulder-length—and wet—blond hair with a towel. She wore faded jean shorts, a T-shirt from Mama Lu's, a taco shop in Traverse City, and a tired smile.

"Hi." Her voice was warm but stretched tight with apology. "You're here about the dogs, aren't you? I am so sorry about the noise; it wasn't supposed to happen. It really wasn't. Anyway, I was just going out to take care of them, and we'll be gone by tomorrow noon."

Something about this felt . . . weird. I smiled. "Can I come with you? I love animals." Which was true in general, although in particular I mostly loved a cat named Eddie.

The woman blinked at me. "Um, sure. Why not, I guess?"

We traipsed through the living room, dining room, and kitchen and out into the backyard, and by the time she'd quieted the dogs I'd learned that her name was Sarah Laurenz, that the dogs were her sister's, and that Sarah had them at their vacation rental because her sister had wound up with emergency surgery due to a burst appendix and wasn't able to take care of anyone but herself for six weeks.

"So I didn't have much choice," Sarah said. "She's my sister, you know?"

"And you're a good one," I said.

"Yeah, well." Sarah patted Ringo's head, and her smile had a slightly evil tint. "I'm sure I'll think of a way to make her pay for this."

Laughing, I said, "There's nothing like siblings."

"Not even close."

"Um, Sarah, I have a confession to make. I'm not a neighbor. I work at the library." I gestured in that direction with the top of my head. "And your sister's dogs have, ah, ventured in our direction."

Sarah closed her eyes. "Give it to me straight. What have they done? Whatever the damage is, we'll cover the cost."

As far as I knew, the only out-of-pocket expense had been fixing the irrigation system, and I was pretty sure Gareth had done most of that himself. Still, there had been some cost, so we exchanged cell numbers. Then I pulled up a security image Josh had sent me and showed it to her.

She peered at it. "Can you send that to me? Because I am so looking forward to sending this to my sister when I bring the boys back to her. Can I tell her the city police want to arrest the dogs?"

I laughed. "I can get you in touch with Joel Stowkowski. He works for the city's police department. If he has time, he might come out and take mug shots for you."

"That would be perfect," Sarah said fervently.

I knew I should get back to work, but I also wanted to get enough information from Sarah to make sure I could track her down once they left town. She seemed nice enough, and I wanted to trust that she'd be in contact about paying for the dog damage, but I wouldn't be doing my job if I didn't make sure.

"Where are you from?" I asked casually, nodding at her T-shirt. "I see you've been to Traverse."

She looked down at her shirt. "Oh, we live in Traverse. I'm a native, my husband's from Ypsilanti. I work here, actually," she said, plucking at her shirt's fabric. "At least for now. I'm partnering with a friend of mine to open our own restaurant next spring."

I respected entrepreneurs more than almost anyone else in the world. They had far more courage than I did. "Well, that's exciting! What kind of place? And where?"

"We're hammering that out right now," Sarah said. "That's why we came to Chilson for a couple of weeks, so I could be here to talk to my partner and we could drive to Traverse together to look at potential locations."

"Your friend lives in Chilson?" I looked around, as if someone else were about to materialize at any second.

"Outside of town, but yeah. Maybe you know her? She works at Three Seasons."

"Could be." My skin was starting to tingle with anticipation, because I was pretty sure I knew what was coming. "What's her name?"

"Misty Overbaugh."

Chapter 22

W ell, that's that," I said to myself. The confirmation that Misty's future restaurant wouldn't open until next spring at the earliest, along with the knowledge that it would be in Traverse City, which was more than an hour away and wouldn't in any way, shape, or form be competition to Chilson-area restaurants, took Misty completely off the suspect list.

I breathed a huge sigh of relief. All along, I'd had a hard time believing that Misty could have betrayed Kristen by adding triticale to the ice cream cones. And never once had I truly thought that she'd killed Remi Bayliss. Still, it had been a possibility. She'd had clear opportunity for the cones, and I'd never found her an alibi for the murder. But there was absolutely no motive.

I'd never have to tell Kristen that her head chef had intentionally endangered Three Seasons guests, or that her head chef had killed someone. And if I was careful, Kristen wouldn't even learn that I'd had Misty on the suspect list.

The conversation spun out in my head.

Kristen: "You thought what?"

Minnie: "That Misty, to help boost her restaurant's reputation, added triticale to the ice cream cones to ruin Three Seasons' reputation, then later killed Remi to help destroy Angelique's."

Kristen: "Are you insane? Misty would never do anything like that. Besides, her new place is in Traverse and won't open until next year. None of that makes any sense. Are you sure you weren't dropped on your head as an infant?"

The fictional conversation made me think harder about the relationship between Misty and Kristen. They'd been friends for years before Kristen had lured her away from a downstate restaurant with the promise of high wages throughout the Up North summers and winters off. They acted more like coworkers than employer and employee, and Kristen almost certainly knew all about Misty's plans to leave. Hadn't Misty said as much at one point?

I pulled out my phone and started texting.

Minnie: *Hey. Does Kristen know about your plans for a start up in Traverse?*

Misty: *Sure. She's been pushing me that way for more than a year, saying if I don't do it now, I might never do it. Why?*

Minnie: *Just curious. Thanks!*

Huh. Well, even if I'd figured all that out days ago, I still would have felt obligated to do my due diligence and make super sure Misty was innocent. Just in case. And now I had. And she was.

Now that Misty wasn't part of the conversation regarding suspects, I needed to learn more about the two still on the list. I also needed to talk to Deputy Wolverson about what I'd learned. Sure, he probably wouldn't care all that much, and I might find it hard to keep my irritation level down throughout, but talking to him was the right thing to do.

And I would talk to him, just as soon as I found out a little bit more. Because right now I hadn't learned anything that was close to the proverbial smoking gun. If I went to him now, he'd give me a long-suffering look, say thanks for stopping in, then ask what Rafe and I wanted for a wedding present.

So how did I find out more about Des Pyken?

I pulled my phone from my pocket. Yep. Long past the time I'd told Holly for my return. But what was another few minutes in the grand scheme of things?

After sending her a quick text that I had info about the dog vandals and that I'd be back as soon as possible to talk to Graydon about it, I headed back downtown.

Des had been there earlier, so maybe he still would be. If so, I'd initiate another conversation, this one more pointed, asking about Three Seasons and ice cream cones and Remi Bayless, and see how he reacted. If I couldn't find him, I'd try to track down Bianca Koyne and see if she could tell me anything about the sale of Seven Street.

Now that I had steps to take, a couple of knots inside me eased a slight bit.

I was helping Kristen. I was actively working to find Remi's killer. I was doing something, and even if none of it moved the needle on identifying the killer, at least I could tick things off the list that I'd tried.

First things first. I hurried downtown to see if Des's vehicle was still parked at the curb.

It was, but he was also climbing into it.

I broke into a jog, slowed to a fast walk, then to a slow stroll. No way was I going to catch up to him.

"Des!" a female voice called. "You forgot this!" Bianca Koyne, clutching a small pile of papers, darted out from a doorway. It led to an upstairs coworking space that was rented by the half day to anyone who needed temporary office space with high-speed Internet and virtual-conference meeting capacity.

"I'd forget my head if it wasn't screwed on tight," he said, laughing. "Thanks. See you next week." He climbed into his car and started it.

"Hey, Bianca," I said, coming up to her and watching Des pull out and into traffic. "Looks like he gets out of parallel parking spaces as smoothly as he backs into them. I saw him park that huge thing earlier today and it was impressive."

Bianca smiled. "That SUV has automatic parallel parking. Des didn't park it; the computer did."

"Huh." I looked down the street, but he was already out of sight. "My car has automatic nothing. I forget how fancy cars can get these days." I nodded at the thick manila folder she was holding. "Selling a house to live in after he buys Seven Street in a few months?"

"This is for the restaurant itself," she said, smiling and patting the folder with her free hand. "We're set to close on Monday afternoon."

"Oh? I thought that was going to be later in the year. Or even next year."

"Apparently not," she said cheerfully. "Which works for me. Say, what do you and Rafe want for a wedding present?"

For the millionth time, I said that we didn't want anything. And, for the millionth time, I got a laugh and a "No, really, what do you want?" in return.

I did what I could to convince her that we didn't need—or want—anything except their smiling presence, then headed back to work, thinking hard.

Des Pyken had lied to me twice in the space of about three sentences. One had been silly, about the parallel parking; the other had been a bigger lie, about the timing of buying Seven Street.

It made me wonder a couple of things. The first was, Why had he bothered to lie at all? But the second thing was the far bigger question.

What else had he lied about?

That night Rafe and I did outside chores. Well, one chore, really, which was giving the gazebo its third and final—and to me completely unnecessary—coat of paint, while Eddie sat on the ground below us and criticized every brushstroke.

"Mrr!" he called.

"Really?" Rafe asked. "Your mom missed a spot on her side, did she? Huh. You have a great eye, my friend. Nicely done."

"Pretty sure he was commenting on the fact that you just splattered white paint on the tip of his tail."

Rafe stopped and turned around to look. "Oh, man," he said, after he realized that I'd been messing with him and that Eddie's tail was fine. "You got me. Good job."

From my perch on the six-foot stepladder, I looked down and gave him a smug smile. "Can't wait to tell your dad that I've finally learned how to do that."

"Nah, that was a once-in-a-lifetime thing," Rafe said with calm confidence. "And it almost doesn't count because it was Eddie related. He's always going to take your side."

As if. "Eddie takes the side of whoever is closest to the treats."

"There is that."

We painted in companionable silence for a few minutes. I studied the part of the gazebo that had three coats of paint and compared it to the part that only had two. Three coats undoubtedly protected the wood more and, though practically invisible, did look better. I sighed because there was now something I had to do. "Rafe?"

"Yes, my little lily pad?"

I sighed again. "You were right and I was wrong. I'm sorry."

"Good to know. About what?"

"Not telling." I grinned. Maybe someday I would, but I didn't see it happening anytime soon.

"Mrr!"

I looked down. Eddie was at the base of my stepladder, his front paws on the first step, his back paws still on the ground. "Stay," I commanded. "Good boy."

"He's only trying to help," Rafe said.

Sure. Like a toddler wants to help Dad or Mom

clean the house. "So I'm down to two suspects," I said.

"That's what you said at dinner." Rafe climbed down and moved his stepladder to the next unpainted section, saying, "But then Kristen called, remember?"

I did indeed. Kristen had declared that she'd solved our wedding officiant problem and that she'd get us the final details in a couple of days. When we'd started pressing her for a name, a small human had started shrieking at an impossibly high decibel level, and the call had ended. "Anyway," I said, "Misty is out. Not only is her new place not going to open until next spring, it's in Traverse City, so there is absolutely no reason for her to ruin the reputation of Chilson's restaurants."

Rafe nodded. "The opposite, if anything. Her new place might get tainted with the drama from up here if word got around about where she's been working."

It was a good point, and one I hadn't grasped until that second. "For a middle school principal, you're pretty smart."

"Oh, geez," he said. "Don't go setting that bar so high. I'll have to spend all my energy living up to it and I'd way rather sit around and watch baseball. Who else have you eliminated?"

"Harold Calkins and Parker McMurray. They both have solid alibis."

"So we're down to Des Pyken and Cherise."

I nodded, then froze in place. Although I hadn't moved, there'd been an odd bump against the stepladder. What the . . .

It was Eddie, of course. "Mrr!" he said, rubbing the side of his face against the bottom rung. "Mrr!"

"Anyway," I said, ignoring my cat because what was there to say, "yes, we're down to Cherise and Des as suspects."

"Who's most likely?"

"Not supposed to have favorites," I said severely. "This is just-the-facts land. No opinions. Information only. Straight data."

Rafe nodded. "Right. But who do you think is most likely?"

"Honestly? It's a tie." I sighed. "Cherise could easily have done the triticale cones, but why would she have killed her own employee? Des, same thing. The triticale, yes, but why would he kill Remi?" Being a liar sent him far down in my estimation as a human being, but that didn't translate to being a murderer.

"Did Remi know Des?" Rafe asked.

"Not as far as I know." When I'd asked Cherise that very question, she'd shrugged and said she had no idea. "The Lee knife connects the triticale to Remi's murder, but what's the connecting motive?" Though killing off key employees had been my original theory, I'd heard nothing about any other restaurant worker being attacked or threatened.

What I needed was one solid bit of information about either Cherise or Des, one piece of evidence that Ash could take to the prosecuting attorney, one thing that would prove the killer's identity without a doubt. The problem, of course, was how to find the crucial bit.

"Mrr," Eddie said, thumping his head against the ladder yet again.

"Keep doing that," I told him, "and you'll wind up with a dent in your forehead so deep that . . ." My voice trailed off.

Rafe's paintbrush paused. "Problem?"

"Nope."

I smiled, because the next day was a bookmobile day, and I knew exactly how to take my next investigative step.

The painting chore went on for two hours longer than I'd hoped, and an hour longer than I'd expected. The sun had just slid down behind the tree line, and the almost full moon was lighting the yard with a golden glow. I was past tired by the time we'd cleaned all the brushes and put everything away, so it wasn't until the next morning, after Rafe had already left for work, that I had a minute to double-check my stroke of genius from the night before.

"Not that I'm doubting myself," I said to Eddie as I pushed away yesterday's newspaper and fired up my laptop. "But it never hurts to make sure."

Eddie, sitting upright on the kitchen island stool next to me, rotated so that his back was facing me.

"What's with the aloof act?" I asked. "What did I do wrong this time? Go ahead. Tell me. I promise I can take it."

His little kitty shoulders heaved a heavy sigh.

"Sometimes," I mused, "I really think you're trying to tell me something more than 'Fill my food bowl' or 'Time for new treats.' What is it you're trying to tell me this time? 'Best-ever chicken salad recipe'? No, wait. You have the answer to who robbed the Isabella Stewart Gardner Museum back in 1990. It really is a pity I'm too stupid to understand you."

Eddie gave me a hot glare, jumped down, and stalked off.

Cats.

I opened the county's website and ran a property record search for Gerald Denton, called Dent by everyone who knew him. Then I ran one for Remi Bayliss and leaned forward, squinting at the results.

They both had addresses on Sturgeon Road. Dent and his wife, Shirley, lived on a twenty-acre parcel in the southwest quarter of section twenty in Zicklin Township. Remi Bayliss had a three-acre parcel in the southeast quarter of section twenty-one, same township.

I used the website's distance function to measure the distance between the two. Dent and Shirley lived just over a mile away from Remi. It was too far away for them to be considered neighbors, but in a sparsely populated area, it was common for people on the same stretch of road to know each other. Over and over again on the bookmobile we heard people say things like, "Oh, sure, we know them. They have a place up the road. Painted their house last year."

Plus there was a new bike path that ran parallel to Sturgeon Road. The path had been in the planning stages for years and had been finished just that spring. A few residents were still disgruntled about the invasion of privacy, but most people loved it, and I remembered Dent and Shirley saying now that they were both fully retired, they were enjoying the evenings of walking the path and getting to know their neighbors better.

If Dent or Shirley didn't show up at the bookmobile, I'd have to invent a reason to stop at their house, but luck was with me because a few hours later, they climbed the steps together, bickering good-naturedly about what they were going to cook for dinner.

"Too hot to cook inside," Shirley said, flapping the front of her T-shirt, which couldn't have made much of a breeze, because she wasn't any taller than I was.

Dent rolled his eyes. "So you want me to slave over a hot grill, is that what you're saying?"

She smiled at him. "For an old man, you're pretty smart."

"Who are you calling old?" He bridled but winked at Julia and me. "Seems to me your birth certificate has a date that's a year older than mine."

"And what proof do you have?" his loving wife challenged. "Do you know where our birth certificates are?"

His blank look was classic.

Julia tsked at him. "You're doomed, mate," she said, in what I thought was a New Zealand accent. "Best go along with what she wants. Happy wife, happy life, yeah?"

He grinned, then slumped a bit as he looked at me. "Minnie," he said. "So sorry to hear that you were the one to find Remi Bayliss. That must have been hard."

I shook my head in a sort of yes, sort of no direction. "No, but then I didn't know her. And now . . ." I paused, then shrugged. "In some weird way, I kind of feel like I should know more about her. How well did you two know her?"

The couple exchanged a glance, and Dent nodded at his wife. "Shirl stopped in more than I did."

"A few times," Shirley said, tucking her short white hair behind her ears. "When she went on vacation, or to visit her family. She didn't have any pets, but she did have some lovely houseplants."

"Remi wasn't from here, was she?" I asked. Her obituary had been bare-bones. That she'd worked at Angelique's and that she'd graduated from a downstate high school. The names of her parents and siblings had been listed, and they all lived in Florida, Illinois, or Arizona.

Shirley shook her head. "No. She grew up in Warren and moved to the west side of the state after high school. Grand Rapids."

A zing went through me. "Oh?" I asked casually. "Did she always work in restaurants?"

"All she ever did," Dent said. "Always trying new recipes. Sometimes we'd get her castoffs."

"Do you know where she worked, in Grand Rapids?"

"Oh, goodness." Shirley pursed her lips. "A number of places. Let me think. There was one with an Italian name. Bistro Bella Vita, I think. Sorry," she said. "I can't remember any others."

Dent snapped his fingers. "She managed a place that turned into a small chain. It's the owner's last name. I hear he's going to open a place up here. Pike? Piker? No, that's not it. But something close."

"Pyken?" I asked.

"That's it!"

Des beamed at me, and my zing burst into a full-fledged idea. I did my best to calm my racing heart. "Did she ever talk about opening her own place?"

Shirley smiled. "You know, I asked her that very question, not long ago. She laughed and said the only way she'd ever open a restaurant was if a fairy godmother waved a wand and gave her a stack of cash. That no way would she go into debt for a restaurant; it was far too risky."

I made murmurs of understanding and general sympathy for losing a neighbor, and shifted the conversation to the new-to-them authors we'd recommended, Walter Mosley and Silvia Moreno-Garcia.

But all the time we were talking, I found it hard to keep my mind from drifting back to the conclusions that came to me in that sudden zinging flash.

Cherise hadn't had anything to do with Three Seasons, or anything else.

It had been Remi and Des, working together.

And Remi had wound up dead.

Chapter 23

By the time I detached Eddie's carrier from the bookmobile's floor at the end of the day, I had a solid theory, one that finally made sense of everything.

Des had come up with the idea to make triticale ice cream cones. With his former manager living and working in Chilson, he'd reached out to Remi and paid her enough money to persuade her to make the cones, which she'd done, using Angelique's triticale. Or maybe she'd bought it herself; there was no way for me to know. She'd used her small Lee knife to slice open the plastic wrap that had sealed a box of cones, extracted the originals, replaced them with the triticale version, and resealed the box, accidentally dropping her knife on the floor during the process.

Then one of three things had happened. Remi had turned on Des—maybe blackmailing him, maybe threatening to tell the police—and he'd killed her. Or maybe he'd planned to kill her all along to cover up the stunt with the triticale. He was a man who planned ahead, so it was entirely possible. Or maybe he'd gone to the kitchen just to talk to Remi, they'd argued, and he'd grabbed the knife and killed her in a fit of rage.

The only problem was this new theory that interlocked all the pieces was one hundred percent conjecture. I had no proof. None whatsoever. And no matter how many ideas I considered—and that included the wacky ones Julia had dreamed up, which ranged from following Des Pyken until he committed another crime to interrogating his mother—I'd come up with only one way to find solid evidence.

Get inside Remi's house.

The sheriff's office had undoubtedly gone through it, but they didn't know what I knew. If I called Ash and told him about Remi working for Des, how soon would he be able to get out there to take another look? It was quitting time on Friday. The whole weekend was straight ahead, and I didn't want to lose the slight momentum I had. Plus, every day that went by was one more day that Three Seasons stayed under a cloud, and one more day that Remi's murder went unpunished.

Once again, I saw that knife handle. Shutting my eyes didn't make it go away. The reverse, actually, so I gave that up to find that Eddie was looking at me. "What?" I asked.

His yellow-eyed gaze was calm but not helpful.

I tapped the steering wheel. Shirley had mentioned that she checked in on Remi's house when Remi was out of town. Did Shirley have a key? Or, like so many people in rural areas, did Remi hide a key somewhere for neighbors or family to use?

"Only one way to find out," I said to Eddie. "Hope you don't mind going home the long way."

"Mrr."

"Excellent." I sent Rafe a text about where I was going, and twenty minutes later, we arrived at Remi's place, parking on the concrete pad next to the house. There was a small stack of bricks next to the pad, and I ached with loss for Remi, that she hadn't been able to finish whatever landscaping project she'd planned.

"Stay here," I told Eddie, sliding my keys into my pocket, and shut the car door in the middle of a "Mrr." The day's temperature was mild, the car was parked in the shade, and I'd rolled down the windows a bit. "You'll be fine," I said through the one-inch gap. "Quit with the histrionics."

I ignored the higher decibel level of his next "Mrr" and got to work.

There were all sorts of places that people tended to hide house keys. Under or in a flowerpot, behind a porch column, inside a garage. Remi's house was a small ranch, circa 1960s. Its front door had no porch, and there was no garage. A tiny shed held some promise, so I headed that way, going around the left side of the house and its side door.

I glanced at the door and stopped. There would be no key hidden in the shed, under the stoop, or anywhere else.

Remi had a keypad.

I muttered a mild curse and, sighing, climbed the few steps to the door. Muttering to myself a bit,

I tried tapping in numbers, but since I had no idea what numbers Remi might have programmed into her lock, or even how many numbers this kind of lock required, it was a pointless exercise.

Then something Josh had once told me bubbled to the surface of my memory.

"People are lazy," he'd said, rolling his eyes. "You wouldn't believe how many morons never re-program the security stuff they buy. I don't get it. What's the point of buying security tech if you're never going to change it from one-two-three-four?"

Could it be that easy?

I flexed my fingers backward, entered the straight four-digit code, and heard . . . nothing. In hopes that Remi had purchased the quietest keypad lock ever, I tried the handle and . . . nothing. Still locked.

"Hang on," I said. "What if . . ."

This time I breathed on my fingertips for luck, then entered a straight six-digit code: 1-2-3-4-5-6.

The deadbolt made a solid *snik!* kind of noise, and I was in.

My first impression of Remi's house was that her taste was vastly different from mine. Rafe and I tended to decorate with books and cat hair. Remi, though, had made careful choices on everything. The walls were a soft dove gray trimmed with bright white, the floor a wood laminate warmed with area rugs in bright abstract colors. Maps from all over the world were tacked to the walls with bright brass thumbtacks, and the furniture was an eclectic mix of wood, leather, and rattan.

I looked at the inviting spaces and felt a pang that the person who'd created this happy and comfortable home wasn't here to enjoy it. That her life had been taken away from her. "I'm so sorry, Remi," I murmured.

The only thing I could do for her now was to put her killer in jail. I needed to stop spending my time on regrets and start doing what I'd driven out here to do. Find some evidence and tell Ash and Hal Inwood about it. I wasn't exactly sure how to spin the story of why and how I'd ended up in Remi's house, but I'd come up with something.

It was a small house, so it didn't take long to determine that there was little in the master bedroom except what you'd expect. A bed, a nightstand, a dresser, and a closet full of clothes, shoes, and other personal items that I wasn't about to touch.

The tiny second bedroom served as a guest room and home office, with a laptop, printer, and little else. Remi must have kept her financial records on her computer. I turned it on, but it was password protected, and this time 1-2-3-4-5-6 didn't do a thing.

I returned to the living room. Remi's single bookcase was filled mostly with cookbooks, along with a few family photos. Her oak coffee table held a small stack of newspapers, a pile of cooking magazines, and a manila folder.

The folder was thick with papers. I opened it, expecting to see the financial paperwork her study had lacked, but instead found draft versions of a business plan. Remi's business plan. For a restaurant.

My mouth dropped open as I scanned the contents.

Concept, sample menu, management team, location, design, target market, market overview, marketing plan, financials. Otto, my aunt's husband, a former accountant, currently dabbled as a financial consultant and investor, and everything I'd learned from him indicated that Remi had a rock-solid plan.

"Huh," I said, closing the folder. The financials showed a substantial investment from Remi herself, a six-figure investment. Was it possible that she'd saved and invested wisely her entire adult life? Of course it was. Was it possible that she'd inherited money? Yes, it was. And was it also possible that she'd made the triticale cones, taken them to Three Seasons, and been paid well by Des Pyken to do so?

It most certainly was.

After putting the folder back where I'd found it, I passed through the dining area and into the kitchen. Cream-colored cabinets, brushed-nickel pulls, laminate countertops in a marble-ish pattern, backsplash of subway tiles that complemented the countertop color. She had a number of appliances on the counter, most of whose function I understood, though not all. And she had a knife block that was filled with the distinctive multi-blue handles of Lee knives.

Which was surprising and a bit disappointing, because if all her Lee knives were here, she couldn't have left one at Three Seasons. Or one at Angelique's to later end up killing her.

"Well," I said into the silent house, and pulled open the utensil drawers, more to do something, anything, than for any other reason.

And there, right in front of me, was a lumpy flat roll of canvas with a single name stamped on the side. Lee.

Slowly, I took it out of the drawer and laid it on the counter. I unsnapped the cover, flipped it back, and unrolled the bundle. Nine sleeves for nine knives. But there were only seven knives in the case. Both the largest and the smallest were missing.

I stared at the knives, trying to come up with a reason for the set to be here and not at Angelique's. Was there any reason for Remi to take only one knife to work? If she had taken any knives, wouldn't she have taken the entire set? Did anyone carry around a long-bladed—and extremely sharp—knife without a protective case? It didn't seem very likely that Remi would do that.

So why would . . . I pulled in a sharp breath.

The only reason the knife set would be here was if someone had returned it. And the most likely person to do that was Remi's killer, who I was ninety-nine percent sure was Des Pyken. He'd put the knives in Remi's house to confuse things. To divert attention. To do what he could to misdirect.

Which meant he'd been here. Remi's killer had stood in the exact same spot I was standing.

My skin prickled.

It was time to take pictures of the paperwork and the knives and get out.

I pulled out my cell phone and snapped quick photos. The set of travel knives on the counter, photo of the knife set returned to the drawer. Manila folder on the coffee table, manila folder opened to reveal the graceful logo of Remi's Bistro that was on her business plan's cover, the plan's summary page, and the financial page.

Everything was put back as closely to its original location as I could manage, and I was closing the back door behind me when I heard a vehicle make a turn onto Remi's driveway.

Dusk was just starting to deepen, and the vehicle's headlights were on high, blinding me. I put up my hand to shield my eyes and watched it approach the house and park right behind my car, so close it almost touched, which was weird because there was plenty of driveway room for two vehicles to park side by side.

I was beginning to get a bad feeling about this.

For a moment I considered rushing back inside, locking the door, and calling 911. But what would I say? That I'd snuck into the house of a murdered woman to look around and now someone had parked behind my car so I couldn't leave? That would get a deputy out here in, oh, about an hour. And maybe this was a neighbor. Or a relative. Someone who'd seen my car and was wondering about the unauthorized person at Remi's house. Maybe it was Dent and Shirley. Maybe—

The driver's door opened. Des Pyken stepped out. "Minnie Hamilton. Funny seeing you here."

Fear crushed my breath. A few heartbeats later, my lungs yelled at me and I sucked in the life-giving air. "Des," I said mildly, walking down the steps and toward the safety of my car. "What brings you out this way?" I chirped my doors unlocked. "And it's nice to see you, of course, but I really have to get going. My fiancé is making dinner and—"

Faster than I would have thought possible, Pyken lunged toward me. With one hand he swept the keys out of my right hand. With the other he grabbed my cell phone from my left hand, hurled it to the concrete driveway, and smashed it with his heel.

The glassy crack shocked me. My shock almost immediately turned to fury. "What did you do that for?" I asked, my voice tight and loud.

"Cut the crap," Pyken growled. "You know exactly why I did that. You've known for some time."

"No," I said as politely as I could manage. "I really don't. And I'm really uncomfortable with this situation, so give me my keys and I'll call destroying my expensive cell phone an accident." I held out my hand.

This was, very possibly, the stupidest thing I could have done, but I'd held out a hope that Des would respond to the polite gesture.

He didn't.

Instead, he grabbed my wrist and spun me around, pulling my arm up behind my back. This was exquisitely painful, and I heard myself give an involuntary whimper.

"Yesterday," he said into the back of my head. "You knew yesterday that I'd killed Remi."

"No, I—"

"You had to," he insisted. "There's no other reason to ask about Three Seasons and Angelique's at the same time."

Sure there was. I'd been fishing for a reaction in hopes of learning something. How was I to know he'd turn that into proof that I knew what I was doing?

"You're coming with me," he said.

I was absolutely sure that wasn't a good idea. Not from my point of view, anyway, so I pulled out the one thing I remembered from my classes in self-defense and let all my weight sag while simultaneously stomping hard on his instep.

In the classes, this got the Bad Guy to yelp with pain and let go, at which point you ran like crazy and hoped the Bad Guy was in too much pain to be right behind you.

"Oww!"

Pyken yelped, just like in the classes, but so did I, because he hadn't let go of my wrist, and letting my weight sag wrenched my shoulder something fierce.

"You little—" Pyken gave my wrist another yank and steered me toward his car. "This way. Right now."

He pushed me over to the rear bumper, held my wrist with one hand, and used the other to fumble with his key fob and unlock his trunk.

"You really don't want to do this." Panic started to leak into my voice and I started to talk too fast. "One murder, well, maybe that was an accident. There could be extenuating circumstances. It could happen to anyone, really. But two murders? There's no chance of explaining that away. None at all, and when I turn up missing, there's . . . no, no. You really don't want to do that."

My babbling talk went even faster, because Pyken was pulling a bottle of beer out of his trunk. And holding it like a weapon. "Whoa," I said, trying to pull away from his grasp and getting nowhere because he was still holding my wrist and he was also pinning me against the bumper. "Let's talk about this, okay? We can come to some sort of agreement, right? Why not—"

He swung the bottle at me. I tried to pull away from the blow, but it caught me full on the back of my head.

Pain exploded. My legs gave way, my arms went loose, and my whole body went slack.

Off in the distance I heard Pyken say with satisfaction, "That's more like it." The beer bottle went flying into the shrubbery and he rolled me forward into the trunk, flipping my limp legs up and over.

The trunk lid came slamming down, cutting off every last bit of the fading light, and the last thing my fuzzy brain heard was a distant "Mrr!" before everything went black.

Chapter 24

I slowly swam up into consciousness, but it was the weirdest waking up ever, because I had no clue where I was, what I was doing, or what I'd done to myself. There was carpet . . . against my face? That didn't make any sense. And why did my head hurt so much? And what had I done to my shoulder? Why couldn't I remember any of it? The last thing I remembered was . . . was . . .

For a moment I felt nothing but sheer, unadulterated panic, because I couldn't remember anything. Not where I was, not what I was doing, not what day of the week it was, not even my own name. My life was a black void. I was a void. I was nothing.

"Breathe," I murmured. "Breathe."

For once, I listened to myself and breathed in and out. In and out. Gasping breath by gasping breath, the panic receded and my sense of self returned.

My name was Minnie Hamilton.

I was about to marry Rafe Niswander.

We lived in Chilson, Michigan.

My job as assistant library director was the best in the world.

I was bound for life to a black-and-white cat, and—

My eyes widened as my memory flooded back.

Where was Eddie? Had Pyken taken him, too? If he'd hurt Eddie I was going to make it my life's mission to destroy him, both personally and professionally. I would make mincemeat out of his reputation and call in every favor I could to ensure that no one in Chilson would ever do business with him.

But first, I needed to get out of his trunk.

The space was dark, lit only the slightest by a glow from the taillights, which wasn't the red I'd expected, but a red mixed with white.

Hang on. White lights? The car was going . . . backward?

I closed my eyes and tried to feel the car's direction, something that should have been easy, but my thumped-head status was making things difficult. Underneath me, I could feel brakes being applied. The car slowed and momentum rolled me toward the back seats.

Yup. We'd been going backward. And, from the way I'd also been slid to the side, we'd turned.

I felt the car's transmission shift and then I was rolled the other way.

So, going forward now.

The timing of the car's reverse direction and then the turn clicked in my head. I must have been unconscious for just a few seconds, because this sure felt like Pyken had backed out of Remi's driveway and onto the asphalt road, then . . . I mapped it out in my still-fuzzy head . . . then right. East. Away from Chilson, and toward . . . what? Where did Sturgeon Road go?

Nowhere, is where it went. At least not any place that might have bright lights and people who might hear me calling for help. The opposite of that, actually. To the east was the Mitchell River, and the hundreds of acres of rocky river valley. State forest, almost all of it. Unspoiled wilderness and a perfect place to . . .

"No," I said. Des Pyken was not going to knock me on the head a second time, this time much harder, and toss me into the woods for some poor hiker to find next spring. I had too many things left on my to-do list. If only I had my cell phone. But I didn't, so wishing for it wasn't productive, and—

Hang on. Cars had internal trunk releases. Mine did, anyway, and my car had to be at least ten years older than this one. All I had to do was find this one, yank it, and work up the courage to jump out of a moving vehicle.

First things first.

I patted around for a T-shaped plastic handle. Any shape of handle, actually, as long as it worked. On the trunk's lid, the sides, the base of the trunk. It had to be here, somewhere. Just one little handle, and I'd be more or less free.

My fingers found a promising rectangle of plastic and I started to feel a huge wave of relief. But there was no handle. "No," I whispered, holding the raw end of a cable. "No, no, no."

Pyken had cut the trunk release. I was well and truly trapped.

I squirmed around, trying to ignore the throbbing of my head and the shrieking of my shoulder, and tried to think. I had no cell phone and nothing in my pockets except an elastic hair tie, which might conceivably serve as a weapon if he got close enough for me to snap it into his eye, but I'd far rather keep my distance. The only other thing I had was my belt, and that had the same distance problem. Using the flats of my hands, I patted around, looking for a tool, a weapon, for anything that might help.

Wait. There'd been interior bins on each side, hadn't there?

I scrabbled left and felt for a lever, one of those disc ones that twisted. There! Righty-tighty, lefty-loosey, and pull!

Flinging the cover aside, I reached in.

And found nothing. Not even a pair of jumper cables.

My hopes started to drift southward, but I squirreled myself around—hooray for being small enough to enable maneuvering inside a locked trunk!—went to the other side, and found a second bin.

With tools.

A smile broadened across my face. There was a crescent wrench, a small and nearly useless hammer, but there was also a screwdriver. Tools. Excellent. All of those could come in handy.

Sweeping all the tools out of the bin, I grabbed the screwdriver and rotated myself around. If I couldn't kick out a taillight, I could do my best to break it from the inside. It was still summer; maybe there'd be people out and about who would see what was going on. Better yet, maybe there'd be a passing conservation officer who'd note the broken taillight and pull Pyken over.

Please, let there be a passing conservation officer.

Tink!

Tink!

Tink!

Piece by tiny piece, I poked out bits of taillight. Tiny pieces of hard plastic fell out and away.

The road bumped underneath me, turning from asphalt to gravel, signaling that we were deep into the state forest lands. I whacked at the taillight faster and faster, harder and harder. When the car came to a stop, more than half of it was gone. But no one had pulled us over. No nice police officer was coming to save me.

I was on my own.

The car's engine turned off. Pyken got out and came around to the trunk. He popped the lid.

"Out," he said.

I'd curled myself into a fetal position, my back to him, and didn't respond.

"Out!" he roared. "Or I'll drag you out!"

Fine with me. No way was I going to willingly walk to my death. Feigning unconsciousness was the only card I had left. If he truly thought I was out cold, there was still a chance I could get myself out of this.

"Didn't hit her that hard," he muttered. "She must have a thin skull." An index finger poked me in the back. I didn't move and kept my breathing light and shallow.

Pyken sighed, then big hands grabbed my armpits, slid me around, and hauled me up and over the trunk edge. "For a little girl, you are freaking heavy," he said, panting.

I desperately wanted to give him a tart response that involved the fact that he hadn't needed to put me in the trunk and the fact that maybe it was him who was weak, not me who was heavy, but I kept my mouth shut and my mind focused on keeping every muscle in my body limp.

Grunting, Pyken dragged me by the armpits, my feet dragging in the dirt, my head lolling to one side. I opened my eyes a crack and saw that the daylight was almost entirely gone. Only a thin line of dark blue marked the western horizon. To the east, the moon was just starting to show itself. Illumination, but not exactly light.

I closed my eyes, just in case Pyken could somehow see my face, and went back to concentrating on playing possum. Letting myself be hauled around like a sack of salt was less comfortable than I would have imagined, if I'd ever imagined it, which I hadn't, but it was better than being dead, and that was next on the agenda unless I could figure a way out of this.

As we went deeper into the woods, Pyken's breaths turned into heaving gasps. Just as I was starting to hope for a well-timed heart attack, he gave me one final heave up and over a log.

"There," he said, panting. "That'll have to do."

Oh so carefully, I opened my eyes to tiny slits. The light of the rising moon was just enough to see Des Pyken, leaning forward, head down, hands on his thighs.

It was now or never.

I leaped to my feet and started to run, but before I got even a step away, a big hand grabbed my ankle.

No!

Instinctively, I flung myself to the ground, rolling and twisting and kicking.

The hand fell away.

And I ran.

"Come back here!" he shouted.

Seriously? How stupid did he think I was?

I ignored him and kept running as fast as I could. Which wasn't as fast as I would have liked, because there wasn't that much light and the last thing I wanted was to crash hard into whatever, knock myself out, and give Pyken easy pickings in the Minnie Hamilton department.

"Stop! I won't hurt you!" he called out.

The man had a screw loose if he honestly thought I'd pay attention to anything he said. He'd already thumped me on the head, tossed me into his trunk, and dragged me deep into the woods. How did any of that translate into "won't hurt you"?

I kept on running, but even in the hundred yards or so I'd gone, I could feel Pyken gaining on me. In the dim light of the rising moon, I could make out the largest objects. Trees, rocks, and nothing else.

But I had to find somewhere to hide. I had to come up with a plan. I had to get away. My wedding dress wasn't returnable, for one thing. Plus Eddie would never forgive me. And Rafe . . .

I shook it all away.

Run, Minnie. Just keep on running. You'll figure something out. You always have and you always will.

So I did. Scrambling over fallen logs. Hurdling small rocks. Dodging around trees. I kept on, but

Pyken was getting closer and closer. It wouldn't be long and he'd be grabbing at my ankles again, and then—

And then I saw my opportunity.

A rock. A rock big enough for an efficient-size human to hide behind. If I could hide there long enough, Pyken would run past and farther into the woods, and I'd zip out and go the opposite way, far enough to lose him forever.

I cornered the rock and tumbled down to my hands and knees, trying so very hard to keep the noise of my heaving lungs to myself. If Pyken saw me, or heard me, I was toast.

Heavy running footsteps flew past.

Then they slowed.

I felt around on the ground for something, anything, that would help. I found lots of small and useless sticks. Dirt. Leaves. Pebbles . . . rocks . . .

"Don't move," Pyken said.

I froze. Then I unfroze, because why should I do what he told me to? He was about to kill me, and I was not about to go quietly into that particular good night.

"Move and you'll just make it harder on yourself." His footsteps, rustling in the detritus of old leaves, went to my right. "Sit tight and it'll all be over soon."

I listened to him but didn't really hear what he said. He was still moving to the right. If I stayed quiet, would he walk far enough that I could slip away, undetected? Though my breaths slowed, my heart beat loud and fast in my eardrums. A beam of light danced over the trees. He must be using his phone's flashlight to hunt me down.

"Come on," he said impatiently. "You're right here. I know you are. Just come on out and we'll get this over with."

He moved left, and I realized what he was doing—walking a grid. He was walking back and forth across the area where I was hiding, looking behind every log, and up every tree as far as I knew. Just my luck that the man who was trying to kill me had watched a lot of cop shows.

"Why delay the inevitable?" he asked.

Pyken's grid search was bringing him closer and closer to me. The inevitable was indeed about to happen.

"It's not going to make any difference in the end," he said, sounding almost reasonable. "So you stay alive a few more minutes. They're not exactly quality minutes, are they? What's the point?"

My hand was tight on the baseball-size rock I'd found. I had one chance. Just one.

"There are only so many places you can be," Pyken said, his voice close now. "I heard when you stopped running, you know. You're not far."

Slowly, oh so slowly, so slowly that my movement wouldn't have caught his attention, I sat back on my heels, pulled my arm back, and waited. The moon was rising now, and I could just make out his shape moving toward me. All I had to do was wait for the right moment.

"I have excellent hearing, did you know?" he said. "Ears of a bat, the doctors tell me. In the ninety-ninth percentile. Comes in handy. That's how I knew Remi was planning on turning me in. I heard her that day, back in the kitchen, talking. Said she didn't know there was enough triticale in those cones to land anyone in the hospital. Said she thought I should be stopped before I really hurt someone." He laughed. "So much for that theory. She didn't give me any choice, though. I had to kill her."

He was close now, close enough that even I stood a good chance of hitting my target. Leaning in, using all my weight, I hurled the rock straight at his head. I heard a thudding smack and a grunt of pain. Not five feet away, he fell to his knees.

But he didn't go all the way down.

Uh-oh.

"You little—" He lunged toward me.

I was already moving, scrambling to my feet, backing away, but he caught my foot with an iron grip.

"Now I got you," he snarled. "You'll pay for that."

Instinct screamed at me to kick and writhe and roll. I ignored all the atavistic impulses and fumbled for the hammer I'd slid into my waistband— Pyken's own hammer from the back of his own car—and held it firm and tight.

Pyken gripped my ankle hard and started dragging me from behind the rock, cursing as we went.

Hard as I could, I swung the hammer at the back of his hand.

"AHH!!"

His scream of pain filled the forest and his grip fell away. He curled into a fetal position, cradling his damaged hand.

I fought the impulse to run and jumped to my feet, a solid distance away from Pyken. I unbuckled my belt and pulled it out. I stood on his ankles, eliciting another scream of pain, and leaned over him, looping the belt around his good wrist.

The bones in his ankles cracked a bit, since I continued to stand on them as I pulled his arm around his back, and he yelled again. He yelled a little more when I pulled his bad arm around, then subsided to whimpering when I wrapped the belt around both wrists, incapacitating him.

I stood there for a moment, panting with the effort. "That'll hold you until I get the sheriff deputies out here," I told him, then jogged off, not waiting for an answer. Though I didn't know exactly where I was going, the rising moon told me in what direction the road lay, and that had to be enough.

The frenetic energy that had helped me escape Des Pyken suddenly wore off. My feet were heavy, my eyes burned with fatigue, and I suddenly remembered that I'd been thumped on the head.

How far was that road? Was I going the wrong way after all? Tears stung my eyes and I wondered if it might be best to just curl up somewhere and sleep for a few days.

A familiar voice drifted through the trees. "Minnie? Minnie! Where are you?"

"Rafe," I whispered. And suddenly I had the energy to fly to him, and into his arms.

Chapter 25

After a happy lifetime of hugging, I released Rafe and looked up at him. The moon's light made him almost glow, and I didn't know how I could ever love him more than I did in that moment.

"Do you want to call nine-one-one," he asked, "or should I?"

I took the phone from his hand and did the deed myself.

"A deputy is on the way," the dispatcher said. "Can you get to a safe place?"

I gripped Rafe's hand and never wanted to let go. A safe place? I was already there. "Yes," I said. "We'll be in a pickup on the side of the road, doors locked."

The dispatcher asked for a more precise location. Since I'd arrived at this particular spot in the trunk of a car, I handed the phone back to Rafe, and he told the dispatcher what she needed to know.

That done, we walked in the slanting moonlight, hand in hand, back to the road.

After I grilled Rafe about Eddie's safety, I had one huge question. "How did you find me? And don't say it was my magnetic personality that pulled you to me, because I won't believe a word of it."

"Dang. You're onto me."

"Truth and nothing but, please."

"It was a combination of things," he said, and I felt, more than saw, his shrug. "When I didn't hear back from a text I sent about dinner plans, I called, and still nothing. The text you sent with Remi's address got me out here. I found your car, your cell phone, and Eddie. He was outside the carrier. Did you let him out?"

"No." I sighed. "The latch must be broken again."

"Well, anyway, he was at the back window, clawing at the glass, trying like crazy to get out of the car. When I opened the door, he zipped out and started galloping down the road. I had to get into the truck to chase him down."

The image made me smile.

"When I caught up to him," Rafe said, "he was sniffing at this little piece of plastic. I got out and looked, and saw it was a chunk of taillight plastic, too clean to have been in the middle of the road for more than a couple of hours. The only thing I could figure was you were leaving a kind of a breadcrumb trail. I grabbed Eddie and got back in the truck, and we followed the plastic bits."

I was shocked. "That actually worked?" The entire effort had been of the last-ditch variety, and now that I was looking back on it, it had been as much something for me to do so I didn't panic as a realistic attempt to signal anyone. "Really?"

"Eddie's eagle eyesight helped," Rafe said. "At least it sure seemed that way. Every time he saw the truck's headlights reflecting off a piece he started howling, you know how he does, and when we didn't see any more pieces, I parked and started walking. And here you are."

We reached the truck and I climbed in to snuggle my furry friend. I repeated his name over and over again, murmuring thanks and endearments and feeling the comfort of his purrs.

A sheriff's SUV roared toward us, lights flashing and sirens blaring, followed quickly by a second one, and it wasn't long before a sputtering Des Pyken was led out of the woods in handcuffs, protesting that he was the victim, asking why they didn't arrest me, that I was the one who'd hit him, tied him up, and left him alone in the woods.

Happily, no one believed him. Eventually the Minnie hairs left behind in Pyken's trunk, along with the bits of my blood found on the bottle he'd used to whack me on the head, torpedoed any chance he had of twisting his story around to implicate me.

But all that came later. The third sheriff's vehicle that arrived had contained Deputy Ash Wolverson and Detective Hal Inwood. After Pyken was put into a back seat, and as we stood in the lightwash of the vehicles, Hal took one long look at me.

"We'll interview you tomorrow morning," he said. "Right now you're going to the emergency room. No arguments. You have blood oozing down onto your forehead."

"No, I don't." I reached up and felt the sticky goo. "Oh," I said stupidly. "When did that start?"

Rafe told Ash what I'd already told him about the location of my car keys, asked Ash to deal with my car, and ushered me into the truck. He did his best to keep me awake, but I fell asleep half a dozen times before we got to the hospital, another half a dozen times in the emergency room, and another half a dozen times by the time we pulled into our driveway.

My beloved half-carried me inside the house and up the stairs. I murmured something about wanting to take a shower, but he ignored that request and, instead, gently washed my face and hands with a warm washcloth and put me into my sleepwear of choice, his oldest, softest Chilson High School T-shirt.

The last thing I remembered before drifting off to sleep was the unmistakable feel of a cat jumping on the bed and settling down next to me.

"Mrr," he said softly.

"Love you, too, pal," I whispered.

And then I was out.

First thing the next morning, Rafe and I sat on one side of the interview table. Detective Hal Inwood and Deputy Wolverson sat on the other, with Sheriff Richardson herself leaning against the wall next to the doorway, her thumbs hooked over her tool belt, looking every inch the competent and professional law enforcement officer that she was.

"The emergency room people said I'm fine," I said. "No major concussion, and my shoulder is strained, is all. So what happens now?"

What happened was a long series of questions about the events of the night before. I answered them as accurately as I could and got only slightly irritated with Hal when he seemed to disbelieve my statement that I didn't know the exact timing.

"Didn't you look at your watch?" he asked.

I held up my naked wrist. "Don't wear one. Never have."

He muttered something that sounded a lot like "Millennials. I'll never understand them," and moved on to a discussion of my rock-throwing skills. "If you'd hit him in the head, you might have done some serious damage."

I stared across the table and felt my face start to grow hot. "Are you criticizing or applauding? Because it sure sounds like—"

"What Hal meant," Ash cut in, "is that we're glad you're safe. Right, Hal?"

The detective went back to muttering, but this time I couldn't make out any of the words. He also didn't ask any other questions, so I figured it was my turn.

"What is Pyken saying?" I asked. "Is he still saying I'm the one who should be arrested, not him? Have you taken the knives from Remi's house to compare with the knife that killed her? And what about the ice cream cones? Did you look in his house for triticale? Three Seasons is innocent of everything and people need to know that."

By this time I was leaning forward, my hands flat on the table. Rafe gently pulled me back into my seat. "Give them a minute," he said softly. "It hasn't even been twelve hours."

"Thank you, Mr. Niswander," Hal said. "Mr.

Pyken has admitted a limited involvement with the triticale cones, but he claims that Ms. Bayliss is the one who increased the amount of grain, making the cones far more dangerous than his recipe called for. He also claims that Ms. Bayliss was trying to blackmail him about the triticale, and that's why he confronted her that day. He claims her death was an accident."

"What?" I shot out of my seat. "Please tell me you're not buying that. He told me flat out that he killed her! He's lied about everything from when he's buying the restaurant to parking his car. You can't—"

Hal shook his head. "At this point there is no evidence to back up his claim, and a substantial amount of evidence indicates that he is lying."

"Oh. Okay." Slowly, I sat down again.

Ash looked at Hal, who nodded. "There are also," Ash said, "a lot of people who are telling us that Des Pyken is a habitual liar. Former business partners, former landlords, and two ex-wives are all ready and willing to give statements to that effect."

Huh. That was interesting. And was something I should have thought about looking into myself.

In the weeks that followed, we also learned that Pyken, in defiance of the clear wishes of Harold Calkins when he'd sold Seven Street, had every intention of doing a complete rebrand. The triticale had been Pyken's idea from start to finish, and he'd snuck around Three Seasons, looking for a way in, until the night Misty left the back door unlocked, at which time he'd had Remi make a quick batch of triticale-laden waffle cones and smuggle them in. He'd also paid a friend to post hundreds of bad restaurant reviews. It had all been part of his plans to set himself up for future success.

But that came later. Right then, Rafe took my hand. "Is there anything else? We came here first thing, and this one"—he tipped his head at me— "needs breakfast."

The sheriff levered herself off the wall. "I've heard varying stories from my officers about how you found each other in the woods last night. Now I'd like to hear from the two of you."

Rafe and I looked at each other. To think that I might owe my life to Eddie was one thing. To think I might owe it to his howling was something else altogether. But there was no backing away from it. The sheriff's gaze, though calm, compelled the truth.

So we told her. Halfway through, her lips started to twitch and she stepped out of the room. I could have sworn I heard muffled laughter, but when she stepped back in and motioned for us to continue, her face was blank.

At the end, I said, "Then I heard Rafe calling my name, and you know the rest."

"Hmm."

Sheriff Richardson's thoughtful focus made me sit up a bit straighter and put my chin up. "Any questions?" I asked as blandly as I could.

"One comment," the sheriff said. "Next time you go on vacation, keep me in mind for cat-sitting duty." She nodded and swept out, leaving the men with their mouths hanging open, and me with a wide smile.

Rafe and I walked out of the sheriff's office into the bright August sunshine. I pulled in a deep breath of fresh air and felt another pang for Remi Bayliss, for all the summer days that were taken away from her. Then and there I made a vow to come up with a small way to celebrate her life, and to do it every year on her birthday. I'd ask Cherise. We could even do it together. A special dessert, maybe, or—

"Hey." Rafe elbowed me. "Breakfast first or new cell phone first?"

"Food," I said, though two blocks later, I wasn't sure I'd made the right decision. There was a line of people out the door of the Round Table, which meant at least a half hour wait, and hunger was vying for breathing as my topmost physical need. I slowed. "Maybe we should—"

Rafe tugged me forward, around the line, and inside. He gave a short, sharp whistle, and caught Sabrina's attention.

"You," she said, giving me a hard glare. "Get in here."

Uh-oh.

I tightened my grip on Rafe's hand and tried to get him to stop. "She's being scarier than usual. I don't want to go in."

"Don't be such a fraidy-cat," he said, still pulling me forward. "What's she going to do, bite you?"

My guess was, if the mood struck her, absolutely yes, but I gave up resisting and let myself be led to the back corner booth, a place typically occupied by Sabrina's husband. Bill, who did financial things my non-math brain had never been able to comprehend, used that booth as his unofficial office. Today, however, it was occupied by two of my favorite people in the world, Kristen and my aunt Frances.

I looked at them, at Rafe, over at Sabrina, then back. "Who . . . I mean . . . what?"

"Sit," Kristen said, patting the seat next to her. "My guess is you haven't had nearly enough coffee yet this morning. No? I didn't think so."

Sabrina bustled up, putting a thermal urn and two fresh mugs on the table. "Today," she told me, nodding, "I won't tell you what to order. Get anything you want. No charge."

As she moved off, I felt my mouth drop open. "What happened to her? And why are you two here?" I swung around.

"What do you think, Frances?" Kristen asked, rolling her eyes. "Sleep deprivation?"

My loving aunt studied me. "Maybe. Could be that bang on the head."

I took the mug that Rafe had filled with just the right amount of cream and coffee and sipped until they finished their dissection of my character. "Just tell me what's going on, okay?"

Rafe leaned forward and held my free hand. "Minnie, this is the only way Sabrina knows how to thank you."

"For what?"

Kristen heaved a huge sigh. "Head wound combined with sleep deprivation. Only thing that makes sense."

My outside face must have shown the interior annoyance I was starting to feel, because Aunt Frances smiled and said, "Everyone in town knows what you did last night. That you figured out who it was that killed Remi, tried to destroy Three Seasons, and did his best to bring down the reputation of every restaurant in the area. You saved them all, Minnie, and were nearly killed yourself in the process."

Her voice, which normally registered deeply in the pragmatic scale, broke a bit. She coughed it away and continued.

"No restaurant in town will take your money until September," she said. "Everything's on the house."

"This one, too," Kristen said, pointing a finger at Rafe. "When he's with you, anyway. Not that he deserves it."

Rafe nodded. "Given."

"And," Kristen went on, "as another reward, I will now tell you the name of your wedding officiant. Sophia Aguilar, the district court magistrate."

I stared. "A magistrate can marry us?"

"Sure can."

"How do you know that?"

She shrugged. "Sophia is a Monday lunch regular. You wouldn't believe the stories she has."

"But why didn't . . ." My voice trailed off as I thought back to my conversation with the court administrator. She had been starting to tell me something, but I'd ended the call after she'd said the judge would be out of town.

Sabrina came by. I ordered a full-out breakfast of eggs, bacon, hash browns, and sourdough toast with orange marmalade, and she didn't bat an eye. It was truly a new world.

"Two more things," my aunt said. "One, I've rounded up half a dozen retired teacher friends, along with Barb McCade, and we'll all help out at Gennell Books until Blythe can find employees to hire."

"Really?" Happiness bubbled up inside me. "That's wonderful! Thank you so much!"

Kristen noted the color of my coffee and handed me more creamer. "And you should know that I've come to the—in retrospect, obvious—conclusion that I need to hire a full-time manager for the restaurant. It'll take the right person, but I have all winter."

I sipped my coffee and felt a wave of contentment wash through me. Like Aunt Frances was always saying, given enough time, things tended to work out.

Epilogue

ONE MONTH LATER

R afe pulled me close. "Ready?"

We were alone in the middle of the floor, waiting for our wedding dance music to start. Almost everyone Rafe and I knew surrounded us. Kristen was hoisting a champagne glass in our direction. Our parents, siblings, cousins, aunts and uncles, nieces and nephews, were all beaming.

So were our friends and coworkers. They were all here. Ash and Chelsea. Graydon, Julia, Holly, Josh, Hunter, Donna, Kelsey, Gareth, and half the library board. High school and college friends. Teachers from Rafe's school, and all of his staff. Downtown business owners, neighbors, and marina rats. The McCades were in their finery and the irascible but lovable Max Compton from Lakeview Medical Care Facility had wrangled a tux from somewhere. Tabitha Inwood was grinning at me, her husband Hal was doing something with his face that looked almost like a smile, and Sheriff Richardson was a vision in a flowing dress and high heels.

Our wedding, held in the library's community room, had gone off without a hitch. My aunt had bedecked the space with flowers and netting and swags and swaths in fabrics I couldn't possibly identify, and the visual result had been stunningly beautiful. The wedding had ended up as standing room only, and I was glad our circle of friends didn't happen to include the fire marshal.

Afterward, we'd endured the obligatory picture taking, then zipped down to the marina, where a tented reception area was waiting, with the bookmobile and the book bike parked nearby. Kristen and her staff had used the bookmobile for food prep, and the book bike's baskets were the designated location for wedding cards.

From what I could tell, everyone had actually done as we'd asked and not bought us a thing. But in the receiving line outside the library, almost everyone had told us that in lieu of a present, they were making contributions to the bookmobile's endowment fund and the school's fund for new technology.

On the far side of the dance floor was a table that held the last remnants of our wedding cake. Its design had been a collaborative effort by Kristen and Cookie Tom, and it had been gorgeous. Classic layers in multiple shades of blue, dark at the bottom, lightening to white at the top, echoing the waters of Janay Lake. The whole thing was draped with frosting flowers so lifelike Kristen had had to stand up and publicly demonstrate their edibility.

Now dinner was over, the cake was eaten, and we were ready to get the party rolling in a serious way. I nestled in closer to Rafe. My friend for more than twenty years. My husband for the rest of my life. "Am I ready? Not really. You know how much I like being the center of attention."

"Buck up, buttercup." He kissed the top of my head. "A few more hours and you can go back to being a mild-mannered librarian with a side hustle of capturing killers."

"Well, if you put it that way."

Rafe's friend and part-time deejay, Tank, started the music, "Still the One" by Orleans, and as my husband whirled me around the dance floor, I saw nothing but him, felt nothing but him, thought of nothing but him.

We were married, and everything was going to be okay.

Tank called up our parents to dance. He called Kristen and Scruffy. He called for Rafe's best man and his wife and the rest of our small wedding party. He called for any other family members, and we started switching partners. I danced with my dad, with Rafe's dad, with Otto, with my nephew. Rafe danced with his mom, my mom, his aunts, and all the other female relatives.

When he and I came back together, we were flushed and laughing, and I was ready for a short break. If I was going to dance all night long, I needed to pace myself.

Tank fired up "Uptown Funk" by Bruno Mars. "Are we ready to party?" he yelled. Whoops and shouts filled the air and chairs emptied as people ran to the dance floor.

"I'll be right back, okay?" I gave Rafe a soft kiss and slipped out of the tent.

My heeled shoes made a light tapping noise as I

hurried to the house. I opened the front door. "Eddie? Buddy, where are . . . oh. There you are."

He'd materialized out of nowhere and was bumping the back of my leg.

"Sorry about not paying enough attention to you," I said, leaning down to scoop him up. "It's been a busy day. Rafe and I got married, remember?"

My cat burrowed his head into the crook of my arm and, for a change, didn't say anything.

The door opened. "Figured this was where you went," Rafe said, coming close. "I say it's time for our first hug as a married couple in our house."

"Don't," I said, backing away. "You'll get cat hair all over your suit."

He pulled me to him with one arm and petted a purring Eddie with the other. "We're officially a family now. Cat hair is part of the deal."

Tears stung my eyes. If happiness was on a scale of one to ten, I'd just reached eleven. "Hear that, Eddie?" I whispered. "We're a family."

Our cat looked up at Rafe, then focused his laser-like gaze on me.

"Mrr."

Ready to find
your next great read?

Let us help.

Visit prh.com/nextread

Penguin
Random
House